LOVE IN SPADES

FOUR KINGS SECURITY BOOK 1

CHARLIE COCHET

CONTENTS

Love in Spades	v
Acknowledgments	vii
Chapter 1	1
Chapter 2	21
Chapter 3	33
Chapter 4	49
Chapter 5	79
Chapter 6	107
Chapter 7	125
Chapter 8	147
Chapter 9	171
Chapter 10	189
Chapter 11	209
Chapter 12	227
Chapter 13	239
Chapter 14	259
Epilogue	275
Up Next	283
A Note From the Author	285
Also By Charlie Cochet	287
About the Author	291

Love in Spades

Copyright © 2018 Charlie Cochet

http://charliecochet.com

All rights reserved. No part of this book may be reproduced or transmitted in any form or by any means, electronic or mechanical, including photocopying, recording, or by any information storage and retrieval system without the written permission of the author, except for the use of brief quotations in a book review.

This is a work of fiction. Names, characters, places, and incidents either are the products of author imagination or used fictitiously. Any resemblance to actual persons, living or dead, business establishments, events, or locales is entirely coincidental.

Cover content is for illustrative purposes only. Any person depicted on the cover is a model.

Cover Art Copyright © 2018 Reese Dante

http://reesedante.com

Edited by Desi Chapman

Proofing by Lori Parks

Formatting provided by LesCourt Author Services

www.lescourtauthorservices.com

Assistant Leslie Copeland lcopelandwrites@gmail.com

LOVE IN SPADES
FOUR KINGS SECURITY BOOK 1

CHARLIE COCHET

ACKNOWLEDGMENTS

To all my readers for supporting me on this new adventure, and those who said they'd follow me anywhere. You continue to awe and inspire me. Thank you.

The lovely folks who have helped me grow as an author and a business woman. For helping me learn about this ever-changing industry and everything that goes with it.

For my fellow authors who offered their support, guidance, and advice. Who have made this journey possible and continue to prove what an amazing community we have.

My friends and family who continue to hold me up, encourage me, inspire me. None of this would have been possible without you. I am so very blessed to have you in my life.

LOVE IN SPADES

Ex-Special Forces soldier Anston "Ace" Sharpe is fighting a different battle these days—one involving the world of private security across the state of Florida. As part owner of Four Kings Security, Ace and his fellow Kings tackle everything from armed transport and investigations to cyber intelligence and executive protection. Cocky, fearless, and brash, Ace isn't afraid to take risks.

After years of working alongside his father, Colton Connolly is ready to take the helm at Connolly Maritime, but his father's retirement is put on hold when Colton begins receiving death threats. If that isn't bad enough, his father signs a contract with Four Kings Security to provide Colton with round-the-clock protection, despite his adamant refusal. Colton's life has been turned upside down, the last thing he needs is a shadow, especially in the form of infuriating, sexy-as-sin Ace Sharpe, who seems to be on a mission to drive Colton mad.

Sparks fly the moment Colton and Ace meet on a sultry night club dance floor. But getting involved with a client, even one as fiery and beautiful as Colton Connolly, is a line Ace is unwilling to cross. Colton might be attracted to Ace, but he'd been burned before. He might be willing to put his life in Ace's hands, but not his heart.

As the Florida nights heat up, so does their passion, and Ace and Colton are faced with a difficult choice—take the plunge and risk it all, or play it safe and walk away?

If Ace can keep a deadly threat from robbing Colton of a future....

ONE

"GODDAMN IT, Ace, get your ass back here!"

King's indignant shout came through Ace's earpiece, and it made his lips curl into a wicked grin. He hit the accelerator, and his Chevy Camaro Zl1 convertible roared like a wild beast. With the wind whipping through his hair, he tore down Anastasia Park Road, his vehicle mere feet from the black SUV trying to outrun him. Did they really think they were going to escape *him*?

"You're not Vin Diesel in a fucking Fast and Furious movie! You're going to get yourself killed!"

"It's like you don't even know me," Ace shouted with a laugh, swiping his Glock from the holster under his arm. He leaned to the left and fired a warning shot, which hit the left taillight. The SUV swerved, regained control, and then lurched forward at full speed.

"Did you just open fire in a *state park*? Jesus fucking Christ!"

"Language, buddy. What would Momma say?"

"Don't you bring your mother into this!"

"There's nothing but road and trees. Besides, you need to be watching your blood pressure, old man."

"Old— *Fuck you*! I'm a year older than you."

"Technically, two years older." Ace leaned over again, this time shooting out the right taillight, making the SUV swerve again. *Amateurs*. "My birthday's not for another two months, which puts you at forty-one while I'm still in my thirties."

"Would you stop shooting!"

"Why?"

"Why? *Why*? The 'why' should be obvious, you little shit!"

Ace tried hard not to laugh. King made it way too easy. "Like I said, there's no one out here, so relax. I'll have them before they reach A1A."

"When I get my hands on you—"

After some scuffling, Red's smooth rumble came over the line. "Ace? You gotta stop, buddy. Let the police handle it. Fifteen minutes. They'll be with you in fifteen."

"No can do, pal. My client, my problem."

"Yeah, I get that, but, Ace, you're not liable if the product you're contracted to transport gets hijacked before you arrive to transport it."

Fuck that. Didn't matter that when he'd arrived at the client's house, the client was screaming at a black SUV burning rubber, making off with the man's million-dollar antique firearms collection. The point was, it was *his* client, and no fucking way was he letting these assholes get away with this shit on his watch.

"Ace?"

Ace smiled at the sound of his cousin's thickly accented voice, part of the Hispanic heritage they shared thanks to

Ace's Cuban mother. "Hey, the family's all here! Hi, Lucky. How's King?"

"Pacing the office and saying something about you sending him to an early grave. Por favor. Can you please not give our best friend and boss an ulcer, please?"

Ace snorted out a laugh. "King's like a fucking Florida roach. Indestructible. A *tank* landed on him, and he's still alive. Remember that?"

Red and Lucky erupted into barks of laughter, loud and boisterous. Man, he loved these bastards.

As expected, King was back on the line snarling at him. "Now you listen to me, you arrogant pain in my ass. You better do whatever the fuck you set out to do and not get dead, or I am going to hunt you down and murder you!"

"Well, that makes no sense. How can you murder me if I'm already dead? I mean, I guess maybe if I was dying and then you strangled me, or if—"

"Ace!"

"Got it. Get the job done. Don't get dead. That should be our new motto. I can see it now, right beneath the Four Kings Security crest. Clients will love it."

"*You—*"

"Gotta go. Don't let Red eat all the donuts, and tell Lucky he still owes me fifty bucks." He could hear Lucky cursing him out in English and Spanish before Ace disconnected the call. Time to put an end to this. He'd given the assholes two warnings, which they chose to ignore.

"Three strikes and you're out." With the opposing traffic lane empty, Ace floored the accelerator and pulled up beside the SUV. The driver looked at him, and Ace waved, gun in hand and a big smile on his face. He motioned for the guy to pull over, but was flipped off for his trouble.

"Okay, have it your way." Ace prepared to shoot out one of the tires, but the guy wrenched the steering wheel, and Ace slammed the brakes. "Fucker tried to slam into me! So that's how it is, huh?" Ace stroked his steering wheel. "Don't worry, baby. No one's gonna hurt you. Daddy's gonna take care of it." Pedal to the metal, he charged forward into the empty lane and sped past the SUV until he was several feet ahead. They were getting close to A1A and, more importantly, traffic. He jerked his steering wheel, the Camaro spinning until he was facing the opposite direction. He put the car in reverse and slammed the accelerator down, grinning at the stunned driver of the SUV as he whizzed by before moving into the lane and putting them almost nose to nose. Ace *whooped* loud, adrenaline rushing his system. Who did these guys think they were dealing with? Defensive driving was a staple of Four Kings Security. And the years Ace had spent driving all manner of vehicles over every kind of terrain didn't hurt either.

Movement from the passenger seat drew Ace's attention. The guy stuck the MP5 out the window, but before he could aim, Ace shot out one front tire, then the other. And unlike Ace's car, which was equipped with run-flat tires, these guys had shit. The SUV's driver lost control, careening off the road and into the shrubbery. Ace spun his car back around and followed, then hit the brakes when the SUV lurched to a stop. He put the car in park, unfastened his seatbelt, and got out. He was about to walk toward the SUV, when he heard King's nagging voice in his head. With a grunt, he removed his double holster and snatched the tactical vest off the passenger seat. He quickly strapped it on, secured his Glock, popped the trunk, and pulled out his Taser shotgun.

Once the trunk was secure, he headed off into the dense shrubbery, shotgun at the ready. The only noise around him was from A1A traffic in the distance. He stalked toward the SUV, making sure to remain crouched low in the dry and dead overgrowth. It was after noon, and although the temperature was in the low eighties, the seventy percent humidity and glaring sun were trying to bake him. His black T-shirt was already sticking to his back, and sweat beaded his brow, the weight of the tactical vest certainly not helping. Having hunted through worse conditions, he barely registered the discomfort.

The SUV rocked, and the two front doors opened. The driver and his companion dropped out of the vehicle into low crouches. The driver held a handgun close to him, his companion the MP5. They darted to the end of the SUV, and the driver opened the trunk. A large armored crate sat in the back, and Ace shook his head. Were they planning on using a bunch of antique firearms?

"Fuck," the driver hissed. "It's got some kind of high-tech lock."

No shit. These guys were obviously new to the whole hijacking gig. Did they really think a gun collection worth millions of dollars was going to be shoved in any old box? Ace recognized the crate, and that particular brand of awesome was equipped with biometric locks and a fingerprint scanner, so these dudes were shit out of luck. Ace steadied his breathing and crept into position right behind the two men. He'd seen all he needed. Gingerly he stood and aimed the shotgun at them.

"Any heart conditions I should know about?"

"The fuck?" MP5 guy and his companion jumped like spooked cats. They spun around, staring at him before their eyes dropped to the shotgun in his hands, their expressions comically bewildered. It was probably the bright yellow sections of the gun that were throwing them off.

"The fuck is that?" the driver asked, motioning to the shotgun.

"You didn't answer my question. Heart conditions. How's your ticker?"

The two men exchanged glances before the driver shook his head. "My heart's fine."

"Mine too," the other replied.

"Glad to hear it." He fired the shotgun in quick succession, hitting the driver's companion first, then the driver, the 500 volts of electric shock dropping them to the ground, giving Ace roughly twenty seconds. Sirens filled the air, and by the time the police arrived on the scene, Ace was leaning against his car, arms folded over his chest, with the two men zip-tied on the ground by his feet.

Four squad cars skidded to a halt, and Ace waved at them. One very tall, very annoyed-looking officer wearing aviators got out of his car. He swaggered over to Ace like a cowboy from an old western, or more like a cowboy from Texas, since that's what Officer Mason Cooper had been in another life. Mason towered over Ace, long legs, broad chest, and thick biceps, his large hands resting on his utility belt. He moved his aviators onto his head, his full lips—which Ace knew firsthand tasted very nice—pulled into a thin line.

"Good afternoon, Officer Cooper," Ace said, grinning wide.

"Fifteen minutes," Mason growled, that slow Texan drawl of his bringing back memories of them in bed together, naked, all that hard muscle pressed against Ace, his sexy rumble making Ace's toes curl. "You couldn't wait fifteen goddamn minutes?"

Ace squinted at him. "Is that a rhetorical question?"

Mason's ice-blue eyes narrowed. He grabbed Ace's arm

and started hauling him away from the car before calling out over his shoulder. "Get 'em outta here. I need a word with Mr. Sharpe."

Ace held back a smile at Mason's manhandling. "Well, this brings back memories."

Mason grunted, making sure they were far enough from the other officers before he released Ace, his low timbre doing lovely things to Ace's groin.

"You okay?" Mason raked his gaze over Ace, his eyes darkening with lust. He tugged on one of Ace's vest straps. "You listened."

Ace rolled his eyes. "Yeah, well, it was either that or have King nag at me about it."

"I like how you were more concerned about King naggin' at you than the possibility of ending up with a bullet in you."

"I believe the two are not mutually exclusive. Remember when you arrested Red?"

Mason groaned. Loudly.

"Yeah, how's that 'not being nagged by King for the foreseeable future' working out for you?"

"How many times do I gotta apologize for that? I was doin' my goddamn job. I shouldn't have to apologize! It was my first day. I didn't know who the fuck y'all were. I answered a B&E, Red was there and strapped. How the fuck was I supposed to know he'd been hired to babysit the property? It wasn't until King arrived at the precinct and everyone lost their fuckin' minds because I'd apparently pissed off the Second Coming that I was told about y'all."

Ace doubled over, laughing at Mason's traumatized expression. Like he was having flashbacks of first meeting King. It had not gone well. The thing was, Ward Kingston only lost his shit with those he considered family because his emotions got the better of him, but with everyone else? He didn't even have to talk. It was impressive. King gave off this weird vibe of familiarity, like he suddenly morphed into whatever guy the person he was dealing with had a soft spot for. He became their big brother, their beloved son, their favorite cousin, a long-lost love, and then they were eating out of his palm and they'd do anything not to disappoint him. It was something in those deep blue eyes of his and the way he smiled.

"I'm glad you find my distress amusing," Mason mumbled. He glanced over his shoulder before turning his attention back to Ace. "So, what you up to this weekend?"

"Providing King doesn't murder me? FYI, if you can't find the body, flex those manly muscles in front of Lucky. He'll sing like a canary."

Mason scoffed. "No offense, but your cousin's a manwhore."

"Why would I get offended? He wears the status with pride."

"Besides, you know I ain't interested in Lucky." His blue eyes softened, and Ace swallowed hard as he looked away.

"Coop...."

Mason let out a sigh. He nodded before letting his head hang. "I know. Doesn't hurt to try, though, right?"

"That's where you're wrong, Coop," Ace said, gently poking Mason over his heart. "It does hurt. We tried, remember?" Mason Cooper was a great guy. Problem was, after almost a year of dating him, Ace knew as much about him now as when they'd first met. Mason had secrets. Lots of them. He also had major trust issues. The fact he couldn't bring himself to confide in Ace—someone who made his living operating with complete discretion—after almost a year, made it clear they had no future together. Ace could have dug into Mason's past or run a thorough background check, but he respected Mason, and looking into him without his permission would have been an unforgiveable breach of whatever they'd had. Having access to the information, didn't give him the right to use it.

The sex had been amazing, and the intimate moments even better, but Ace needed more. The problem was he cared about Mason, which led to them hooking up several times after their breakup. Having Mason shut him out each time he tried to get close had become too painful, so he'd done what he did with every guy who made him feel like he'd want more—he left them before they could leave him. They could be friends. Nothing more.

"I reckon you're right," Mason said quietly. "It was good, huh?"

Not trusting himself to speak, Ace nodded. He patted Mason's shoulder. "I'll follow you to the station." He spun on his heels, walked backward to his car, and winked at Mason. "Gotta call this in. I'll be sure to tell Lucky you asked about him."

Mason's laugh when he flipped Ace off made him smile. Whatever demons Mason was battling, Ace hoped the guy found some peace. He deserved to be happy.

Ace helped two officers haul his client's crate into the back of Mason's squad car before he climbed behind the wheel of his Camaro. "Thanks, officers!" Ace waved as he waited for Mason to get into his car.

Watching the man walk by was always a treat. As soon as Mason was on the move, so was Ace. Since his client's property was now in police custody, Ace wouldn't be letting it out of his sight until his client arrived at the precinct. It would take some time for the property to be released from evidence, then Ace would transport it as agreed. Soon as he was done, he'd drive off to his home away from home. Of course, that meant having to deal with his less-than-thrilled brother-in-arms. If all else failed, he'd do what he'd been doing for years when it came to pissing off King. Hide.

Ace peeked through the open blinds of his cousin's office. Lucky was at his desk, and the room appeared devoid of one large fire-breathing King. Ace slipped inside and closed the door quietly behind him, then peered out the window to check the hallway outside one more time before closing the blinds. Lucky's lips quirked up, but he didn't move his eyes away from his laptop screen.

"My life hasn't flashed before my eyes, so I'm guessing he's busy?" Ace headed for Lucky before a noise outside in the hall had him diving behind his cousin's desk. Just because he didn't see King, didn't mean King wasn't close. They'd had years of training and honing their skills in the art of invisibility, among other things, all of which proved extremely useful for their current careers. Unfortunately when his boss was ex-Special Forces like Ace was, the chances of getting away with anything were slim to none.

"You made it to my office in one piece, you know? So I would say that is very likely."

Ace cursed under his breath. He checked his watch. "Has he eaten lunch? You know how hangry he gets if he doesn't eat lunch."

Lucky leaned back in his chair. "He was about to have lunch, but then he found out you'd gone all Vin Diesel."

Ace scoffed. "Don't be ridiculous." He smiled evilly. "It was more Mad Max."

"I would advise you not tell him that. Also, it was Bibi's BLT."

Ace let his head fall against the desk's edge with a groan. "I'm fucked."

"Sí. Muy. You know how much King loves Bibi's BLT, and how much he *hates* when the tomatoes make the bread all soggy and gross. He is right; it is very disgusting."

"Wait." Ace looked up at him. "What else did she bring?"

"For Red, his favorite—steak and aguacate tacos. For me, the carnitas, and for you, un Cubano."

Ace's stomach growled, and he all but drooled on himself. Damn it, Bibi's sandwiches were foodgasmic. "And, uh, where's my sandwich?" Like he didn't already know.

Lucky's grin was wicked. "In King's office."

"He's holding my sandwich hostage?"

Lucky nodded. "He's a little terrifying, you know?"

Suddenly Ace perked up, and he smiled wide, hopeful. "Where's Red?"

Lucky groaned and shook his head. "Come on, bro. Don't send Red to do your dirty work. That's just, like, wrong."

"But Red's the only one who's safe from King's wrath. No one can resist that big, sappy smile of his. He's like a big puppy. Who gets mad at a puppy?"

"King will know you sent him, and then he's going to be even more pissed. He might even tell Tía."

Ace gasped. "You really think he'd tell my mom?" Who was he kidding? King would totally tell on him, and his mom would take King's side too. Lucia Olga Sharpe had claimed the Kings, Joker, and Jack as her own, and after discovering King had lost his parents while he'd been deployed, she'd gone full-mode Cuban mom on him, mothering him as if he were her own. Since Ace *was* her own, he reveled in her smothering King with motherly love. King adored her, no mistake about that, but she also drove him crazy. God help him if he didn't call at least once a week to keep her updated on his health, his love life, the latest gossip, and a complete rundown of his meals for the day. Ace being around for that phone call so he could laugh his ass off was always worth King passing him the phone when he was done so Ace could be interrogated.

The door opened, and Ace stiffened.

"We've got a meeting with a potential client in twenty minutes," King growled. "I know you're there, Ace."

Ace popped up from behind the desk. "Can I have my sandwich?"

"I ate it."

"You ate my sandwich? What the hell? That is so not cool!"

"Neither is your agenda of driving me crazy. Tell me something—do you put it on your calendar? When you come into the office, do you sit at your desk, check your calendar, and say, 'Oh, look at that. Today is Drive-King-Batshit-Crazy Day.' Is that what you do?"

"You're very dramatic. I particularly liked the way you looked at your hand as if you were looking at a calendar. You should consider a career in improv."

King narrowed his eyes. "My office. Now."

"Fine, but only because I'm concerned about your health."

"Thanks. I appreciate that," King grumbled as Ace followed him down the hall toward King's office.

"That's me. Mr. Considerate."

"I'm impressed you managed to say that with a straight face."

Ace beamed at him. "I've been practicing."

"You're the most exhausting human being I've ever come across." They walked into the office, and Ace dropped into the chair next to Red, his fist held out for a fist-bump but his smile aimed at King. Red chuckled and fist-bumped him.

"I love you," Ace told King.

"I love you too, now shut up."

Lucky's grin was ridiculous as he took the seat next to Ace. "You two are so cute."

Ace and King both grunted.

"Okay, everyone shut up. In fifteen minutes, we'll be meeting with Mr. Paxton Connolly II, the current president and CEO of Connolly Maritime Enterprises and Worldwide Shipping Solutions. This is a family-owned business that's been around since the early 1900s. It employs over five thousand employees worldwide, with a revenue of over two billion dollars. Their company provides everything from liner services to freight logistics, ocean and inland transport, and project management. Due to health issues and advisement from both the family doctor and his ex-wife, Mr. Connolly will be retiring, and his son, Colton Connolly, will be taking over. Colton has been working alongside his father since college, being groomed to take over the family business. Colton is the reason Mr. Connolly is meeting with us."

"Someone has a problem with Colton taking over?" Red asked.

King shook his head, surprising them. Usually when they were approached by a company like Connolly Maritime regarding a changeover of that magnitude, it meant corporate unrest.

"According to Mr. Connolly, everyone loves Colton.

The company has one of the best employee benefits packages in the state, followed by the lowest employee turnover rate, and that's thanks to Colton. They've watched him grow up in the company. There's no one better to take over. The reason Mr. Connolly is meeting with us is because his son has been receiving death threats."

Ace was confused. "I thought you said everyone loved Colton?"

"The threats haven't been in regard to the company, or the takeover, but to his being gay. My first thought was a disgruntled employee, but when I spoke to Paxton Connolly, he rejected the idea immediately. It made no sense to him that someone would have a problem with his son now, when Colton's been out and proud since high school. Paxton is very supportive of his son, and Colton's sexuality has never been kept from, or been an issue with, the company. I've read the threats, and it's clear someone's taken a personal interest in Colton, and the threats have been steadily escalating."

King swiveled in his chair and clicked a tiny remote. The flat-screen on the far wall of the office came to life, showing six printed letters. They got up and approached the screen to study the letters that had been sealed in evidence bags and scanned.

"The ink, paper, and font used are generic. No fingerprints or residue of any kind was left behind. Whoever handled these was smart," King said, returning to his desk. The rest of them followed.

"Colton hasn't been taking the threats seriously, and Paxton wouldn't even be aware of what was happening had an intern in Colton's office not accidently opened a delivery meant for his boss. Inside the box was this letter." King handed them each a photocopy of a printed letter that looked similar to the ones on the screen.

SINCE YOU LOVE COCK SO MUCH, I'M GOING TO CUT YOURS OFF, SHOVE IT DOWN YOUR THROAT, AND WATCH YOU CHOKE TO DEATH ON IT.

"Jesus." Ace shook his head. He dropped his copy onto King's desk like he might catch something. "You said it was inside a box. Was there anything else in the box?" Whatever it was, he felt sure he wasn't going to like it.

King nodded, showing them a crisp color photograph of what looked like a large phallus covered in blood, and the three of them recoiled. "It most likely belonged to a large animal, possibly a horse."

"Oh God, that's disgusting." Ace gagged and shoved the photo away.

"That is one sick fuck," Lucky murmured.

"For the last three months, the letters have been arriving twice a month, different days each time. Paxton Connolly and I have spoken at length, and he's ready to sign a contract but wants to meet you all first. One of you will be Colton's personal security, but I want the three of you working this. Red, Jack's going to take over the risk assessment you were scheduled to do for Mr. Garcia. Lucky, I know you were looking forward to going down to South Beach to work the LGBT film festival, but I need you on this, so I'm sending—"

"Don't say it," Lucky groaned.

King didn't bother hiding his amusement. "Joker."

"Fuck! King, that was supposed to be *my* gig, bro." Lucky crossed his arms over his chest, his pout fierce. "Fine, but if he throws it in my face, I'm going to punch him."

"As long as it's off the clock," King drawled before turning his attention to Ace. "Jack is going to make the transport once your client's property is released from evidence. I'll be contacting the client after our meeting."

Ace nodded. He hated leaving things unfinished, but King wouldn't have made the call if it wasn't important. King's phone beeped.

"Yes?"

Jay, King's executive assistant came on the line. "King, Mr. Paxton Connolly is here."

"Show him in, please."

They all stood when Jay opened the office door, and a tall, broad-shouldered, handsome man with silver interspersed with his blond hair walked in. Lines formed at the corners of his gray eyes when he smiled.

"Thank you so much for meeting with me on such short notice, Mr. Kingston." Paxton nodded to the rest of them. "Gentlemen."

King thanked Jay, who promptly closed the door behind him, before taking Paxton's outstretched hand. "Please, everyone calls me King. Let me introduce you to the rest of the Kings. This is Russell 'Red' McKinley, Eduardo 'Lucky' Morales, and Anston 'Ace' Sharpe."

They took turns shaking Mr. Connolly's hand. The man looked genuinely pleased to see them.

"It's a pleasure to meet you all. I've heard nothing but great things about Four Kings Security. When I consulted with my head of security, he recommended your company without hesitation."

"We're glad you came to us, Mr. Connolly," King said, showing Paxton to the chair directly in front of his desk. Red and Lucky resumed their seats, and Ace pulled up one of the extra chairs lining the office and placed it next to King's desk facing Paxton and the others.

"If you don't mind my asking," Ace said, needing to know, "is there a reason you didn't hire your current security company for this?" Connolly Maritime already had a security company on the payroll. They were a little old-school, with a few loose cannons, but they were a good bunch.

"I don't mind at all. We've been with our current security company for decades, long before Four Kings. They've been invaluable to us, but as my son pointed out at our last board meeting, Connolly Maritime has grown exponentially over the years, and with the changes in the market, and technology, comes the need to take our security to the next level. I've already spoken to our security manager. Our contract with them will end on very amicable terms. Every trusted counsel I've sought gave me the same response. If you want the best, hire the four Kings. My hope is once the threat to my son is taken care of, we can discuss continuing our business relationship. If you can protect my son, I'm confident you can protect our company."

If Four Kings Security could secure a contract with Connolly Maritime, it would be huge. They could look into moving forward the expansion down south and open the office in Miami ahead of schedule.

"We'd be honored to represent you and Connolly Maritime. First, why don't you tell us a little about your son," King said. "I'm assigning your son's protection to Ace, Lucky, and Red." He motioned to the three of them. "But one of them will personally provide round-the-clock protection to your son. To determine which one of them would be the best fit, I need to know a little more about Colton."

18 CHARLIE COCHET

Paxton nodded. "I love my son. He's a good man, and I couldn't be prouder of him. Speaking frankly, he can also be a little shit. Stubborn as the day is long. I wish I could say he gets it from his mother, but that would be unfair of me since he gets his stubbornness from me. From his mother, he gets his temper. His business sense is second to none, and he has a way with people, but when you get on his bad side, look out. He despises insincere flattery and personal questions, warm one minute and freezing your balls off the next. I already approached him with the idea of hiring private security for him over this, and he was completely against it. This is going to piss him off to no end. If there's one thing my son won't stand is loss of control. Whoever you send in, he'll see as a threat to that control, and he will fight it with everything he has."

Ace cleared his throat. "Permission to speak freely, sir?"

"Ace," King warned.

"It's okay," Paxton said, putting up a hand. "You boys say what you need to say. No minced words."

"Your son sounds like a pain in the ass." Ace ignored King's heavy sigh and the way he closed his eyes, clearly summing patience.

Paxton scoffed. "Understatement."

"That's why I'd be perfect for the job."

King sat back and moved his gaze to the ceiling. It was clear he agreed, but that didn't mean he had to like it. The room was quiet, all eyes on King. Several heartbeats later, he leaned forward, his gaze meeting Paxton's and his fingers laced together on his desk.

"I won't lie to you, Mr. Connolly. Ace's methods are somewhat... unorthodox."

"Meaning?"

Ace grinned. "Sir, I'm an asshole at the best of times, but I'm damn good at what I do. My job will be to protect

LOVE IN SPADES   19

your son, not coddle him or kiss his ass. If he wants a fight, he'll get one, and believe me, he won't win. I *will* protect him, by any means necessary."

"In other words, you're not going to take his bullshit."

"Not if it interferes with me doing my job."

"Good. We've already established a way to make this contract watertight, with an added clause stating he can't fire you or cancel the contract. Anything and everything will have to be authorized by me."

"Yes, sir."

They all turned their attention to King, and Ace held back his smile. He could see the exact moment King made the decision. His friend actually flinched. It was subtle, but it had been there.

"Ace is correct. If your son is difficult to work with, Ace is the best King for the job. He'll take lead on this, be your son's personal security, assemble a team, and get started as soon as the contract is signed."

"Excellent. I've forced him to take some time off under the guise he's got vacation time he needs to use, but because he's a stubborn pain in the ass, he's informed me he'll be working from home a good deal of the time. For all I know, he'll show up at the office. Kid's always done whatever the hell he wanted anyway."

Ace liked the guy already. Too bad Colton was going to *hate* Ace. It seemed like the guy had finally met his match.

TWO

WHEN HAD his life become such a mess?

Colton closed his eyes, allowing the alcohol and pulsing beat of the music to wash over him. This was exactly what he needed. How long had it been since he'd let himself have some fun? It seemed like all he did these days was work and, as of late, argue with his parents.

They only want what's best for you.

He promptly told the little voice in his head to shut up. Yes, his parents loved him, and he never forgot how fortunate he was to have such accepting parents or how privileged he was. He had no doubt everything they did was because they wanted what was best for him. The problem was, no one ever asked *him* what he thought was best for him. If he wanted something that didn't fit within the constructs of what was expected of him, he had to fight for it. His mother thought him "headstrong," his father "difficult," but the truth was, he only wanted to be himself, not the version of him everyone else wanted him to be. It had taken a long time to figure himself out and get his life in order, but when he had, he'd been as happy as the next guy.

Then some sick bastard figured he'd try and take control of Colton's life. If that wasn't bad enough, his father kept insisting he hire a private security company. Not happening.

Colton leaned against the bar and smiled widely at Seth when he had the man's attention. The large mountain of a bartender with rippling muscles sauntered over. He wiped the bar's surface in front of Colton before leaning his arms on it.

"What can I get you, Mr. Connolly?"

"Good evening, Seth. Tequila, please. Something nice."

"You got it." Seth winked at him before turning and reaching for a bottle of Don Julio 1942 Anejo Tequila—a very nice choice indeed. He poured the golden liquid into a Himalayan salt tequila glass, returned the bottle to the shelf, and placed the drink in front of Colton, with a wedge of lime on a black napkin. "Here you go, beautiful."

"Thanks." Colton returned Seth's smile before throwing back the tequila and following through with the lime wedge, aware of Seth dropping his eyes to Colton's lips. Seth had made his interest known quite some time ago, and although Colton didn't mind the flirting, he had no intention of getting involved with anyone he did business with. Seth was a stunning man—all chiseled jaw, rich olive skin, and soft brown curls—but he was employed by Frank Ramirez, the owner of Sapphire Sands and a good man Colton considered a dear friend, one who trusted Connolly Maritime with the import of the club's alcohol.

A couple of shots later—and a little more flirting—Colton was feeling better. The club was packed tonight, but then it was always packed. Colton had been coming here since he'd turned twenty-one. It was familiar. Safe. All the employees knew who he was, and—with the exception of a couple of flirts like Seth—he was treated as if he were family. Every year on the club's anniversary, Colton hosted the Sapphire Sands Charity Masquerade Ball. The ticket price for the event was outrageous, but none of the guests who attended minded the hefty price since the profits all went to an LGBT charity. It was a night of elaborate costumes, with an exquisite meal prepared by a celebrity chef, and incredible entertainment that went on into the wee hours of the morning. Colton looked forward to it every year, and as the benefactor, he hadn't missed one since its inception.

"Is Frank in?" Colton asked Seth.

"Yeah, he's in the office. Want me to call him for you?"

Colton shook his head. "I'll drop by the office and say hello. Thanks, Seth."

"Anytime, Mr. Connolly."

Colton had every intention of getting drunk off his ass, dancing, and forgetting his troubles for a while, but first he'd see Frank. His friend would be pissed if he found Colton was in the club and no one had told him. Thirteen years ago, the guy had appointed himself Colton's unofficial big brother, despite Colton's attempts at the time to get into Frank's pants. At twenty-one, Colton had found the thirty-one-year-old former firefighter turned club owner a walking wet dream. It had been very annoying, not to mention sexually frustrating, at the time. While his brain had been focused on getting laid by the stud with pitch-black hair and honey-colored eyes, Frank had been building a friendship between them without Colton even realizing, a friendship Colton was eternally grateful for now that he was wiser and older.

Deciding to stop by the men's room first, Colton walked in to the elegant black marble washroom to the sound of sniffing. A young man paced one end of the bathroom. He was a little overdressed for a night at the club. It was possible he'd come to meet friends after work, but something told Colton that wasn't the case. He was young, late twenties at most, with fair hair he'd clearly been running his fingers through—as it was now sticking up at odd angles—and blue-green eyes. Pretty.

Colton had finished his business and washed his hands, when the sniffling turned into tears.

"Hey, do you need help?" Colton asked gently, making his way over. The young man gave a start. He'd clearly been so lost in thought he hadn't even been aware Colton was there.

"Oh God, I'm sorry. Crying in the bathroom. This is so cliché and embarrassing. I should go home, but I forgot my wallet, and that asshole was supposed to have been my ride home, but then he probably wasn't even going to take me home. Man, even that sounds cliché. I'm a walking cliché. I can't believe this is happening to me. No, of course it's happening to me. It's exactly the kind of thing that would happen to me." The more he paced, the more distraught he seemed to be getting.

"What's your name?"

"Joshua." He wiped at his eyes and pressed his lips together, most likely to hold back more tears.

"Joshua, why don't you start from the beginning."

"It's pathetic. I'm pathetic. I really thought...." He shook his head, fresh tears welling in his eyes.

"You're not pathetic. You're upset. Tell me what happened."

"Long story short? I got a new job as an assistant for a big law firm downtown, and I thought I'd been hired because I am damned good at what I do. Turns out I was hired because I was a 'hot piece of ass.' My boss's exact words." Joshua took the tissue Colton handed him. "Thank you. He brought me along tonight to meet an important new client. Asshole wanted to fuck me in the back rooms. When I said no, he kept trying until I pushed him. He got pissed and told me not to bother coming to the office tomorrow, how I was nothing but a hot piece of ass."

"He fired you because you wouldn't let him fuck you?"

Joshua nodded. "I even moved because he asked me to. He said I needed to be closer to the office in case he needed me, and he'd make sure the firm reimbursed me. I had to dip into my savings, but with my new salary, it would be okay. I could pay that back in and finally start paying off my student loans, and now I don't even know how I'm going to pay my rent next month or my car payment. I won't even be able to afford health insurance." His bottom lip quivered before he broke off into a sob. "Oh God. What am I going to do?"

Colton gently laid a hand on Joshua's shoulder and gave a reassuring squeeze. "You're going to thank your lucky stars you're no longer working for that bastard. It's going to be okay, Joshua. I promise." He pulled out his wallet and one of his business cards, which he handed to Joshua. "Call that number tomorrow morning and speak with Nadine, my executive assistant. She'll be waiting for your call. One of our other executive assistants is leaving for a job in New York in a couple of months. In the meantime, he can train you on his duties. The pay and perks are very generous, and the company offers full health insurance coverage. We would love to have you at Connolly Maritime if you're interested."

Joshua's jaw dropped, and his blue eyes went huge. He

moved his gaze to the card in his hand, then up to Colton. "You.... Did you just offer me a job?"

Colton nodded. He shoved his hands in his pockets. "If you're interested." Joshua's gaze turned wary, and Colton chuckled. "Google me. I can wait. Two *n*'s, two *l*'s in Connolly."

Joshua worried his bottom lip between his teeth, his eyes back on the card in his hands.

"Go ahead. I won't be offended. I like that you're not taking my word for it."

With a nod and a small smile, Joshua pulled out his phone and tapped away at his screen. Colton knew what he'd find. He'd been featured in *Forbes Magazine* more than once, along with a host of other magazines and websites connected to the business world. There were pictures of him at charity events, parties, tournaments, races. The more Joshua scrolled through the information on his phone, the wider his eyes became.

"Oh my God." His head shot up, and he gaped at Colton. "You really are Colton Connolly. My boss has talked about you."

Colton scrunched up his nose. "I don't think I want to know."

"He was hoping to get himself invited to the White Party on Fisher Island."

"What's your boss's name?"

"Ted Booker."

"Yeah, Ted Booker is never getting an invite. The White Party on Fisher Island is hosted by an old family friend and current business associate. Booker will be lucky if he's allowed on the island." Most people had no idea how much power and sway Connolly Maritime had in the state of Florida. Colton wasn't one to throw his weight around, but if it was to teach a man like Ted Booker a lesson, then he'd happily do it.

"You could have your pick of anyone you wanted for this job. Why would you help me? You don't even know me."

"Intuition. I have a good feeling about you, Joshua. You're not going to let me down, are you?"

Joshua shook his head emphatically. "No, sir." Tears welled in his eyes again, and he threw his arms around Colton. "Thank you so much, Mr. Connolly! I swear I won't let you down."

Colton chuckled and patted Joshua's back. "I know you won't. Everything's going to be fine."

"Oh, so you won't let me fuck you, but you'll let this guy all over you?"

Joshua spun around with a gasp, then took a quick step behind Colton.

Colton assumed the tall handsome man with an ugly sneer was Joshua's ex-boss, Ted Booker.

He squinted at Colton. "Do I know you?"

Colton smiled wide. "Colton Connolly, of Connolly Maritime." He enjoyed the way Ted's face drained of color. "And I would appreciate you showing my employee a little respect."

Ted stared at him. "What?"

"Joshua is the newest member of Connolly Maritime. It would seem his previous employer couldn't see his value. Oh, and the White Party? Not going to happen."

Ted took a step forward, and Colton blocked his path. The man was red with embarrassment and indignation, his fury aimed at Joshua.

"What did you do, you little slut? Did you get on your knees for him and suck his dick to get a job?"

Colton put a hand out to stop Ted from advancing. "You need to walk away, Ted. *Now*."

"Or what?" Ted snarled.

"You've already lost face. If you don't walk away and leave Joshua alone, I'll make sure you lose more than that."

Ted reeled back as if he'd been struck. "Are you threatening me? Over that—"

"Careful," Colton warned. "I won't ask twice."

"What the hell is going on in here?" Frank stormed in along with two of his security personnel, his dark brows drawn together as he looked from Ted to Colton.

Ted spun to face Frank and thrust a finger in Joshua's direction. "I want that little shit thrown out on his ass! He's been spreading lies about me and putting my business at risk because he didn't get what he wanted from me."

Frank glanced over at Colton, who discreetly shook his head. With a sigh, Frank stepped closer to Joshua, his tone gentle when he spoke. "Sweetheart, talk to me."

Joshua melted under Frank's gaze, and Colton held back a smile. He knew that look well. It was hard not to go weak in the knees when Frank Ramirez looked at you with those soulful eyes. Like nothing in the world could hurt you while he was there. Frank opened one arm for him, and Joshua walked into his embrace, settling against Frank with a small sigh. He lifted his face so he could meet Frank's gaze, and when he spoke, his voice never wavered.

"You can check the security cameras. Mr. Booker brought me here under false pretenses. When he pulled me into one of the back rooms, I made it very clear I wasn't interested, and even after clearly saying no, I had to push him away for him to get the hint. Then he fired me. Mr. Connolly was here while I panicked, and when he found

LOVE IN SPADES   29

out what happened to me, he offered me a job at his company."

When Frank lifted his gaze to Ted, Colton almost felt sorry for the guy. Almost.

"Mr. Booker, are you not familiar with the word *no?*"

"He's lying," Ted insisted.

"If I check my security feed, I'm not going to see you pulling this young man into the back, then?"

"He went willingly," Ted spat out. "He wanted it."

Colton cringed, and he saw the exact moment Ted grasped how screwed he was. He'd put his foot in it. If he hadn't, Frank's murderous glare would have made it obvious. As someone who'd spent his adult life trying to save people, Frank did not take kindly to Ted's words. He addressed his security personnel, his narrowed eyes still on Ted.

"Get this piece of shit out of my club." Frank thrust a finger in Ted's direction. "If you ever try to set foot in here again, I will personally beat the shit out of you, and if you so much as come near—" His expression softened when he looked down at the young man tucked against him. "What's your name, sweetheart?"

"Joshua."

Frank turned his attention back to Ted, his face once again transformed into a mask of disdain and anger. "If you go anywhere near, Joshua, you'll be dealing with me."

"And me," Colton added. He didn't know much about Joshua, but something told him the young man could use a little care and support. Something about him brought out a protective streak in Colton, and if the way Frank was holding on to Joshua was anything to go by, Frank felt the same. It was incredible, how quickly people could form a connection. One minute they were strangers, the next they were friends.

Ted begged and sputtered apologies as he was dragged out of the bathroom.

"Dick," Frank muttered. He turned to Joshua and held him out at arm's length, looking him over. "Are you okay?"

Joshua nodded. "Thank you... um...."

"Frank Ramirez. I own Sapphire Sands."

"You own the club?"

Frank chuckled at Joshua's wide eyes. "Yes. Now, what would you like to do next? Do you want me to call you a car to take you home?"

Joshua seemed to think about it. He opened his mouth to reply, but Frank cleared his throat.

"Or, you could hang out with me for a while in my office. There's a comfortable couch if you're feeling tired. Are you hungry?"

Joshua nodded, his cheeks flushed.

"Okay, how about you wait for me in my office, and I'll stop by the kitchen, have them make you something special. Seth will make you whatever you want to drink. On the house. For having to deal with that prick. I don't allow that kind of behavior in my club."

Joshua looked stunned. He looked from Frank to Colton, who nodded, then back to Frank before dropping his gaze to his fingers.

"You really don't have to, Mr. Ramirez. You've done so much for me already."

Frank placed his fingers to Joshua's chin and lifted his face so their eyes could meet. "Please, let me take care of you for a little while, Joshua."

Joshua nodded, and Frank smiled warmly. He used the

LOVE IN SPADES   31

radio clipped to his belt to call one of his men, who happily escorted Joshua from the bathroom.

"Don't forget to call the office," Colton called out to Joshua.

"I will! Thank you so much, Mr. Connolly."

When they left, Colton leaned against the wall, his arms folded over his chest, and his wide smile aimed at Frank. "You're adorable."

Frank narrowed his eyes at Colton before walking out of the bathroom, Colton on his heels.

"Where do you think you're going so fast, Mr. Ramirez?"

"Shut up." The noise of the club exploded around them, and Colton followed Frank into the kitchen.

"You were very sweet with him."

Frank spun on his heels and squinted at him. "What are you doing?"

"Me?" Colton blinked innocently. "He's clearly smitten with you. I remember the feeling. It's your arms." Colton playfully squeezed Frank's biceps, which were straining against the black suit jacket. He looked incredible as always in his tailored black suit with a black button-down shirt and black tie. Colton dropped his arms and laughed at Frank's glower. "You make people feel safe, Frank, and Joshua clearly needs that."

"He's too young," Frank muttered.

"You're not an old man. For Christ's sake, you're forty-three."

Frank scoffed. "Which makes me ancient to most of these guys."

"Ridiculous. Look, it's obvious Joshua's not had it easy. I think he dodged a bullet with that asshole Booker." Frank opened his mouth to argue his case some more, but Colton held a hand up to stop him. "Think about it. Now I'm going to go get stinking drunk in your club. Go take care of that sweet young man, and if he happens to want to take care of you, maybe consider it, huh?"

Frank's frown was deep. "Why are you going to get stinking drunk?"

The man never missed a beat. "That's a conversation for another night," Colton said, patting Frank's cheek. He turned and headed for the doors leading out to the club before Frank could stop him. "I promise I'll tell you all my secrets then."

Frank scoffed at that. "I already know all your secrets."

"Then you can tell me some of yours," Colton called out as he opened one of the doors.

"Yeah, yeah. Let someone know when you're ready to go and they'll call you a car."

"Love you, Frank!"

Frank waved him off, and Colton laughed as he headed back to the bar. Time to have some fun and forget the Teds of the world.

THREE

"WE SHOULD HAVE CALLED. We owe it to Frank."

As always, Red was the voice of reason, and normally Ace would have agreed, but this time they had a slight conflict of interest.

"Frank probably already knows we're here," Lucky grumbled through Ace's earpiece.

Which was also true.

"He's obviously busy," Ace replied, scanning the club, "or he'd be out here already. Let's find Colton. If we have any problems, we'll talk to Frank. Oh, and whoever Frank finds first gets to break the news." His friends' curses made him smile. "Let's do this."

Ace liked Frank. A lot. The man often broke bread with the Kings, and together they drank to their mutual heartache, but as it turned out, Frank and Colton went way back. The two were close friends. If Frank had to choose between Colton and keeping his contract with Four Kings Security, no doubt Colton would win. Frank was as loyal as they came. Of course, Ace wasn't above using that friendship to get Frank to cooperate. If Paxton didn't know about the threats to his son until recently, chances were Frank probably didn't know.

They'd arrived at Colton's Ponte Vedra mansion only to be informed by Asha, Colton's household manager, that her employer wasn't home. If that wasn't bad enough, the man was out clubbing. No security. Not even his driver. They were *not* off to a good start.

The heavy bass of the sensual beat reverberated in Ace's chest, his heart seeming to pound along with the music as he waded through the sea of sweaty, gyrating bodies. Beautiful go-go boys with sinewy bodies danced on plinths raised high above the crowd, wearing nothing but glittering blue high-top sneakers and tiny sparkling blue shorts that accentuated their pert round asses. Their flawless-looking skin shimmered with pale blue glitter as they moved suggestively to the rhythm. Unable to help himself, Ace paused long enough to admire the sleek, dark-skinned beauty on the plinth closest to him, earning him a wink and a kiss blown his way from lush, lip gloss covered lips. Ace groaned and quickly reminded himself he was here for business, not pleasure.

Walking through the crowd of scantily dressed men in various stages of undress—and drunkenness—was like walking into a bull pen with a huge target painted on his back. Hands slid over his arms, neck, face, and ass. If he stopped for too long, someone's fingers would find their way into his hair. Men smiled at him, blew kisses, and murmured dirty promises. Sapphire Sands was not a club for window shopping. The backrooms weren't filled with men chatting over drinks. The club encouraged guests to let their freak flags fly, offering total discretion. It was members only, and to be a member, you had to have major cash or clout. The four Kings held companywide membership, a perk offered by Frank, thanks to his contract with Four Kings Security, a contract that would continue as long as no laws were broken. The Kings didn't involve themselves with businesses linked to illegal activities, which meant no drugs or solicitation allowed.

Sex was certainly happening in all corners of the club, but it was consensual and no money exchanged hands. Frank Ramirez prided himself on running a tight ship.

Getting through the crowd was slow, especially when Ace kept getting stopped by men hoping to hook up. Lucky's voice came through his earpiece.

"Have I mentioned lately how much I love my job?"

Ace chuckled. "Remember you're on the clock, so hands off the pretties."

"You suck."

"I do. Long and hard. But not right now."

"Dick."

"Really, Lucky?" Red laughed. "You know if you open that door, he's going to walk right through it."

"This is like trying to find a needle in a—what do you call it? Hayloft," Lucky grumbled.

"You mean haystack," Ace offered.

"Yeah, that. Haystack. A very sexy, half-naked haystack. ¡Santo cielos! Perdóname, madresita mía."

"I don't even want to know what you've found that you're asking your mother for forgiveness. How about you find me Colton Connolly?"

"Triplets, Ace. *Triplets*. Hola, mi amor. Ay, pero que belleza. ¿Sí? Yo también. Te lo prometo."

"Lucky," Ace warned.

"Right. Work."

It was like letting a wolf loose in a henhouse. Thankfully, Lucky valued his job, and his life, more than whatever orgy he was undoubtedly wishing he was in the middle of right now. No orgy was worth King's wrath if he found out they'd fucked around while on the clock. Not that such a thing had ever happened, or would happen. As crazy as Ace drove King with his actions sometimes, he *never* crossed that line, the one that would put the Kings' professionalism or reputation into question. They were too damned good at what they did to be distracted by a pretty face or spectacular ass. Ace came to an abrupt halt, and for the first time since opening Four Kings Security, he found himself repeating those words in his head.

He'd found Colton Connolly.

There was no missing him. Not because he was jaw-droppingly gorgeous with a face that screamed classic Hollywood and a body that tried to make Ace's dick spontaneously combust, but because he was wearing a red shirt so blindingly bright—not to mention so tight it looked painted on—that it was impossible *not* to see him. The scarlet button-down shirt stood out against his tanned skin and black dress slacks. When he straightened to his full height, he towered over almost everyone. At six foot five, his body wasn't bulky, but lean with a trim waist Ace could easily wrap his hands around, a waist currently being gripped by a heavily muscled man plastered to his back while a shorter man was pressed to his front. The man at his front wedged his hands between Colton's ass and the other guy's groin. Another five men danced around them, circling like sharks, waiting to get a piece of Colton. Mr. Colton Connolly clearly did not know the meaning of lying low.

Ace pressed the PTT button on the concealed microphone clipped to the inside of his jacket sleeve. "I've got eyes on Colton. I'm going in. Stand by."

"Copy that," Lucky replied.

"Copy that," Red echoed.

Ace gently pushed men out of his way, his eyes on Colton, who moved his hips in a way that should be illegal. His lips were parted, and his arms were up and around the neck of the man behind him. Colton's legs were impossibly long, and Ace could easily imagine them wrapped around him, those long fingers caressing, squeezing. Colton's skin was slick with sweat, a wave of fair hair falling over his brow. The man oozed sex and sophistication.

Okay, get ahold of yourself.

Ace approached the men, and when he reached them, he spoke loud enough to be heard over the music. "Excuse me." He stood just over the shoulder of the guy at Colton's front, his height allowing Colton to see him. Their eyes met, and time slowed, everything going out of focus except for Colton, who stood bright and vibrant in front of him like some ethereal god. Fuck, he was stunning. Ace sucked in a sharp breath at the intensity of those striking blue-gray eyes, and the world came crashing back. Colton's gaze dropped to Ace's lips, and his tongue darted out to lick his bottom lip.

"Oh yes, please."

Ace hadn't expected the deep rumble dripping with sex that was Colton's voice. It sent a shiver through him, and he found himself coughing into his hand to regain control.

"Can I talk to you in private for a minute?"

Colton shook his head, shouting over the music. "No, but you can dance with me." He kissed the cheek of the man who'd been humping his leg, then pushed him to one side, grabbed Ace, and dragged him in front of him, their bodies pressed together. At six foot one, Ace was hardly a short man, but Coltan had four inches on him, which was certainly a new experience. Ace needed to talk to the guy in private, or better yet, convince Colton to leave with him. He hoped Colton wasn't the kind to cause a scene. Colton shoved his knee between Ace's legs and grabbed his ass.

Shit, the guy was stronger than he looked, and horny as hell, judging by the raging hard-on pressing into Ace.

"Fuck." Ace was so close he could feel Colton's hot breath on his skin. He closed his hands around Colton's wrists and moved the man's hands away from his ass, bringing them up to trap them between them. Colton splayed his hands against Ace's chest, his lips curled up sinfully.

"Fucking comes later," Colton purred into his ear, sucking Ace's earlobe into his mouth.

A tremor went through Ace, and he stiffened. This wasn't happening. Whatever reaction he was having to this man had to stop. Colton was a client. His safety was paramount. Ace flipped the switch and stepped back, Colton's wrists still in his grip. When he spoke, his voice brooked no argument.

"Mr. Connolly, I'm not here to dance. I need to speak with you. It's important."

"Do we know each other?" Colton raked his lustful gaze over Ace. His eyes were glassy, and his movements made it clear he was more than a little drunk. "I would definitely remember you, handsome. My God, look at your eyes. There's like three different colors in them. I bet you hear how beautiful they are all the time. No, we definitely haven't met, or I would have been all over that," he said, motioning to Ace's general person. "I'd really like to get my hands on you."

Damn. Okay. No. "Colton, my name is Ace. I'm from Four Kings Security. Your father hired me to protect you."

It was like someone dumped a bucket of ice water on Colton, and those stunning eyes turned to steel. "My father sent you?" Colton's voice was clipped, and he jerked his wrists from Ace's hold. He crowded Ace, jabbing a finger against his chest.

It took everything Ace had not to grab that finger and drop Colton to his knees, though he'd bet the man would look delicious on his knees. *Stop it.*

"I'll tell you what I told my father. I don't need babysitting," Colton spat out. "And I sure as shit won't allow a bunch of trigger-happy mall cops to tell me what to do."

Ace refused to be baited. "Colton, your father is concerned about your safety, so he hired the best. I promise you, we'll get through this, but I need you to come with me."

"Fuck off," Colton snarled, turning to leave, but Ace caught his arm. Colton whipped around, and Ace expected him to throw a punch. Instead, Colton smiled, though it didn't reach his eyes. Ace braced himself as Colton slid his hands up Ace's chest, his voice husky as he spoke into Ace's ear. "You're not going to leave, are you?"

Ace shook his head. "Not without you."

"You want to guard my body?" Colton took hold of Ace's hand and pressed it to the rock-hard cock straining against his dress pants. "What else do you want to do to my body?" He slid his other hand slowly down Ace's chest toward his belt. "Is it included with your services, or does my father have to pay you extra?"

Ace pushed Colton away from him, ignoring Colton's breathy laugh. Flipping Ace off, Colton turned and headed through the crowd. Ace stayed close to him. He hit his microphone's PTT button.

"I've got Colton. He's not cooperating. Red, you know what to do. Lucky, meet me by the door. I'll be there with Colton as soon as I can. Everyone else, remain in position, continue to secure the area, and keep an eye out for Frank."

Ace received immediate confirmation from his team. The last thing they needed was for Colton to cause a scene, but it was looking more likely with every step he took away from Ace. If someone hired Four Kings, they were serious about their protection, and although clients weren't thrilled about the intrusion into their lives, they understood it was necessary and cooperated fully. Colton didn't want their protection, and he clearly had no intention of cooperating.

Colton slipped between two men at the bar, where he was served immediately, the barman's smile wide as he passed Colton a glass of amber liquid. He leaned in to say something to Colton, who laughed and said something in return, clearly flirting. Colton downed the liquid in one gulp as the large man to Colton's left turned to face him, eyes darkening with lust as he raked his gaze over Colton.

"Hey, sexy." The man's muscles had muscles, his white T-shirt straining over bulging biceps. He leaned in close and reached for Colton. Ace snatched his wrist before he could make contact.

"Hands off," Ace warned, releasing the guy when he jerked his arm away.

"He with you?" the guy asked Colton, his eyes on Ace.

Colton threw back a shot of something. He smacked his lips together, then ordered another before he turned his attention to the big man and slid a hand up the guy's broad chest. "Ignore him. He's nobody."

"Kinda pissed for a nobody," the guy said, glancing at Ace who stood silent and still, waiting.

"He's my bodyguard."

The guy laughed. "That right? Well, if you don't want to be his Whitney, you can sure as hell be mine."

Colton laughed. He slipped his arms around the guy, who whispered something in Colton's ear. Colton nodded, and the man licked his lips, his hands gliding around to grab Colton's round ass, making Colton groan.

"We need to go," Ace said, taking hold of Colton's arm. Colton pulled himself out of Ace's grasp and took the large man's hand in his, but instead of leaving, he leaned in to murmur in Ace's ear.

"I'm not going anywhere yet. Unless you'd like to suck my dick instead. No? Then fuck off."

Ace didn't know what pissed him off more, the fact Colton thought he could talk like that to him or how fucking turned on it made him.

Colton grinned knowingly. "Coming?"

Ace gritted his teeth, his hands balled into fists at his side.

"I didn't think so."

If that's how Colton wanted to play it, Ace was all in. He followed the two men toward the back of the club, through a set of thick black curtains that led to a narrow hall with rows of curtained-off sections to each side. The music drowned out the moans and grunts. Colton led his hookup into an empty room, releasing the man's hand before he turned to Ace, who'd taken up position outside to wait.

"Oh no. That won't do. What if he tries to hurt me?" By this point, Colton's words were slurring. Despite his soft tone, his eyes were filled with anger. "Now be a good little mall cop and stand inside the curtain."

Ace stood guard inside the now closed curtain, his jaw clenched tight as Colton allowed himself to be pushed up against the far wall. Colton moaned as the man slobbered all over him, kissing his neck, under his jaw, his face. Colton put his arms up above his head, his eyes on Ace as the man unfastened Colton's pants, and yanked them down, moaning at the skintight red boxer-briefs. He pulled them down, and Ace looked away before he could see anything. He ignored Colton's chuckle. It was quickly followed by a decadent moan. The noises that followed had Ace clenching his jaw so tight he was afraid he'd break something. Either Colton was getting the best fucking blow job in the history of blow jobs, or he was purposefully playing it up to piss off Ace. If Ace had to guess, he would say the latter.

"Oh fuck, yeah. Suck my dick just like that. Oh God, your tongue feels amazing on my balls."

Instead of getting mad, Ace had to fight back a laugh. He had to give it to Colton. The guy was a spitfire. He was determined to get his way. *Little shit.* Ace schooled his expression as he focused on the black wall ahead of him, and not on Colton writhing, gasping, and groaning on his right. It was like listening to porn. Ace had his hands clamped in front of his groin. He steadied his breathing and focused on his job. Whatever reaction Colton was hoping to get out of Ace, he wasn't getting it, and it became obvious when he shouted dramatically.

"Oh God, I'm going to come!"

Ace pressed his lips together in a thin line to keep from barking out a laugh. Well, someone was a bit of a diva.

"You gotta let me fuck you."

Colton hummed thoughtfully before looking to Ace. "Hey, got a condom?"

Ace knew exactly what Colton was trying to do, and it might have worked on someone else, but not him. He reached into his jacket pocket, pulled out a condom and a packet of lube, and tossed both over his shoulder as he turned toward the curtain.

"Don't be long. Car's waiting." Ace reached for the curtain as Colton called out.

LOVE IN SPADES   43

"Where the hell do you think you're going?"

Ace concealed his smile. "Outside. My job is to protect you, not help you get off."

"Don't you walk away from me," Colton said indignantly, coming to stand in front of Ace. He zipped his pants up, his red shirt half-in, half-out of his waistband. He was so riled up, he was practically vibrating. Colton's skin was almost as red as his shirt, and he raked a hand through his already disheveled hair.

Ace couldn't help his chuckle. Looked like Mr. Colton Connolly was a little too used to getting his way.

"Are you laughing at me?" Colton fumed.

"I'm amused you think I take orders from anyone, much less you."

Colton's eyes went wide before he stumbled forward and poked Ace in the shoulder. "You're fired."

"That's the beauty of contracts. They're binding. You can't fire me. Only your father can." Ace gave Colton his best shit-eating grin. "Now, you have a good time. Oh, hold on." He reached into his jacket pocket and pulled out a small pack of tissues. "Here you go."

If looks could kill, Ace would have disintegrated then and there.

Colton spun on his heels and stormed off. Ace quickly followed, turning to shrug apologetically to the big guy, who stood wondering what the hell was going on. Colton thundered back into the main part of the club and headed straight for the bar. Ace caught his arm before he could reach it.

"I think you've had enough. Time to go."

"You're right. I have had enough. Enough of *you*." Colton tried to pull himself out of Ace's grip, and maybe if he wasn't so drunk he might have actually managed it, instead of tripping over his own feet. Ace took hold of Colton's other arm to steady him. "Get your hands off me."

Ace sighed. "Colton, I'm here to help."

Since he couldn't get away from Ace, Colton changed tactics, pressing his body to Ace's. "I've heard about you *Kings*. Bunch of has-beens who couldn't cut it in Special Ops turned security guards."

Ace slammed Colton up against the wall. "Now you listen to me, because I'm only going to say this once. You fuck with me all you want, but you say one goddamn word about my brothers, and the only threat you're going to have to fear is *me*."

Colton's lips curled into a satisfied grin. "Ooh, big words for such a little man."

Ace's eyes welled up at the memory of his fallen brothers, and he shoved away from Colton, hating he'd exposed his one vulnerability. "We came home because we lost half our unit. Good men torn away from their families. From their children and loved ones. They were heroes who fought for this country. Show a little respect."

Colton swallowed hard and looked away, shame washing over his face. "I'm sorry," he said quietly, wiping away the wetness in his eyes. "You're right. That was uncalled for."

Ace nodded. He hardened his gaze and rounded his shoulders. "We're leaving."

"I apologize for my callous words regarding your brothers-in-arms. That doesn't change anything else. I don't want you here. I won't have anyone controlling my life. Not that sick bastard, not my father, and certainly not an entire team of armed men."

"Too damned bad," Ace growled, infuriated with himself for letting Colton get to him. He knew better than

LOVE IN SPADES   45

to respond to provocation, and yet he had. "Are you going to cooperate?"

Colton crossed his arms over his chest, chin lifted defiantly. "No."

"Okay. We'll do things your way." He grabbed Colton's arm, ignoring the man's yelp as he hoisted him up into a fireman's carry.

"What the hell?" Colton struggled against him, but Ace was stronger, and sober. He carried Colton through the crowd, which thankfully moved out of his way.

"Put me down, you Neanderthal!"

They passed the bar, and Colton yelled out at the bartender he'd flirted with earlier. "Seth, call Frank!"

Shit. He had to get Colton out of here fast. "Excuse me. Boyfriend's had a little too much to drink." Ace winked at one particularly large man who looked like he was about to step in to help Colton out. "I forgot our anniversary," Ace said loudly. The man looked uncertain.

"He's not my boyfriend," Colton yelled furiously. "I wouldn't date this man if he were the last dick left on the planet!"

Everyone around them howled with laughter, and Ace cringed. "Come on, baby. Don't do me like that. I promise I'll make it up to you." Ace patted Colton's ass, earning him an infuriated scream from Colton and a laugh from everyone around them. "Let this be a lesson to you, boys. Remember your anniversaries!" He carried Colton toward the front door when someone dropped a brick wall in front of him.

No, wait, it was Frank. Ace smiled at him. "Hey, Frank. How's it going?"

Frank's eyes were comically wide as he looked from Ace to Colton and back. "The fuck is going on?"

"I don't have time to explain right now," Ace said, starting to feel Colton's weight. "But I'll call you."

"First he brushes me off, and now you?" Frank crossed his beefy arms over his chest, and Ace was sure he'd hear fabric tearing any minute now.

"Frank, tell this brute to put me down!"

"Ace, put him down," Frank growled.

"I can't. I've been hired to protect him, and since he doesn't want to cooperate and he's drunk off his ass, I'm taking him home."

Frank's head snapped to Colton. "You hired the Kings to protect you? Jesus Christ, Colt, what the hell have you gotten yourself into?"

"One," Colton said, holding out two fingers. Seeming to notice, he put one down. "One, I didn't hire them. Two"—he kept one finger up—"my father hired them. Wait, that's part of one, so, one A. Two, I'm not drunk."

Frank shook his head before turning his attention to Ace, who winced.

"Frank, buddy, I love you, man, but Colton here is no delicate flower."

"Are you saying I'm fat?" Colton yelled right into Ace's ear.

Ace groaned and moved his head away. "And now I'm deaf. Thanks, Frank. Look, I'll have him call you when he's sober. His dad hired the Kings to protect him, so you know it's serious. I have to get him home."

"Don't do it, Frank," Colton said.

"Shit." Frank rubbed his hands over his face. He looked worriedly at Colton. "Tell me. Is it true? Your dad hired them to protect you because you're in danger?"

Colton waved a hand dismissively. "It's nothing. Some sick bastard sending me shit."

LOVE IN SPADES   47

Frank seemed to think about it, then let out a resigned sigh. "I'm sorry, Colton, but you mean a lot to me, and I'd never forgive myself if I let you out of here without the Kings and something happened to you. You're in good hands. I promise." His gaze turned hard when he looked at Ace. "Keep him safe. If you need anything, let me know."

"Damn it, Frank!" Colton tried to wriggle free, but Ace held on tight, thanking Frank as he hurried out the club door. Red was in front with the SUV, and Lucky opened the back door for him. Ace bent over, shoved Colton inside, then quickly climbed in after him and slammed the door. Colton tried to open his door, but Red had control of the locks.

"Get us out of here," Ace told Red as soon as Lucky was in the passenger seat. They all strapped in, and Ace reached for Colton's seatbelt only to have his hand smacked away.

"I can put my own seatbelt on," Colton snarled, jerking the seatbelt toward him. "You're an asshole. Did anyone ever tell you you're an asshole? I can't believe Frank. Let me out of here."

"You do realize you're trying to open the door of a moving vehicle while wearing your seatbelt?"

"Shut up," Colton snapped. He turned his attention to the front. "Who are you?"

"The guy driving is Red," Ace replied.

Colton moved his gaze to Lucky, who was smartly keeping his big trap shut. "And who are you?"

"That's Lucky."

Colton moved his narrowed gaze to Ace. "I wasn't asking you, was I? Ace, Red, Lucky. What are you? Vegas rent boys?"

"Are you asking me or them?" This had to be the most fun he'd had on a job. Colton was shitfaced. His cheeks were red, his eyes glassy, and he was swaying. Here was a man who was about to take over a multibillion-dollar company, and he was acting like a drunk college brat. It was highly entertaining.

"I'm looking at you, aren't I?"

"I'm not really sure." Ace couldn't help but tease. He pointed at Colton's left eye. "This eye's looking at me, but that one's looking a little uncertain."

Colton slapped his finger away. "I hate you."

"You don't know me."

"Thank God for that."

Ace chuckled.

"Is this how you treat all your clients?"

Colton went off on a tirade, which Ace easily tuned out. He texted King to let him know they had Colton and were on their way back to his house. The car suddenly fell silent, and he looked up to find Colton slumped against the window, mouth wide open as he drooled on the glass.

"Did he run out of oxygen?" Ace checked the man's pulse. "Nope, still alive."

"This is not going to be easy," Lucky said, meeting Ace's gaze in the rearview mirror.

"No, but it might be fun."

FOUR

HE WAS DYING.

At least it felt that way. Colton buried his face against his pillow. Why was his head trying to collapse in on itself? He shut his eyes tight before slowly cracking one open, then the other. The curtains to his room were thankfully still drawn. The last thing he needed was blinding sunshine coming through the wall of glass doors and floor-to-ceiling windows on both floors of his bedroom. He adored his bedroom and spent more time up on his second floor sitting area than he did in his living room, especially when the cooler weather allowed him to curl up in front of the fireplace surrounded by the sounds of the crackling fire and the ocean outside his open doors.

The moment his broker showed him the pictures of the house, he'd fallen in love. Two-and-a-half floors of high ceilings, wall-to-wall windows, and balconies outside almost every room. The vast amount of white gave everything a clean, elegant, and spacious look. It also brightened everything up, which he loved, but not at this moment. Bright white was not favorable to a hangover.

With a groan, he dragged himself to sit up, his bare feet hitting the plush carpet. He frowned down at his white undershirt and red boxer-briefs. When had he stripped out of his club clothes? And how the hell had he gotten home? Considering his hungover state, it was no surprise last night was somewhat of a blur. He remembered being at the club, trying to drown his sorrows in alcohol and male bodies. One particular male body flashed through his mind clear as day, and he hung his head with a groan. Of course his brain would hang on to *the* one guy he wanted to forget most, and his cock was in cahoots with his brain. Colton glared at his dick.

"Traitor."

Pushing to his feet, he lumbered into his bathroom and flinched against the brightness when he stepped inside. Grumbling, he brushed his teeth and splashed water on his face before getting undressed. Removing the only two items of clothing on his body shouldn't have been as difficult or painful as it was. As soon as he was naked, he stepped into his shower and turned on the water as cold as he could stand, in the hopes of getting rid of his morning stiffness and the images of mesmerizing gold-green eyes, a chiseled jaw, and pouting lips. The man had freckles, for fuck's sake, strewn across his nose. Colton remembered wanting to taste them, among other things. Who the hell gave that man the right to be so beautiful?

"No. You are *not* doing this," he scolded himself. His painfully hard erection had other plans, and Colton took himself in hand with a moan as he vividly recalled the gorgeous man who'd stolen Colton's breath the moment he'd stepped in front of him. Ace. Fuck, he was gorgeous. Square-jawed, lush lips, intense eyes, and a hard body. Too bad he was off-limits. Considering Colton had no intention

LOVE IN SPADES   51

of seeing Ace again, what could it hurt? Leaning one hand against the stone tile wall, he closed his eyes, letting the cool water sluice over him as he stroked himself, his bottom lip between his teeth.

Why was it his mind had no trouble conjuring what Ace felt like against him, the way his body molded perfectly to his? Those strong calloused fingers closing around his wrists and that low gravelly voice sent a shiver through him. His breath hitched, and his hand moved quicker over his searing flesh as he pumped his cock, pleasure rippling through his body. He knew nothing about the man who'd intruded on his life, but the more Colton tried to put Ace out of his mind, the more his brain tormented him with flashes of a cocky grin, long lashes, and the way he'd manhandled Colton. Fuck, he didn't even know that kind of thing turned him on, and from what little he could recall, Ace hadn't been completely unaffected. That was another tidbit of information his brain had decided to retain.

"Fuck." Colton gasped, feeling his muscles pull and tighten as his orgasm built and exploded in a white light in front of his eyes as he came hard, his body trembling. He dropped his head against the tiles and closed his eyes. "Happy now? Got it out of your system? Good. It's over."

He finished showering, turned off the water, and dried himself before heading back into his bedroom. From his walk-in closet, he picked a slim-fitting taupe button-down short-sleeve shirt with striped cuffs, black slacks, and a brown belt that went with his brown brogues. Feeling better already, he fixed his hair, grabbed his wallet, keys, and a pair of aviators that matched his outfit, and headed downstairs in search of breakfast, and more importantly, coffee.

Maybe it had all been a dream? The details were rather fuzzy, so it was possible. He remembered parts of being in a car with two other men. Maybe they'd dropped him off? Once downstairs, he neared the kitchen and the sound of voices, one of them a familiar low sexy growl that went straight to his groin.

No. No way. He hurried into the kitchen and came to an abrupt halt at the sight of the sinfully beautiful man leaning against the breakfast bar counter, a mug in his hand. Colton's eyes were drawn to the man's right hand, and the small black spade tattoo between his thumb and index finger. He was dressed in black military cargo pants, a black baseball cap with the white Four Kings Security logo, black boots, and a black T-shirt that stretched obscenely over his muscular chest and biceps. Across from him sat the two men who had been in the car last night, both sporting card suit tattoos in the same spot as Ace on their right hands, one a red heart, the other a black club. One was big and broad with auburn hair and warm hazel eyes. Next to him was a slightly smaller, leaner Hispanic man. Colton remembered him speaking Spanish at one point to the other men. His hair was black, his jaw stubbled, and his eyes deep chocolate brown. The three men studied Colton intently. It was unnerving.

"Good morning," Ace said cheerfully. He pointed to the espresso machine. "There's coffee."

Colton narrowed his eyes. "You kidnapped me."

"No. We—your security detail—escorted you home." Ace picked up a tablet, then held it out to Colton, who marched over and snatched it from him. His stomach dropped and his ire rose with every word he read. It was a contract between his father, their company, and Four Kings Security. *Oh, that sneak.* If it had been between him and Four Kings, Colton would have been able to do something about it, but his father had brought the company into it, and company policy covered hiring outside security for Connolly's executives should the need arise. How could his father do this to him?

"I'd like to discuss the changes we need to make around the property."

"Changes?" Colton's head shot up and he stared at Ace. When he spoke, his voice came out quiet. "You want to make changes to my home?"

Ace's gaze turned sympathetic. "I promise you, we'll only make changes to what we consider essential, and no one will invade the privacy of your bedroom. Any changes we make are a direct result from the risk assessment we've conducted. It's necessary to maintaining the security of both you and those under your employment here on the property. Your security system is good, but not up to our standards. We'd like to install thermal cameras and new biometric keyless locks that operate with approved retina scans and fingerprints. The new system will electronically monitor anyone entering and leaving the property and will keep an electronic roster we can access from anywhere. We already have three specially equipped SUVs on-site, one outside the property, one parked at the front of the house, and one at the back, ready twenty-four hours a day for a quick getaway. We'll provide additional transport as needed. In case of noncompliance, changes can be made on your behalf. It's in the contract. But I would rather run things by you and get your input."

Ace gently took the tablet from Colton's hands, which was smart considering Colton's hands were shaking. They'd come into his home, and now they wanted to take control and make changes. If he refused, they'd been given the go-ahead to continue.

"Your panic room has been inspected and would need

updating with the new system, but we also have a safe house ready in case of emergency evacuation, the location of which is disclosed only to me and my security team. Your home will be stocked with emergency supplies, including satellite radios and shortwave radios. You already have a top-of-the-line power generator, which is great. I'll be showing you some nonlethal approaches to stopping and detaining someone. It helps keep the lawsuits to a minimum. If we deem it necessary, I can arrange lessons in close-quarter combat. King is running a thorough check into everyone at Connolly Maritime and anyone who does business with you. He'll let us know the moment any red flags pop up. Nadine provided me with your schedule, so I'd like to sit down with you to discuss some of the concerns I have on events with a high-risk factor."

Colton walked to the cupboard, took out his favorite coffee mug, and made himself a latte while Ace continued to tell him how they'd be stripping Colton of his freedom piece by piece. Once his latte was done, Colton took a sip, then left the kitchen, heading to the stairs, Ace on his heels.

"Colton, I know this might seem extreme, not to mention inconvenient, and I'm sorry, but we're talking about the very real threat to your safety. It's my job to do whatever it takes to keep you safe."

Do whatever it takes. Colton flinched at the words. It wasn't the first time he'd heard those very words, and they'd destroyed him. Never again. He took the steps two at a time, stalked into his office, and slammed the door in Ace's face. He locked it, ignoring Ace's knocking.

"Colton, please open the door. Let's discuss this."

After placing his mug on his desk, Colton picked up the phone and called the only other person who would have known about this.

His mother.

"Colton, my darling. Are you—"

Her soft voice filled with concern made Colton explode. "How dare he do this to me!"

"Sweetheart, he's your dad. He loves you."

"He promised me he would never interfere in my life like this."

"This is different. He's trying to protect you, and quite frankly, I'm glad. When were you planning on telling me?"

"It's nothing," he grumbled, feeling guilty for worrying her. They hadn't always seen eye to eye, especially after she'd divorced his father. He'd been in high school at the time, struggling with teenage angst and coming to terms with his being gay when his mother decided she'd throw divorce on top of everything. A long line of therapists had tried to help him understand that although his parents had fallen out of love with each other, it did not mean they didn't love *him*.

"Nothing?"

The hitch in his mother's voice brought him out of his thoughts, and he braced himself. He needed far more caffeine for this, and his headache wasn't helping any. Usually he could count on his mother to agree with him, since she had a tendency of being against whatever his father said, sometimes simply on principal. He should have known better since it concerned his safety.

"Some psychopath is threatening you to the point your father felt the need to hire one of the best security companies in the state, and you expect me to believe it's nothing? It is *not* nothing." She let out a sigh. "Honey, it's okay to be scared."

"I'm not scared," Colton snapped. "I'm livid. I will *not*

let anyone control me or my life. Not Dad and not some sick fuck!"

"Colton, please."

He took another sip of his latte, his gaze going out the window, and he gritted his teeth at the uniformed figures scattered around his property. God only knew how many more there were. Did his father hire an entire goddamn army? "My house is crawling with armed men."

She paused before speaking up, her tone playful. "You always did like a man in uniform."

Colton arched an eyebrow despite the fact his mother couldn't see him. "Excuse me?"

"Any of them sexy?"

As she said the words, Ace appeared outside his balcony doors. "No, they're arrogant, infuriating, and make me want to hit something," Colton ground out through his teeth.

Ace motioned to himself then inside the office. Colton flipped him off. To his horror, Ace opened the door. *Are you kidding me?* Damn it. He must have forgotten to lock it.

"Mom, I need to go."

"Honey, please, have a little faith in your father."

Colton promised to call her back later, then hung up. He marched over to Ace, until their chests were nearly touching. "Get the hell out of my office."

Ace pointed down to where he stood outside the door-frame. "I'm not in your office. Also, we need to have a talk about you leaving doors unlocked."

Unbelievable! He was going to strangle the man's thick tanned neck. "I'm pretty sure I fired you."

"Yeah, we've been over that, remember? You can't fire me."

"I didn't agree to this."

"You don't have to. It's tied to your contract with Connolly Maritime. You know very well they're within their right to mandate executive protection for any company asset at risk."

"You think you're so damn clever," Colton sneered, heading for the door. "Well, you and your men won't be staying. My father is overreacting. I'm going down there to speak with him, and you'll be packing your things when we get back." The contract he'd read stated Ace would be providing personal round-the-clock executive protection to Colton, meaning the man would be in his face practically every waking hour every day for who the hell knew how long.

"Colton, can we please discuss this? Just a few minutes, and I can explain why we want to make the changes I mentioned earlier. We're not trying to take over your life. I know it may feel that way, but all we want to do is make sure you're as secure as possible. Why are you so against this?"

Colton threw open his office door. "I don't have to explain myself to anyone, much less you." On the way to the front door, he did his best to ignore the infestation in his house. They were all over the damned place. He threw open the front door, his jaw dropping at the sight of Ace sitting on the concrete wall lining the tile steps, wearing aviator sunglasses, and a huge grin. How the hell had he gotten there ahead of him? He wanted to punch that stupid shit-eating grin off his stupidly handsome face.

"Good morning, Colton. Where would you like me to drive you this fine morning? I would recommend some breakfast first. It'll help with that nasty hangover."

Colton slammed the door behind him and stomped down the steps, then stopped in front of Ace. He opened his mouth to tell Ace what he could do with his suggestions when his stomach rumbled loudly.

"There's this little hole-in-the-wall café on the way that does a killer guacamole breakfast sandwich stack on sourdough bread. It's just what you need."

"You have no idea what I need," Colton snapped. His stomach growled again, and Ace chuckled.

"Maybe, but I know what your stomach needs. How about it?"

"Fine. If it'll get you off my back."

Ace opened his mouth to reply but seemed to think better of it. Colton narrowed his eyes. He stepped away, and Ace stood. Despite the few inches Colton had on him, he found himself taking an additional step back. The all-black outfit added to the formidable air Ace gave off. His posture and poise screamed former military. It would seem you could take the man out of the military, but you couldn't take the military out of the man. Ace bowed dramatically before motioning toward the SUV parked in the driveway.

Colton turned on his heels and stalked over to the vehicle, then crossed his arms over his chest when Ace opened the back door for him. The more Ace smiled, the more aggravated Colton became. He climbed in and fastened his seatbelt. Damn it. He should have gone around and sat behind the driver's seat so he wouldn't have to see Ace. It was fine. He was fine. He'd only have to put up with it for a few more hours until he convinced his father to cancel that ridiculous contract.

As they headed to wherever Ace was taking him, Colton was informed his household manager and his driver had been given paid vacations. Either Ace, Red, or Lucky would take over the driving using one of their specially equipped SUVs. The car was fitted with ballistic windows, run-flat tires, and a panic button. It was packed with emergency supplies, from a map with clearly marked escape routes stashed in the glove compartment, to food, water, first aid kit, a satellite phone, and radiation detector. In the trunk were a couple of fold-up bikes, and it even had an emergency cell phone hidden in the back in case someone tried to kidnap him using the car and tossed him in the back. The Kings seemed to be prepared for a host of terrifying scenarios Colton preferred not to think about.

Traffic wasn't too awful, and Colton managed to distract himself with the passing scenery outside the SUV windows. The sun was shining bright, the heat and humidity enough to send tendrils of sweat trickling down his back if he stood outside too long. As a native Floridian, his out-of-state friends teased him, saying he should have been used to the heat by now, but nope. He'd never get used to Florida heat and humidity. It was what it was, and he had to bear it like everyone else. Sometimes it was tolerable, and sometimes he wished he could conduct business from inside a pool of ice water.

When they arrived at their destination and Ace opened the door for him, Colton stepped down, stunned by the sight of the street in front of him. No parking, only dirt and asphalt in front of the small building.

"This is it?" Colton scanned the street, some of which was lined with small businesses that were either freshly painted and gave off a bit of a fifties vibe or looked as if they'd been closed for years. Across from the café was an apartment complex, and next door was a brick extension with one closed window. "This is like the town that almost was."

Ace chuckled. "Yeah, it's not the most glamorous street, but trust me. The breakfast sandwiches are amazing." He held the door open, and Colton walked in, removing his sunglasses so he could get a good look at the place.

The man hadn't been kidding when he said hole-in-the-wall. It resembled the inside of someone's kitchen. Old doors lined the counter, and the hanging lights were made of colanders. The tables and chairs were mismatched, and one wall had a section cut out with wood slats running from top to bottom, its wooden pegs displaying various loaves of bread and bagels. In front of it, a display case held several choices of pastries and cake slices. Ace sauntered up to the young woman behind the counter, removed his sunglasses, and flashed that perfect smile.

"Hi, Donna. How are you this beautiful morning?"

The young woman blushed and giggled. "It's even better now that you're here. What can I get you, Ace?"

"Two of those mouthwatering guacamole stacks, and two lattes. I'll take mine iced." He looked over at Colton. "Iced or hot?"

Colton narrowed his eyes. "Now you're ordering my food for me?"

Ace held his hands up in surrender. "You're right. I'm sorry. It's my favorite, and I got a little excited. I overstepped." Ace lowered his hands. "What would you like, Colton?"

"Hm." Colton took his time looking over the menu before finally smiling at Donna. "The guacamole stack sounds delicious. I'll have that. And a latte. Iced, please."

Ace hung his head, and shook it, a smile tugging at his lips in the corner.

Donna rang Ace up, and he winked at her. "We're going to eat out in the garden." He paused and glanced in Colton's direction. "Is that okay?"

Colton held back a smile. "That's fine."

With a smile, Donna disappeared to where Colton assumed the kitchen was.

"This way," Ace said, ushering him toward a door at the end of the room.

Colton lowered his sunglasses, and stepped outside, pleasantly surprised by the garden. It was very pretty, enclosed by a wooden fence, a large tree on one end, and lots of shrubbery and flowers surrounding the area. Two long picnic tables lined one side of the garden, light blue folded chairs sitting on either side and a blue umbrella to keep away the sun. Across from the picnic table was a smaller round table and another picnic table. Colton took a seat at the small round table, and Ace sat across from him. To their right, next to the tree, was a doghouse, and Colton couldn't help his grin when a tall slender beauty with a shiny gray coat and big brown eyes trotted over to him and laid her head on his lap, her slim tail wagging happily.

"Well, hello there, beautiful." He pet her head, scratching behind her ears, laughing as her tail-wagging had her entire butt moving.

"Looks like Misty's found herself a new friend," Donna said on her way over, a mason jar with iced coffee in each hand. She placed their drinks on the table, and Colton thanked her.

"She's gorgeous. Yes, you are. You are," Colton cooed, rubbing her fur.

"She's an Italian greyhound, and loves attention."

"And she will get *all* the attention." Colton smiled brightly at Donna, who let out a little gasp before turning to face Ace and not-so discreetly holding her thumbs up.

Ace laughed but didn't deny what she was insinuating. Before Colton could speak up, Donna whirled around and skipped back inside. Colton glared at him.

"Even though your sunglasses are mirrored—a detail you seem to have forgotten—I know you're giving me the skunk eye."

Colton moved his sunglasses to the top of his head and glared some more. "Better?"

"Your eyes are the same color as her fur right now. Stormy and stunning."

Colton straightened. "Are you flirting?"

"Complimenting. Are we not at that stage in our relationship?"

"We're not at *any* stage because we have no relationship," Colton hissed.

"Really?" The wicked look that came into Ace's eyes gave Colton pause. "I don't know. I mean, you grabbed my ass, rubbed up against me, and put my hand to your dick. I would say that constitutes as something."

Oh. My. God.

Ace let out a bark of laughter. "Oh shit, you don't remember, do you?"

It couldn't—he wouldn't—*oh my God*. Colton's face tried to set itself on fire. "That can't be right."

"About you groping me, coming on to me, or asking me if I wanted to suck your dick?"

Colton covered Misty's ears. "Do you mind?"

"Not really."

Ace took a sip of his latte before leaning his elbows on the table. "Before I told you who I was, you came on to me, pulled me against you, rubbed up against me, and grabbed my ass. After you knew who I was, you thought you'd make me go away by trying to make me uncomfortable with your sexuality. You put on a little porn show, remember?"

"I did no such thing!" Jesus, he was suddenly sweltering. He was about to deny everything profusely, but then he recalled a man he didn't know on his knees in front of him. It all came crashing back, and Colton gasped.

"There it is." Ace chuckled before taking another sip of his iced coffee.

Colton quickly lowered his sunglasses and turned away, ignoring Ace's laughter. His heart hammered in his chest, and he jumped to his feet, pacing the floor.

"Oh God." He'd been all over Ace, but how was he supposed to have known? When he first laid eyes on Ace, his dick had taken over, liking what it saw. He'd assumed Ace was there for a good time or to hook up, like all the other men who'd danced with him.

"Hey, whoa, it's no big deal," Ace assured him, gently taking hold of his arms and stopping his pacing. He moved Colton's sunglasses up to his head, and Colton couldn't even look Ace in the eye. "You're really upset about this. Why?"

"My behavior was completely inappropriate and unacceptable." He closed his eyes and shook his head. "Shit. After threatening that vile man for what he did to Joshua, I go and do something just as horrible."

"I don't understand." Donna headed for them with their sandwiches, and Ace released him. "Come on, sit and talk to me."

Colton nodded, not trusting himself to speak yet. He thanked Donna for his meal and took another sip of his coffee. His stomach rumbled, and Ace pointed to the sandwich in front of him. "Eat something first."

"I think I lost my appetite," Colton murmured. "I threatened to ruin a man for trying to force a young man to have sex, and—"

"And please tell me you're not about to compare yourself to that asshole."

Colton was taken aback by the conviction in Ace's tone and the anger in his eyes.

"Yeah, you were drunk and stupid, but you didn't make me do anything, Colton. No one can make me do anything I don't want to. Trust me." Ace leaned forward, his eyes never leaving Colton's. "You thought I was another guy looking to get in your pants, and after that, you didn't do anything I couldn't handle. I went along with your little game because I wanted to. I needed to get a read on you, and I did." He sat back and bit into his sandwich, then talked through a mouthful of it. "Eat."

Colton wasn't a hundred percent convinced, and he felt miserable about what he'd done, but if Ace said he was okay, Colton would take his word for it. "Fine, but I apologize regardless."

"Apology accepted," Ace garbled around his food. "Eat your sandwich."

"Fine." Colton cut his sandwich in half before picking one side up and taking a large bite. He moaned at the explosion of tastes in his mouth.

"Right?"

Ace looked so damned happy that Colton liked it, and in all honesty, it was damned good. His headache pulsed a little less, and he no longer felt sick to his stomach. It was so strange eating a casual meal with Ace. He knew nothing about this man other than what he'd heard. Plenty of his friends and business associates had hired Four Kings Security at one point or another. The private security company worked everything from executive protection to corporate espionage. They were one of the largest and most prestigious security companies in the state. All he knew was what he'd read in articles or found online, all public information about the six ex-Special Forces soldiers who retired from the military, four of them opening a private security company together and bringing in trusted and highly trained personnel, many of them ex-military or law enforcement.

From what Colton had read, the four Kings had earned their nicknames back during their military service, each one nicknamed after a playing card suit, namely the king cards. Ace was nicknamed after the king of spades. Lucky, the king of clubs. Red, the king of hearts. And King, the king of diamonds. Why they'd been given the nicknames was anyone's guess. When interviewed, the Kings refused to answer the question directly, merely stating it was personal and meaningful to them, enough for them to brand an entire company around those names. Although all four Kings owned the company, Ward "King" Kingston was the man in charge, which Colton found very interesting. Regardless, Colton would acknowledge his father had hired the best, but that didn't mean he was going to accept it.

***

TRAFFIC WAS light on I-295 N, and they reached Connolly Maritime in less than half an hour. Colton was about to instruct Ace where to park when Ace turned right, driving straight to Colton's designated spot inside the employee parking lot. The fact Ace knew where his parking spot was shouldn't have pissed him off as much as it did. He threw open the door, got out, and slammed the door behind him, not waiting for Ace before he stormed across the walkway toward the building's entrance. He went to open the door, but Ace beat him to it and opened it for him with a big grin.

Inside the lobby, Oscar greeted him from behind the marble security desk. "Good morning, Mr. Connolly."

"Good morning, Oscar."

Oscar cleared his throat and pointed to the small device in front of him. Colton frowned down at it.

"What is it?"

"Thumbprint scan. New security measures," Ace said before smiling at Oscar. "Good morning, Oscar."

Oscar nodded. "Good morning, Mr. Sharpe."

"Oh, you've got to be kidding me." Colton rounded on Ace. "Who gave you the authority to make changes in my company?" Ace opened his mouth, but Colton held up a hand. "Let me guess. My father."

Ace smiled ruefully before putting his thumb to the pad. A little green light accompanied a beep. With a frustrated growl, Colton jabbed his thumb against the pad. As soon as the green light appeared and it beeped, Colton headed for the private elevator that led up to the executive suits, ignoring Ace thanking Oscar for his good work on implementing the new security measures. Maybe Colton could catch the elevator before Ace reached him. He swiped his keycard, then repeatedly pushed the call button.

"Come on."

The doors opened, and Colton quickly stepped in. He turned, and Ace was there. *Damn it.* How did the guy do that? It's like he materialized from thin air to torment Colton. Ace stood beside him, and Colton tapped his fingers against his leg. Thankfully, Ace remained silent. As soon as they reached the top floor, Colton thundered out of the elevator and headed straight for his father's office. No one stopped him or greeted him, most likely due to the murderous look he knew he was sporting. His father's door was open, and he glanced up from his paperwork. Colton turned to close the door, intending to leave Ace outside, but Ace was already in the office.

"Wait outside," Colton demanded.

Ace shook his head. "I'm sorry, Colton, but I go where you go."

"We're on the fifth floor in my father's office. There's no one here but him. What, is someone going to parachute in through the window?"

"Maybe."

Wow, the guy actually managed to say that with a straight face.

Colton slammed the office door, then spun to face his father. "Do you see this? This is my life now. He's like my fucking shadow."

Paxton sat back in his chair with a sigh. "Please watch your language, Colton."

"Get rid of him."

"No."

Colton marched over to his father's desk, slammed his hands down, and leaned forward, his voice a low growl when he spoke. "How could you do this? How could you go behind my back like this? Like *him*?"

"Son, this is nothing like that. I tried to reason with you, but you wouldn't take this threat seriously."

Colton threw his hands up in frustration. "My God, Dad. If I freaked out every time someone called me a fag or told me I should die or burn in hell because I was gay, I would never have made it out of high school."

Paxton flinched, and Colton hated that he'd caused it. His father was a good man. What was more, he was supportive. Always had been. Did that mean Colton was supposed to feel bad about what his father had done behind his back? After what Colton's son of a bitch grand-father had done? How long had it taken him to trust his family again after that? He'd known his parents hadn't been involved, understood *now*, but the damage had been done.

Paxton ran a hand through his thick hair. "The fact I went and did this against your wishes despite what your grandfather did has to tell you how scared I am for you, Colton. This sick bastard knows where you work and where you live. Please, it's not permanent. Until the threat is over."

"And how long is that going to be? Days? Weeks? Months? I have a life, a business to run."

"My retirement isn't official for another three months, and if I have to postpone it until I know it's safe for you, then so be it."

"They're going to make changes to my home whether I agree or not," Colton countered angrily. He was losing the battle, he knew it, but he wasn't going down without a fight.

"Because you're not cooperating, Colton. You want input? Work with the Kings. They're here for your protection. Stop fighting them. Wasn't it you who stood in front of the board weeks ago, making your case on bringing in a new, more technologically advanced security firm who could do more than keep up with the growth of Connolly Maritime, who could predict the changing trends and be one step ahead? Did you not propose putting a system in place to run more inspections and perform regular audits of all our client accounts and the freighters coming in on our shipping liners? You proposed an entire security overhaul, Colton, and now when there's a threat, one the company believes requires your protection, you're refusing to cooperate? How do you think that will look to the board?"

Shit. His father had him by the balls, and he knew it. Paxton was right. Colton had never been the kind of man who didn't practice what he preached. He preferred to lead by example. The way the world was going, they had to be smarter about security. Too many companies had crumbled due to cutbacks or laziness when it came to security. As one of the largest shipping and logistics companies in Florida, they couldn't afford to be complacent.

"Okay, fine."

Paxton blinked at him. "Okay?"

"Yes, fine. If this will put your mind at ease, and that of the board, I'll deal with it."

Paxton came around his desk and pulled Colton into a hug, patting his back. "Thank you, son."

The anger drained out of Colton as he returned his father's embrace. "Sure, Dad."

Paxton pulled away to cup his face. "If you need anything at all, you call me, all right?"

"I will," Colton promised. "I better go. I have some work to catch up on."

"Son, take the damn vacation time."

"Maybe. No promises." Colton said his goodbyes and headed for the door. As soon as he'd closed it behind him and they were out in the hall, he turned to Ace.

"Do whatever you have to do on my property and to the house, but I'm not changing my schedule. You want to stay? Do your job and earn your fucking keep. I want this mess over with."

Ace narrowed his eyes. "Yes, sir, Mr. Connolly."

Before leaving, Colton dropped by Nadine's desk to check in with her but was pleased to hear she was in the middle of a conference call with Joshua. He made a mental note to give her a call later to see how it went. After years of working together, he and Nadine were in sync when it came to business matters, and he was sure Nadine would agree that Joshua was a great fit for Connolly Maritime.

Spinning on his heels, Colton turned to head back

toward the elevator when he smacked right into Nolan, their senior vice president and a close friend of the family's. "Jesus, Nolan, I'm so sorry." He put his hand on Nolan's shoulder to steady him. "I didn't see you there."

"No problem. I was going to see Paxton before I headed out to lunch with Annie. She's bringing Lily."

Colton smiled at the mention of Nolan's adorable five-year-old granddaughter. "How is she?"

"A bundle of giggles and hugs like always." Nolan's warm brown eyes got a little teary, but he swiftly wiped the wetness away with his thumb. "Like she was never sick."

"We were all praying for her. She's a strong little girl." It had been horrible seeing how broken Nolan had been while he watched his granddaughter fighting to stay alive. They'd all done everything they could to support him and his family during that terrible time. The whole company had been worried for them.

Nolan sniffed, but his eyes were filled with pride. "Like her mother. We're all so proud of her. Thank you for all you and Paxton did. For the fundraiser."

"You're family, Nolan. We wanted to help however we could."

"You did." Nolan turned his attention to Ace, his friendly smile wide. "Oh, I'm sorry. I'm Nolan Stewart."

Ace returned his smile and took Nolan's hand. "I'm Ace. It's nice to meet you, Mr. Stewart."

"He's my new warden," Colton grumbled.

Nolan looked confused. "I'm sorry?"

"Dad thinks I needed babysitting over some stupid letters."

"Letters? What kind of letters require hiring private security?" Nolan asked quietly. "Colton, what's going on?"

Colton let out a heavy sigh. "Some jackass has been

sending me threatening letters. It's nothing, but you know Dad. He worries, and with him retiring and me taking over, he's not taking any chances. Personally I think he's overreacting, but if it will set his mind at ease...."

Nolan looked horrified. "I'm going to have to agree with Paxton. If there's any chance someone's out to hurt you, Colton, then he was right to hire protection."

"Grandad!"

They all turned, and Nolan dropped to one knee, his arms wide open for Lily, who sped right for him in a flurry of colorful tulle. She launched herself into his arms, and he picked her up, pretending to gobble her up and sending her into fits of giggles. It was hard not to smile from ear to ear like a sap when faced with the adorable little girl. Her mother, Nolan's daughter, kissed Colton's cheek.

"Hi, Colton. It's good to see you."

Colton kissed her cheek in return and squeezed her tight. "You too, Annie. How's hubby?"

"Handsome as ever," Jeremy replied with a wink as he strolled over. *Arrogant* as ever was more like it. Sadly, the man wasn't wrong. He *was* handsome. Too bad he was also a total douche.

Jeremy Lynch was the poster boy for corporate America. He was tall, blond, broad-shouldered, with perfectly straight white teeth, former captain of his football team and prom king—because those were the sorts of things people needed to know—with a vast investment portfolio. He was a member of several distinct polo and yacht clubs, owned several cars that collectively cost more than a small country, and owned his own successful import company. As of two years ago, he was also a client of Connolly Maritime, thanks to his father-in-law, Nolan.

The man was also a bigot who claimed he had nothing

against "the gays"; he simply didn't understand why they couldn't be happy with what they had and stop pushing their agenda in everyone's faces. Colton tolerated him for Nolan and his family's sake. Jeremy tolerated Colton, because he might be an asshole, but he wasn't stupid. How the guy ended up married to such a sweet, kind-hearted woman like Annie was anyone's guess. In the years Colton had known him, he'd never once seen Jeremy think about anyone but himself.

Colton held his hand out to Jeremy, who hesitated for a split second, like he usually did, before he took Colton's hand and shook it, smiling that fake toothy grin of his.

"How are you, Jeremy?"

"Never better." Jeremy beamed. "Did Annie tell you about the new cabin in Aspen?"

Annie's smile dimmed, and she reached for Lily, her smile once again filled with warmth and love as soon as she had her little girl in her arms.

"Lily, did you say hello to Colton and his friend?"

Jeremy scowled at her. "Honey, I'm discussing something with Colton."

"Hello, Col," Lily chirped happily, waving at him.

"Hi, munchkin." Colton tickled her, and she squirmed, giggling loudly. She looked at Ace and shyly hid her face against her mother's neck.

"She's a little shy with people she doesn't know," Annie told Ace.

He chuckled warmly, reached into one of his cargo pants pockets, and pulled what Colton first thought was a box of cigarettes but turned out to be a deck of cards. Why was he carrying around playing cards?

"Would you like to see a magic trick, Lily?"

Lily turned her head, nodding timidly.

LOVE IN SPADES 73

Ace removed the deck from its case, then tucked it back into his pocket. He shuffled the cards, then fanned them out for Lily.

"Pick a card, but don't let me see what it is."

Lily pursed her lips in great concentration before she took one and slipped it out. She kept it close to her chest and peeked at it, then nodded at Ace.

"Okay." He shuffled the deck again, then split it. "Pop it back on there for me." Lily did as asked, and Ace shuffled the cards again before handing them to Colton. "How about giving those a good shuffle for me."

Colton arched an eyebrow at him but followed directions for Lily's sake. She was enthralled, her little body leaning forward and her eyes wide. Colton shuffled the deck, then handed it back to Ace. He turned the deck over, and started going through the cards, his frown deep.

"That's strange."

Jeremy snickered. "Guess we can't all be winners, champ."

Can't all be jerks either, but you seem to do so well.

Ace ignored Jeremy and tapped his lip thoughtfully. "Now where could that card be?" He gasped and pointed at Lily. "You know magic too?" He reached behind Lily's ear, flicked his wrist, and drew back his hand, his expression comically surprised as he showed her the card. "It was hiding behind your ear the whole time!"

Lily gasped and turned to her mother. "Mommy, that's the card! Did you see?"

"Wow, I did!" She tickled Lily, making her squirm and giggle.

"You should do kids' parties," Jeremy said, and Nolan rolled his eyes from next to him. "I'd be happy to recommend you to my friends. Though you might need to wear something a little more colorful."

Colton smiled apologetically at Jeremy. "I'm sure Ace would love that, but he's a little busy running one of the top security companies in the state."

If Ace was surprised by Colton's words, he didn't so much as blink. Jeremy on the other hand was stunned. He looked Ace over, and Colton could see the man's calculating wheels turning.

"Really? Which company?"

"Four Kings Security," Ace replied, tapping his cap and the logo in the center of it, his smile friendly.

Jeremy stared at the logo. "You work for Four Kings Security?"

Ace shrugged. "You could say that."

"So humble." Colton *tsked*. "He's actually one of the Kings."

Jeremy's mouth formed an O, and suddenly he was all over Ace. "Well damn, son. You should have said something." He patted Ace's shoulder and shook his hand again. Jeremy was all about status, and even though Colton had never done business with the Kings, anyone who ran any kind of successful business in the state of Florida knew who they were.

"Dad, we better get going," Annie said, and Nolan nodded.

"Right." Nolan pulled Colton into a tight hug, and when he stepped back, he gave him a pointed look. "You listen to your dad, okay?"

Colton nodded. "I will. You guys have fun at lunch." He kissed Annie's cheek, then Lily's before shaking Jeremy's hand. He started walking away when Jeremy called out after them.

"We'll do lunch, Ace. I've got business to discuss with you."

"Sure thing, Mr. Lynch," Ace replied, giving him a salute as he walked backward.

"Call me Jeremy."

Ace gave him another salute before turning and accompanying Colton to the elevator. As soon as they were inside the empty elevator and the doors closed, Ace turned toward him.

"What was that about?"

"Sorry, but the guy is a pretentious jackass. He loves looking down his nose at people. I've known him for years. I have no idea what Annie sees in him. You should see him at the company parties. The way he kisses my father's ass? You'd think he wasn't such a raging homophobe."

"That so?"

"Yep. He's learned to hide it well. The first time we met was at one of the company Christmas parties. He didn't know who I was, but I was there with a date. Annie introduced us, and the disgust in his eyes is something I'll never forget. Then he told me he'd pray for my soul."

"You're kidding."

"Oh, but it gets better. He had the audacity to ask what my parents thought of my lifestyle. I pointed to my dad and told Jeremy he could ask my father himself. Watching him turn green was the highlight of my evening. After that, he was on my ass like he wanted to ride it."

"And yet he wants to do business with a security company owned by four nonstraight guys?"

"I said he was a bigot, not an idiot. The only thing Jeremy values more than his supposed righteousness is the all-mighty dollar."

"Ah, I see." Ace was quiet for a moment before he spoke up again. "Why did you tell him I was one of the Kings?"

"Because he was judging you."

"And you didn't like that?"

"I may not want you here, Ace, but I won't stand idly by while someone tries to belittle you."

"Because he called me a children's entertainer?"

"No, because he thought you were below him. What someone does for a living is their business. It's not anyone's place to judge, especially when they don't even know the person."

Ace nodded. "I agree." The elevator pinged, and the doors opened. They met Oscar at the security desk, placed their thumbs to the scanners, and were soon on their way to the car.

"Do you mind if I ask what happened to Lily?"

Colton's heart squeezed in his chest. "A couple of years ago, her heart started to fail her and she needed a heart transplant, but she was low on the list. Nolan and his family were preparing for the very real possibility Lily wouldn't live long enough for a heart to become available. We tried everything. Poor Annie was inconsolable, and Nolan was beside himself. His only grandbaby. Anyway, Nolan received a call that a heart had become available, and Lily was prepped for surgery. It was a miracle. Now look at her."

Ace opened the back door for Colton. "I'm glad it all worked out for them. She's a sweet kid."

"She is." Colton climbed in and fastened his seatbelt, sitting thoughtfully as Ace closed the door and went around to the driver's side. Maybe he was being too hard on Ace. The man had been hired to do a job, and that's what he was doing. Outside of being one of the Kings, Ace appeared to be a guy like any other. Well, maybe not like any other, considering the man had been Special Forces, but he'd shown a different side of himself with Lily. Would it kill Colton to give the guy a break?

Ace headed toward the interstate, and Colton frowned. "Where are you going?"

"Home. We still have to go over your schedule."

"You didn't think to ask me where I wanted to go?"

"Seeing as how the only thing you have scheduled for today is work, and you're currently on leave, I'm taking you home. This is why we need to go over your schedule. I need to know your plans. No surprises."

Colton glared at Ace through the rearview mirror. "What if I want to go out?"

"Then we'll discuss it and make the necessary preparations, though you should limit any outside activity that's not obligatory."

It might not kill him to give Ace a break, but that didn't mean he wasn't feeling murderous tendencies.

FIVE

FOR A MOMENT, Ace thought Colton had called a truce. Oh, how naïve he'd been.

On arrival at Colton's Ponte Vedra mansion, Colton was out of the SUV before Ace even put it in park. He ran inside the house, forcing Ace to go chasing him, and then the little shit proceeded to play hide-and-seek with him. He knew Colton was in the house, but the guy clearly knew his property better than Ace. He might have studied the blueprints of Colton's mansion, but Colton had lived in it for years. Ace checked every damn room in the house, growing more and more pissed off by the minute that no one had spotted the guy.

"Ace, I have eyes on Colton," Lucky informed him. His cousin sounded too amused for his own good.

"Where is he?" Ace fumed.

"Eh, the pool."

Ace stormed toward the back of the house and took the steps down two at a time. There in the pool, looking like he didn't have a care in the world, Colton sat on a pool float in the skimpiest pair of bright blue swim trunks Ace had ever seen. He smiled at Ace, his blue-tinted aviators hiding his eyes. Not that Ace needed to see his eyes to know the man was thrilled at having gotten one over on him. He rubbed sunscreen over his chest.

"There you are. I was beginning to wonder where you'd gone. My father's right. I should take some time off, and what's more relaxing than a swim in the pool? Beautiful day for it, don't you think?" He held the bottle of sunscreen up. "Would you be a dear and get my back?"

"What the hell did you think you were doing?"

"What do you mean? I couldn't go for a swim without changing."

"You weren't in your room," Ace replied through his teeth. "You weren't anywhere."

Colton pointed behind him. "I was in the cabana. Where else would I change to get in the pool?"

If the stalker didn't kill Colton, Ace just might. "Cut the bullshit, Colton. You were running from me."

"Maybe you need to be a little quicker."

"Quicker?" Ace inhaled deeply through his nose and let the breath out slowly through his mouth. Since when did he let himself get riled up? No matter how much of a pain in the ass a client could be, he was always calm and in control. He smiled sweetly at Colton. "You know what? You're absolutely right." He stepped up to the edge of the pool and crouched down. "Why don't you hand me that lotion. I'll help you out."

Colton floated over, his grin wide. "See? We're getting along better already." He held out the bottle to Ace, and Ace moved Colton closer, turning the pool float so Colton's back was to him.

Ace popped open the lotion's cap and leaned in to

murmur by Colton's ear, aware of the way the man shivered at his husky tone. "You're right. It's a beautiful day for a swim." Colton looked up at him from over his shoulder, his lips parted sensually. He really was a beautiful man. Ace leaned closer, their faces only inches away, and Colton's cheeks turned a lovely shade of pink that had nothing to do with the sun. It would appear Colton was as attracted to him now as he'd been when they'd first met. Shame Ace couldn't do anything about it. Didn't mean he couldn't have a little fun. If Colton wanted to play dirty, Ace was game. "You look a little warm. Let me help you with that." He dipped his hand beneath the water, grabbed the pool float, and flipped it over with Colton in it.

Colton yelped and flailed before he hit the water. With a laugh, Ace moved away so he wouldn't get soaked. He made sure to stand back from the pool when Colton surfaced, sputtering and cursing. Ace straddled one of the lounge chairs closest to Colton, dropped down onto it, and lay back, enjoying the shade of the umbrella. It was still hot as balls, but at least the sun was no longer trying to melt him.

"Geez, Colton. You should be more careful."

Colton let out a frustrated growl as he wiped the water from his face, followed by his hair. He glared daggers at Ace. "Fuck you, Ace."

"That's against company policy, sweetheart, but it's awfully flattering."

Colton scoffed. "Please. Like you could handle this."

"Well damn," Ace said with a laugh, not having expected that. The guy continued to surprise him, which wasn't an easy feat these days. He also secretly loved the fire Colton possessed. "I see."

"No, I don't think you do." Colton reached the end of

the pool and climbed out like some Bond babe, water dripping from his sleek, well-toned body. He ran his fingers through his hair as he sauntered over and stopped in front of Ace, rivulets of water running down his flat stomach, soaked swim trunks, and long legs.

Ace trailed his gaze up, his sunglasses allowing him to hide the hunger that undoubtedly filled eyes. He made sure not to linger on the bulge between Colton's legs. Fuck, was that as gorgeous as the rest of him? *Look but don't touch.* Ace discreetly gripped the edges of the lounge chair just in case.

Colton dropped one knee onto the chair between Ace's spread legs. "Take your sunglasses off."

"What are you doing?" Ace ignored the request and frowned. "You need to back away."

"Why? Am I getting you wet?" Colton's voice was low and thick. He reached for Ace's sunglasses, and Ace caught his wrists. "I thought you said you could handle me."

"Actually, I didn't address that statement at all."

Colton slid forward, and Ace jerked when Colton's knee brushed against his dick. He should release Colton, but instead his grip tightened on Colton's wrists. What the hell were they doing? Anyone from his team could appear at any moment. The umbrella was the only thing keeping anyone inside the house looking out from getting an eyeful.

"Do you like what you see?" Colton loomed over him, droplets of water falling on Ace, and Ace swallowed hard.

A droplet trailed down Colton's neck, and Ace wanted to follow it with his tongue. Fuck, he needed Colton to not be so close.

"Tell me, Ace. Is it a conflict of interest when you want to fuck your client?"

Ace clenched his jaw tight. "I think you need to step away."

"What if your client wanted you to fuck him?" Colton's smile was sinful, but thankfully, he stood, turned, and started walking toward the cabana. "It's a shame, really. Had we met under different circumstances that night at the club, I would have taken you in the back and let you fuck my brains out. Oh well."

Ace cursed under his breath, adjusting himself as he got up. He'd expected some resistance from Colton, but nothing had prepared him for the sultry minx. What did it say about him that he wasn't putting a stop to this behavior? He supposed their start at the club hadn't helped, but he could have easily snuffed that flame the moment it ignited, but he hadn't. Why? As Colton slipped into a plush white robe, his eyes closed as he lifted his face to the sun and dried his hair with a towel, his long neck exposed. Ace was in trouble if he didn't get ahold of himself. Colton opened his eyes and smiled knowingly at Ace. Fucker winked at him before sauntering off.

It very quickly became clear that although Colton told his father he was going to cooperate, he neglected to mention he would do so by being the most annoying, frustrating human being on the planet. Everything he did was designed to push Ace over the edge. Patience had never been a problem for Ace. He'd spent hours upon hours completely still during special ops. His military career had prepared him for everything and anything his new career might throw his way. It did not prepare him for Colton Connolly, and it sure as shit didn't prepare him for shopping with the man. After four hours of shoe shopping, he was ready to gouge his eyeballs out with a shoehorn.

"Hm. I don't know. Ace, what do you think?" Colton turned to him with two pairs of white shoes.

"They're the same," Ace grunted. At least they were indoors with air-conditioning. He sat on some soft pouf thing, his ass going numb as Colton tried on every pair of designer shoe in the place.

"They are not the same," Colton insisted. "This pair is snow white, and this pair is baby-powder white."

Ace squinted at him. "So, what you're essentially saying is they're both white."

Colton huffed and turned away from him to speak to the cute little blond assistant who kept sneaking less than wholesome glances at Ace when Colton wasn't looking.

"How is it going?" Lucky asked, stepping up beside him.

Ace stood, speaking quietly so Colton wouldn't hear him. "I'm about to strangle him with a pair of shoelaces. I swear on my abuelita's life if he doesn't pick a pair of fucking shoes in the next ten minutes, I'm going to Tase him."

Lucky cackled, the bastard. Did he not understand the extent of Ace's pain? It wasn't like he hadn't accompanied clients on lengthy shopping trips before, but none had ever spent this much time in one damn store. "He's been in this store for four hours, Lucky. *Four* hours. There are no shoes left for him to try on!"

Colton tapped his chin before turning and smiling when he spotted Lucky. "Lucky, you look like a man with taste."

Ace's brows shot up near his hairline. Now he had no

taste? Colton remained oblivious to Ace's telepathic attempts to smack him with the shoe in his hand.

"Snow white or baby powder?"

"Actually," Lucky said, picking up a couple of pairs of shoes Ace was pretty sure Colton had tried on about two-and-a-half hours ago. "I would go for the Jimmy Choos or the Louboutins."

"Those look like slippers," Ace grumbled.

"Because they are, Capitán Obvio."

Ace mouthed the words "I'm going to kill you" to Lucky.

"They're hot this year," Colton supplied before the assistant—who was staring at Lucky's ass like he wanted to crawl into it and take up residence—shot his head up and let Colton know how much the shoes were.

Ace laughed and held up a hand. "Hold up. I'm sorry. For a moment there, I thought you said those shoes were thirteen hundred dollars."

The assistant nodded. "Oh yes. That's the members-only discount."

"Discount," Ace repeated. "Oh my God. I could get ten pairs of shoes for that. Good shoes."

Colton didn't look amused. "Tell me, Ace. Do you own shoes that aren't combat boots?"

"Don't be ridiculous. Of course I do."

"He has sneakers too," Lucky offered cheerfully.

Ace turned to his cousin, who he was going to strangle after he strangled Colton with some designer shoelaces that probably cost more than his rent. "Why don't you go patrol over there?"

"Can you believe he actually wore his old combat boots with his suit to our cousin's quinceañera party?" Lucky shook his head in shame.

Oh my God, he was never going to live that down. Thanks to his Cuban family, there wasn't one person in the whole fucking state of Florida who didn't know about his wearing his damn boots to Marissa's party. It was like six degrees of separation. If anyone knew anyone in his family, they—and everyone they knew—had heard about the damn boots. He had relatives in Cuba, who he'd never even fucking met, calling him to ask about the damn boots.

Colton looked horrified. "You didn't."

"Seriously, it's not that big a deal. We were on leave, I couldn't find my dress shoes, and it was too late to go out and buy a new pair, so I had to wear combat boots."

Colton peered at him. "You only own one pair of shoes that are not boots or sneakers?"

"What the hell would I need dress shoes for?"

"And then," Lucky added, "because we've been close since we were young, it's my fault for letting him leave the house like that, you know? I wasn't even with him! I mean, I met him at the place, but do you think that matters? No. I have to hear it from my mother, his mother, *and* our tía. I'm *still* hearing about it, and Marissa turned thirty years old six months ago. I'm going to be hearing about his damn boots when I'm old and retired. It's going to be my legacy. My grandchildren will be talking about it all like ¿Recuerda cuándo el primo del abuelo se apareció en la fiesta de Marissa con esas botas? Que pena. Pobrecita Lucia." Lucky held his hands up. "Gracias a Dios my mother wasn't wearing her chancletas. It would not have been pretty."

Colton burst into laughter, and then suddenly he was laughing so hard he had to sit down. "Oh my God, I can't. My side hurts."

"You two are hysterical," Ace grunted.

LOVE IN SPADES   87

Lucky grinned at him and shrugged. "What can I say? I live to please others."

"Are you two done? Can we go now?"

Colton wiped the tears from his eyes and nodded. He turned to the clerk, smiling brightly. "Thank you so much for your assistance. Please charge the valet box, belts, and socks to my account."

The clerk nodded before hurrying off. He returned in no time flat with a fancy bag containing Colton's purchases, none of which were shoes.

"Wait, what about your shoes for the White Party?"

Colton waved a hand in dismissal. "Pft, I bought those months ago."

"Then why...?" It dawned on Ace, and he was all but breathing fire through his nose. *Calm. Breathe. Putting your client in a chokehold is frowned upon, and you know King won't appreciate you shoving the client headfirst into the trash bin outside the shoe store.* "I hate you."

"You don't know me." Colton's eyes sparkled with mischief as he threw Ace's words back at him.

Ace stopped in his tracks and stared at Colton as he walked away chuckling to himself. Lucky patted his shoulder.

"Wow. He's good, bro."

Ace flipped off his cousin and stormed after Colton. Thankfully Colton was ready to go home, and when they arrived, he announced he'd be in his room relaxing. Lucky went off to find Red, and a second later Ace received a text from King letting him know he was catching up with Red and Lucky and would meet him in the kitchen in fifteen minutes. Ace sent one of his men to stand outside Colton's room. He didn't know how long his meeting with King would take.

Needing some more caffeine, Ace made himself an iced coffee and sat at the island counter with his drink while he waited for King. He'd washed up his glass when King showed up.

"How's Colton?"

Ace grunted at the mere mention of the man's name. "God, he's *so* annoying. I really want to punch him in the face. Can I?"

King sighed. "No, you can't punch the client in the face."

"But what if I *really* want to? I'll make it quick, I promise. Just a pop." Ace demonstrated with a swift jab. "Won't even make him bleed."

"No."

"You used to be fun," Ace replied with a huff.

"Yeah, well, one of us needs to be the adult."

"Screw you. I'm an adult. I had bran cereal for breakfast this morning. *Bran*. Not even my grandfather eats that shit. It was foul, and considering we've had Jack's cooking, that's saying something." Ace shuddered at the thought. Never again would he get so drunk he thought Jack's turkey, potato chip, banana, and Nutella sandwich was a good idea.

"Are you done?" King asked, arching an eyebrow at him.

"For now. I reserve the right to bitch about him some more later."

"Duly noted." King's rumbling chuckle made Ace smile.

"How's the investigation coming along?"

"We've cleared most of the employees at Connolly Maritime and are looking into Colton's friends and ex-boyfriends. He *really* didn't like me asking for that information."

"Paxton did say Colton hated personal questions."

"He also said the man was stubborn as hell, and he

wasn't wrong. Colton's determined to make things as difficult for us as possible. I'm having to work around him a good deal of the time."

"Have you looked into the grandfather?"

King eyed him. "On his mother's side or father's side? Not that either one will be very helpful, considering they both passed away years ago."

"Father's side. The other day in Paxton's office, Colton alluded to his grandfather going behind his back with something, and now Paxton had done the same. Whatever it was, it really did a number on Colton, and I'm positive it's connected to why he's fighting this so hard."

King looked thoughtful. "Do you think you can get close enough to find out what it is? It might help us understand him better, and maybe find a way to get his cooperation."

"I'll try, but trust is a big issue for Colton, and he barely tolerates my presence as it is. I don't want to do anything to jeopardize what progress I've made with him."

"Okay. If you can broach the subject, do it. Otherwise, we'll continue to work around him. I'll keep digging on our end. Let me know of any changes or concerns. I've already checked in with Red and Lucky, so I'm going to head back to the office."

"Sure you don't want to stick around?" Ace asked, smiling sweetly.

"Why? What are you going to do?"

Ace laughed at the suspicion in King's expression. His best friend really knew him too well. "Colton's got that White Party this weekend on Fisher Island. We're supposed to be leaving in the next couple hours. I've been trying to convince him to cancel."

"Let me guess. He's refusing."

"Refusing is such a mild term. Did you know the man can freeze your balls off with a look?"

King's eyes danced with amusement. "I didn't know, but thanks for the warning." His smile fell away, and he was all business again. "How's the emergency evac plans coming along? I can have an extra team ready for extraction if necessary."

"Thanks. Island security cleared us right away, but that's not surprising, considering our previous and current clients who reside on the island. The teams have escape routes ready, though with the limited transport options available to us, we all know how quick that can go to hell. The SUVs are prepped and ready to go. I wore Colton down and got him to let us helo him in, but he's really *not* a fan. The rest of the team will be leaving ahead of us, and they'll take the ferry onto the island. They're meeting us at the helo pad. We've got a couple of speedboats docked and ready just in case. Lucky's going to lead the team on the island, and Red's going to stay here with the rest of the team in case our perp is planning to take advantage of Colton being away. The island's seclusion and exclusivity can either work in our favor or against us. Red's done checks on all the guests. The list is extensive. We're talking over two hundred guests and their plus ones. Drill's the same as before. Firearms are not permitted, only nonlethals."

"Good work. Keep me informed."

"Always."

King left, and Ace went in search of Colton. When he walked through the downstairs of the house and didn't see him, he knew where to find him, which meant going outside. Unless he believed Colton was in immediate danger, he wouldn't intrude on the man's privacy. Not that it was necessary. All he had to do was go to his room, the balcony of which connected to Colton's balcony. It was the reason he'd picked that particular bedroom. In case of an emergency, there were two ways for him to get into Colton's room. At the moment, they had no such emergency, so if Colton wanted to keep him out, all he had to do was close the doors to his sitting room, and draw the curtains, but Colton loved the ocean view too much to let Ace ruin that for him.

Ace found Colton exactly where he thought he'd be, curled up in his armchair, a book in his hand, and a glass of white wine in the other. Colton didn't bother looking up when he spoke.

"Did anyone tell you you're like a storm cloud? The way you roll in, I don't even have to see you to know you're there. You block my sunlight."

"Ouch. I'm not the only one good at throwing shade." Ace turned one of the rocking chairs, and sat facing Colton, who sighed and closed his book.

"If you're here to try and convince me not to go, don't bother."

"Colton—"

"This event is important to both me and our company. The host isn't just one of our biggest clients; he's a dear friend of the family, and as one of the charity's benefactors, the children's organization I'm contributing to expects to see me there. I'm not cancelling this or the Sapphire Sands Charity Masquerade."

"For now, let's focus on the White Party. It's on an island, which limits our options in case of an emergency."

"It's secure," Colton argued. "No one will be allowed onto the island or into the event without being cleared by security."

"The party itself is on the beach. Out in the open. It's a logistical nightmare."

Colton arched a perfectly shaped eyebrow at him. "I'm sorry, are you telling me the Kings are incapable of securing their client while at an event?"

"I didn't say that," Ace replied patiently.

"Good. Now go get ready. There's a suit hanging behind the door of your room." Colton stood, stretching his long, toned body, and Ace found himself mesmerized, especially when Colton's shirt rode up, exposing smooth tanned skin and well-defined abs. "Are you listening to me?"

Ace's cheeks grew warm, and he moved his eyes up to Colton's, sucking in a breath at the heat he found in Colton's gorgeous gaze. Colton sauntered over, and Ace quickly got to his feet. He took a step back, forgetting the damn rocking chair, and fell back into it. Colton's husky laugh sent a jolt of need through him, and he cursed himself for letting his guard down. It had never been a problem before. Colton was hardly the first attractive man—or attractive gay man for that matter—Ace had worked alongside of. Colton was throwing him off his game, and he couldn't allow that. He had to put an end to it. Now. He coughed into his hand.

"I hear you. Suit behind the door. Gotcha."

Colton stepped out onto the balcony and came to a stop between Ace's spread legs. Swallowing hard, Ace leaned back in the rocking chair, his fingers in a death grip on the chair's armrests. Colton began to lean in, and Ace threw a hand out to stop him.

"What are you doing?" Touching Colton had been a mistake. Ace splayed his fingers against Colton's abdomen, and Colton visibly shuddered. He took the hem of his shirt and slowly tugged it up and out from under Ace's fingers,

LOVE IN SPADES   93

his low groan matching Ace's when his hand lay against Colton's smooth bare skin.

"I like your hands on me, Ace."

I like my hands on you too. It was what he wanted to say but didn't. He had better control than this, or so he thought. The line between him and his clients was never crossed. Why was he finding it so difficult to maintain that line? *Because you want him so fucking bad it hurts.* Ace made the mistake of lifting his gaze to Colton's, and the fiery lust in those stormy blue-gray eyes had him placing his hand to Colton's hips and digging his fingers in. Before Ace had time to register what was happening, Colton was straddling his lap, the fingers of one hand buried in his hair while he caressed Ace's jaw with the other, his lips brushing over Ace's.

"I've never met a man with the power to both infuriate *and* arouse me simultaneously. How do you do it?"

"A talent, I guess." Ace gripped Colton's hips, holding him down against him as he thrust up, his erection rubbing against Colton's, making them groan. Fuck, they were both so damn hard. All he had to do was unzip Colton, wrap a hand around his firm dick, and give it a few tugs. He'd have Colton coming all over his hand in minutes. He thought about licking his fingers clean, then kissing Colton so he could taste himself. *Fucking fuck, that is* not *helping!*

"I've been dreaming about that cock," Colton murmured. He poked his tongue out and flicked it across Ace's lips, making him jump. Colton chuckled before his sexy low drawl was back. "And your mouth. God, Ace, you make me so fucking hot."

Ace shut his eyes tight and worked on controlling his breathing.

"What are you thinking right now?" Colton ground his

hips against Ace's, his arms wrapped around Ace's neck. "Do you want me, Ace? Tell me you want to take me to bed and fuck me so hard I'll feel you for days."

Ace opened his eyes, his breathing steady as he unwrapped Colton's arms from around his neck. He dropped his gaze to Colton's lush lips, a burning need spreading through every inch of his already smoldering body. He'd never wanted anyone as bad as he wanted the sexy man in his lap. Temptation was a real bitch.

"What is it you want from me?" Ace asked, managing to regain some semblance of calm.

Colton ground his hips down again, his lips curled in a seductive grin. "Isn't it obvious? Am I being too subtle?"

"Colton," Ace warned, his eyes all but rolling into the back of his head when Colton moved his hips again. *Fuck.* If he didn't do something, he'd explode.

"My bedroom is right behind me."

"No," Ace growled.

"Because you can't or don't want to?"

Ace threw Colton's words back at him. "Isn't it obvious?"

"Do you want me on my knees, Ace? Do you need me to beg?" Colton dragged his nails down Ace's chest, and Ace could feel the burn despite his T-shirt. "You'd like that, wouldn't you?" Colton's face was the picture of ecstasy as he moaned. "Oh God, yes. Ace, fuck me. Make me come. Bury that big dick inside me."

"That's it." Ace got up, knocking Colton onto his ass, his hands balled at his sides as Colton laughed. "You think this is funny?"

Colton shrugged. "A little."

"Well, it's not," Ace growled, turning to go as Colton

jumped to his feet and grabbed his arm, the smile gone from his face. He almost looked... concerned.

"You're really upset."

And Lucky called *him* Captain Obvious.

"What gave it away?" Ace sneered, his anger melting when Colton cupped his face, his eyes searching Ace's for who knew what. Ace gently took hold of his wrists and moved his hands away. He couldn't have Colton so close to him right now. "I don't play these kinds of games, Colton."

Colton frowned. "Neither do I."

"Really? You could have fooled me."

"I can't seem to control myself around you." Colton pushed away from him with a frustrated growl. "I don't *want* to want you, but I fucking do, and it's driving me crazy." He worried his bottom lip with his teeth. "I thought maybe if I did something about it, I could get it out of my system." He met Ace's gaze. "I could get *you* out of my system."

"I don't shit where I eat, Colton."

"That's... a very unpleasant way to put things."

"It's the truth. I'm not interested in fucking around. This is my career, my reputation, my life. I won't screw that up for a quick fuck, especially with you."

Colton's expression turned indignant. "Why? Am I not good enough?"

With a sigh, Ace closed the gap between them and brushed his fingers up Colton's jaw, smiling at the way Colton melted against him.

"I don't want a quick fuck with you, Colton, because there would be no getting you out of my system."

Colton sucked in a sharp breath, and Ace leaned in to kiss Colton's cheek.

"You deserve more."

Colton's cheeks flushed an adorable shade of pink, and Ace wanted nothing more than to grab him and kiss the hell out of him. As if sensing that, Colton took a step back. Mischief filled his eyes, and Ace braced himself.

"So what you're saying is that you actually like me."

Ace held back a smile and kept his expression stoic. "Well, I don't know that I'd go that far." He turned, loving the sound of Colton's rich, throaty laugh echoing behind him as he headed back to his own room. And yet, he couldn't help the smile that crawled onto his face. He'd never met anyone like Colton Connolly. For the first time in his life, he was unsure.

Colton was beautiful, and an explosive attraction definitely existed between them, but it was an attraction Ace couldn't pursue. He was here to keep Colton safe, and that meant being around the man at all hours, for who knew how long. Getting involved with Colton would bring a shitstorm down on him of epic proportions. If he screwed up, he could cost the Kings the contract with Connolly Maritime. If it got out that he slept with a client, his career could be over, and he'd worked too damn hard to get where he was. As tempting as Colton was, he was off-limits.

In his room, Ace found the suit Colton spoke of hanging from his door. "The fuck?" He grabbed it, marched back out onto his balcony, and went around to Colton's bedroom. "Colton," Ace growled, walking into the sitting room.

"Down here," Colton called up.

Ace hurried down the stairs, ignoring the huge California king bed Colton was sitting on as he removed his shoes and socks. "I'm not wearing this."

"Why? What's wrong with it?"

The man looked far too amused for his own good. "The

price tag for one." How the hell had Colton even known what size to get?

"It's a work expense, and therefore tax deductible."

"It's linen. White linen. Everything is white." The pants, jacket, the shirt underneath. Even the damned belt was white.

Colton squinted at him. "I'm not sure if you're familiar with the whole premise of a white party, but basically, you wear white."

"You don't say." The guy was fucking hilarious.

"And it really wasn't expensive. It's off the rack."

"Oh, it's off the rack. Well, that's okay, then." He narrowed his eyes at Colton, who was clearly trying not to smile and failing miserably. "I'm not your Ken doll."

"Don't be ridiculous. Of course you're not my Ken doll." The glint in his eye was wicked. "You're my personal G.I. Joe."

Ace pursed his lips. "I'm not sure whether I should feel insulted or not. I'll get back to you on that."

"Why don't you go get dressed while you think about it, and try not to hurt that pretty little head of yours."

"Don't objectify me. I'm more than a pretty face and spectacular ass."

"I'm sure," Colton purred. "Please go. We leave in an hour."

"Why is no one else wearing white?"

"Because they won't be seen. You, unfortunately, will be."

"And still with the insults."

Colton laughed. It was loud, rich, and made Ace smile.

"Go. Get out," Colton said, pushing him toward the stairs.

"Fine. Fine. But if I look like an ass, that's on you.

Everyone will be all 'Oh my God, did you see Colton's security detail? He looked like such a dork.' And I'll be all, 'Ha! I told you so!'"

"Well, I can hardly have you looking more handsome than me."

Ace missed a step and almost hit the stairs face-first, but managed to grab the railing in time. He straightened and turned to glare at Colton, who was cackling on the way to the bathroom.

"When did you get a sense of humor?"

Colton stopped outside his bathroom door and looked up at Ace, his grin wide. "When it became clear there'd be no getting rid of you. If you're going to constantly be in my space, I might as well enjoy tormenting you."

"Peachy," Ace grumbled, heading upstairs. The truth was, he'd take playful and flirty Colton over pissed-off Colton any day of the week. This was a whole other side of Colton he was seeing, and he liked it. Maybe a little too much, but that was on him, and he'd deal with it.

Ace showered and dressed, glowering at himself in the mirror. He looked like a douchebag. Not that everyone who wore all white looked like a douche, but he certainly did. Not only were his shoes also white, they were knit Oxfords. *Knit.* He didn't even know they made those. Granted, he knew as much about designer brands as he did about art. Whenever he needed something top-of-the-line for a special occasion, he got Lucky to do it for him. Anytime Lucky tried to talk to him about designer labels, it was like he was speaking a different language. Ace nodded and told him to make sure he looked good. Having a client dress him was a first, and he wasn't sure how to feel about that. Not that he could do anything about it now.

Once he'd dressed and styled his hair, he checked in

LOVE IN SPADES   99

with Lucky and Red to make sure they were on schedule. With everything confirmed, he gave Lucky the go-ahead with his team, leaving him in the living room on his own waiting for Colton. He checked his watch. ETA on the helo was ten minutes. He took a seat on the end of the couch, sat back, and waited. The lighter material of his suit made him very aware of the weight inside his suit jacket's inner pocket. He reached in and removed the intricately designed tuck case of Union playing cards, his thumb stroking the embossed metallic copper artwork. The ache to his heart wasn't as great as it had been once, but it was still there, and always would be, much like the love he had for the man the cards represented.

"Everything okay?"

Ace gave a start and cursed under his breath for allowing himself to get distracted. "Yeah, of course." He quickly tucked the cards back into his inner jacket pocket and stood. Colton looked like he wanted to say something, and Ace was grateful when he didn't. He wasn't ready to talk about what happened to Pip or the others, not with anyone who hadn't been involved or an appointed therapist.

Colton nodded, then motioned toward the glass doors. The balcony had several sets of stairs, the farthest of which led down to the small helo pad on the far end of the property. That was when he *saw* Colton. Jesus. He looked like he'd stepped out of *The Great Gatsby* or something, with his hair neatly parted and slicked to one side, and the white three-piece suit accentuating his broad shoulders and slender waist. He wasn't wearing a tie, the top two buttons of his white shirt open. He was stunning.

"Are you sure you're okay?" Colton asked, his concern touching.

"Great, considering I look like a snowman." He looked

down at himself, and when he lifted his eyes, he was caught off guard by the fiery look in Colton's gaze.

"Actually, you look more like a marshmallow."

The guy actually managed to say that with a straight face. Ace was impressed. "Are you saying this outfit makes me look gooey and sweet or puffy and pudgy?"

Colton laughed softly on the way to the door, Ace right behind him. The whir of the Airbus H135's blades whipped gusts of wind at the nearby trees, but the engine was low-noise, which was key when operating in the city. The Kings had three of these bad boys, all with excellent payload capacity and performance range, the interior of which had been designed with luxury in mind and even included a fully stocked minibar. Underneath it all, they were dealing with technologically advanced beasts picked for their safety features, from their crash-resistant cells to their energy-absorbing fuselage. The rear door and oversized sliding doors boasted fast loading and unloading of passengers and equipment. It was the same type of chopper often used by medical services and law enforcement. Four Kings Security had several pilots on staff, including the four Kings, Jack, and Joker.

The all black helicopter displayed the white Four Kings Security crest proudly beside the sliding door, big enough to be spotted from anywhere. Ace opened the door for Colton and waited, but Colton just stood there.

"I, um, I'm not sure...."

Ace was about to tease Colton, but he'd gone pale. "Shit, Colton, are you afraid of flying?"

"I'm not fond of it," Colton stated carefully.

"Colton, the look on your face isn't because you're not *fond* of flying." It was more like he was about to pass out at the thought of flying. Damn it, he'd pushed the helicopter, believing Colton's resistance was him being difficult, but how the hell was he supposed to know if Colton didn't tell him? "Why didn't you say you were afraid of flying?"

Colton's jaw muscles flexed, his intense gaze meeting Ace's. "I didn't need to give you another reason to believe I'm pathetic."

"What?" Since when did Colton care what Ace thought of him? And why would he assume that's the conclusion Ace would leap to after being told the guy was terrified of flying? "Where's this coming from? You know what, we can talk about it on the way to Fisher Island. I'll have Red bring around one of the SUV's, and—"

"No." Colton breathed in deep and rolled his shoulders. "We're doing this."

"Colton, you don't have to—"

"I do," Colton insisted before climbing into the cabin. After some hesitation, Ace climbed in after him, slid the door shut, and checked it was securely locked. He helped Colton buckle in before he pressed the button to lower the privacy screen. Jack's big boyish grin greeted him.

"Hey, Ace."

"Hey, buddy. Ready to get this bird in the air?"

Jack nodded and handed him a couple of the passive headsets. "ETA eighteen hundred."

"Great. Jack, this is Colton Connolly. Colton, this is Jack. He's like a brother to us Kings. Him and his pain in the ass best friend, Joker, who's down in Miami wreaking his own personal brand of havoc."

Colton waved a quick hello to Jack before he went back to his death grip on his seat's armrests.

Jack leaned back so Colton couldn't see him. He motioned to Colton, mouthing the words "He okay?"

Ace nodded and patted Jack's shoulder before handing

one of the headsets to Colton, who swallowed hard. He reached for it as the helo moved.

"Oh Jesus." He closed his eyes, and Ace put the headset on for him before he put on his own. Once he'd made sure Colton was safe and secure, he buckled himself into his own seat beside Colton and put a hand on Colton's.

"Hey." Ace gave his hand a squeeze. "Colton, look at me."

Colton's lips were pressed together in a thin line, but he did as Ace asked.

"I'm here. I'm with you. It'll be okay."

Colton swallowed hard, then nodded. The helo began its ascent, and Colton threw his other hand over Ace's, his eyes shut tight. The lift off was smooth, but Ace remembered what it felt like the first time he'd gone up in one of these birds. Then the first time he'd had to jump out of one.

"You know, the first time I made the jump, I was shitting myself."

Colton glanced over at him. "The jump?"

"Yeah, out of one of these," Ace replied pointing up. "Well, not specifically one of these. It was a combat helo. I made sure I was at the back. Red was first. He was nervous, but he's the kind of guy who when he sets his mind to something, he does it. You can tell too. He gets this look on his face, like he's concentrating real hard." Ace mimicked Red's stern pouty face, making Colton laugh. "Then he's gone. Next up was Lucky, Mr. I'm-not-afraid-of-anything. Spoiler alert, he's full of shit."

Colton laughed again, and this time it was joined by Jack's husky laugh.

"See, Jack knows. Right, Jack?"

Jacopo "Jack" Lorenzo Constantino wasn't overly big or muscular like Red or King. He was slighter and shorter than

Ace, somewhat shy, and always smiling. People had no idea of the very dangerous, very talented man behind that boyish grin. The phrase "Jack of all trades" didn't do him justice, because Jack didn't just pick up new skills easier than anyone Ace had ever known; he mastered those skills in no time flat. Whatever Jack needed, whatever someone needed him to be, he made it happen. The number of languages he was fluent in was staggering, and along with Joker, the two proved how truly deadly the human mind could be. Unless the skill included cooking. Then the only thing that made Jack deadly in that department was the very real possibility his food might actually kill someone from how bad it was. Jack's Italian grandmother had gotten on the phone with a priest to order an exorcism when she found Jack had used ketchup as a replacement for pasta sauce, or "gravy" as she called it. Ace had been there for the ketchup incident and had never laughed so hard in his life.

"Remember the snake that almost choked him in his sleep?" Jack asked with a laugh.

Colton's eyes went wide.

"Yeah." Ace snickered, shaking his head. "It was actually a piece of old hose." Ace waggled his eyebrows, and Colton gasped.

"You didn't."

"He'd been showing off again and needed to be brought down a peg or two. He's my cousin, so I feel like the responsibility falls to me."

"What did you do?" Colton asked, smiling.

"When Lucky lay down to sleep, Ace snuck up behind him and dropped it on him. I had never seen that guy move so fast. But wait, it gets better. He was so desperate to get away, he tripped over Red and fell into King, who were both asleep. They had no idea what the hell was going on and launched Lucky into the air, where he landed on Joker, who's all of five foot six and a hundred and thirty pounds."

"Poor Joker," Colton said, shaking his head in sympathy.

Ace and Jack went silent at the statement before bursting into peals of laughter.

"What?" Colton asked, bemused.

"Poor Joker? Poor Lucky! Joker's small, was the smallest in our A-Team."

"A-Team? I'm guessing that has nothing to do with Mr. T?"

Ace chuckled. "No. That was what we called our ODA, Operational Detachment Alpha. Our unit. As you can imagine, Joker's got major short-guy syndrome, and I don't blame him. Our drill sergeant was a real asshole to him, but he was determined to make it through with the rest of us. He's one of the toughest bastards I know. Man, when Lucky landed on him?"

Jack let out a low whistle. "Joker gave him a dead leg, and if you've never had one of those, consider yourself fortunate."

Colton shook his head in amusement before turning his gaze to Ace. "So, you started the chaos, and your poor cousin paid the price."

"Oh, believe me, he had it coming."

As Jack regaled Colton with tales of their shenanigans during deployment, Ace absently placed his hand over his heart and the cards tucked inside his inner jacket pocket. How different would their lives have been had things not gone down the way they had that day? Would they have still come home and gone into business together? Would they have stayed and continued to serve? What if they had, and instead he'd lost Lucky, or Red, or King.... They'd come so close to losing him that day. Ace blinked away the wetness in his eyes, grateful for his mirrored sunglasses. Regardless, they'd all left a part of themselves behind, pieces that would always be missing.

Colton's laughter snapped Ace out of his thoughts, and he found himself smiling at the rich, infectious sound. Ace might not be able to replace those missing pieces, but as he watched Colton laugh, tears in his eyes, completely open and genuine, it occurred to Ace he had no reason not to fill those dark voids with love.

SIX

AS SOON AS THEY LANDED, Ace helped Colton out of the helo and thanked Jack, letting him know he'd call if there were any changes. Jack would be staying close by in Miami until it was time for him to pick them up. From the big smile on Colton's face, it was clear he liked Jack, but then who didn't? The guy was adorable. Anyone who spent any time around the man fell hard. Jack was a regular guy, or so he appeared.

Ace finished checking in with Lucky and his team, then they split up as planned. The White Party was both an inside and outside affair, with the party starting inside, where guests mingled as they waited to be called for dinner, which would move the party outside. Beyond the glass doors and the balcony, a walkway led down to the beach, which was set up with tables, chairs, torches, strings of white lanterns, and several open bars.

With Lucky taking care of the rest, Ace focused on Colton and his personal safety. He remained close but far enough to not be intrusive. Anyone who'd hired any kind of personal security would know why he was there. Despite his plain clothes, it was in his posture, his stoic expression, the earpiece, the way he continuously scanned the room and the people in it, and the way his gaze always ended back on Colton. Those who didn't know him, smiled widely at him until it became apparent he wasn't anyone important, and politely excused themselves. Ace never took it personally.

Being a King earned him a certain amount of respect and clout, but he wasn't one of them. If it wasn't for his job, he'd never have crossed paths with the majority of these people. His being there sparked some curiosity from former and current clients in attendance. Colton was an expert at deflecting questions he didn't want to answer, using compliments to steer the conversation away, which was genius, because not one person in this room wouldn't jump at the opportunity to talk about themselves. The party's host, Kurt Terrance, spotted Colton and headed straight for him. He was a very tall, handsome black man with kind eyes and a friendly smile. His hair and trimmed beard were interspersed with gray, and he looked stunning in the designer all-white suit.

"Colton, it's so good to see you." He opened his arms wide for Colton, who didn't hesitate in walking into the embrace, the two of them roughly the same height.

"It's good to see you too, Kurt." Colton pulled back, his smile genuine and wide. "How have you been? Retirement looks good on you."

Kurt laughed heartily. "I can't complain. Cecilia's having the time of her life dragging me all over the world. Of course now that Shantel's pregnant, Cecilia goes where her baby girl goes."

Colton gasped, his face lit up in sheer joy. "Oh my God, you're going to be a grandfather?"

"Yep," Kurt stated proudly, chest puffed up and eyes a little glassy. "My baby's having a baby. Can you believe it?"

"Congratulations, Kurt!" The two men hugged and backs were patted. They gushed over the little bundle of joy that hadn't even arrived yet. Ace could tell the kid would be spoiled rotten, and if Colton's smile was anything to go by, not just by the grandparents.

"Where is Cecilia?" Colton asked, scanning the crowd.

Kurt rolled his eyes, but it was clear he was completely smitten with his wife. "Checking up on Shantel. Poor girl. Her mother loves her, but she's driving her crazy. Checks up on her all hours of the day. She's trying to convince Shantel to come down to Florida for the rest of the pregnancy."

Colton winced. "How's that going?"

"As well as you can imagine," Kurt replied, a deep rumble of a chuckle rising from his wide chest. "After she found that gator in her pool, baby girl got the hell out of the state and never looked back. Can't say I blame her."

Colton laughed, his smile fading when Kurt's expression turned concerned. "And how are you these days, Colton? I noticed the added muscle, and as fine as that young man is, I'm guessing he's not your plus one."

"A precaution," Colton assured him, his smile warm. "You know how it is."

Kurt scrunched up his nose. "Yeah, sadly I do." He shook his head and sighed before meeting Ace's gaze. "You take care of my boy, you hear me, son?"

On instinct, Ace held himself straight and gave a firm nod. "I will, sir."

"Military?" Kurt asked him.

"Green Beret."

Kurt held his hand out to Ace, who took it. "Thank you for your service, son."

"Thank you, sir." Ace couldn't help the way his heart squeezed. "You remind me of our commander. He was a good man. Firm but fair."

Colton's gaze turned sympathetic. "Was?"

Ace cleared his throat and nodded. "He was killed during a special ops mission."

"I'm sorry to hear that," Kurt said, and Ace tried not to squirm under Colton's scrutiny. It was clear he wanted to know more, but thankfully someone approached, but not before Kurt patted Colton's arm. "You're in good hands, Colton, but if you need anything, anything at all, you pick up the damn phone and you call me, okay?"

Colton assured him he would, and then the two were swept up in conversation as several guests joined them. It was fascinating, this other side of Colton. The genuine side. Not that Colton wasn't genuine with Ace, but until recently, the man had, understandably, shown mostly anger and frustration toward him. Now Ace was seeing his softer side. The way little creases formed at the corners of his eyes. His laugh was contagious, and his smile stunning. It was clear that everyone was charmed by him, and how could they not be? Anyone who spoke to him received his undivided attention. The men brought him in for tight hugs, and the women would touch his arm or shoulder as they spoke. He entertained them with humorous stories, seemed to know everyone to the point he complimented each and every one on specific achievements. He reminded them to dig deep into their pockets and donate generously to the children's charity they were here to support.

After an hour, Colton politely excused himself from the group, and Ace followed him as he headed for the bar. "I need a drink. Preferably one with a proof high enough to make me forget about Champ Chambers Jr. and his dick pic."

Ace chuckled, remembering what followed the incident. Chad had motioned Colton to one side and showed him his phone. The horrified expression on Colton's face should have given Ace a clue, but his suspicions that Chad had just done something stupid were confirmed when Colton tilted his head and said loudly, "Oh my God, what is that? Is it dying? Why is it so pale and shriveled?"

Chad's face turned an impressive shade of purplish red before he gruffly excused himself and took off. Colton had resumed his conversation with the group as if nothing had happened, but Ace could tell the man was simmering beneath the surface. If Chad was a smart man, he'd be halfway across the country by now or booking a plane ticket to the other side of the globe.

The color suddenly drained from Colton's face, and Ace stepped closer. His movement seemed to be enough to snap Colton out of whatever trance he'd fallen under, and Colton turned to him, surprising him by closing what distance remained between them. He leaned in, his voice shaky.

"I think I'd like to go for a walk on the beach, get away from the crowd for a while."

Ace was about to suggest against it, but the pleading in Colton's blue-gray eyes was unexpected. He nodded and gently took hold of Colton's elbow, escorting him toward a set of large glass doors that led out onto a wooden walkway they could take down to the beach. Someone moved quickly around them, and Ace placed himself between the man and Colton, a hand out in front of him, keeping the tall blond at arm's length.

"What the hell?" The man scowled at Ace before moving his dark eyes to Colton. "Colton, I need to talk to you."

"I have nothing to say to you," Colton hissed from behind Ace. He placed a hand gently on Ace's shoulder and spoke quietly. "Keep this man away from me."

"Are you kidding me with this?" The harsh laugh was unpleasant, and Ace blocked the guy when he tried to get around him.

"Sir, I'm going to need you to keep your distance," Ace warned.

"Tell your rabid dog to stand aside before I have him put down."

Did Colton know he was squeezing Ace's shoulder?

"Don't you dare talk to him like that."

Ace didn't let his surprise show. Instead, he kept himself between Colton and the man he clearly didn't want near him.

"Are you sleeping with him?"

"What?"

"Is that what you're resorting to these days? Sleeping with the help?"

"Ace, this is Mick 'the Dick' Wellington III. The dick part has nothing to do with his penis and more to do with his being an insufferable asshole, as you've probably guessed."

Ooh, Colton *really* didn't like this guy.

"Damn it, Colton, can we please discuss this in private?"

"There's nothing to discuss. I'm pretty sure I made myself very clear the day I kicked you out and told you to go to hell. Go crawl back under whichever sugar daddy you've attached yourself to." Colton leaned into Ace again. "He's like a barnacle. Nothing short of a blowtorch is going to get rid of him." He straightened and scrunched up his nose. He was adorable. "I watched a video on YouTube of a barnacle. Did you know they are absolutely hideous? Like something out of a science fiction horror movie. Their little beaks open up and these tentacle things come out, and oh God, it's awful." He shuddered, and it took a lot for Ace not to laugh, especially when faced with Mick's scandalized expression at being compared to a barnacle.

"Still a drama queen, I see. Colton, please. We were good together."

Colton's brows shot up near his hairline, and he laughed. "Good together? Are you out of your mind? It was all a lie, Mick. *You* were a lie."

"I loved you. I still—"

"So help me, if you say you still love me, I will use Ace's Taser and tase you in the balls. I'll—" Colton cut himself short, then cleared his throat. He smoothed down his vest, lips pressed in a thin smile. When he spoke, his voice was calmer. "I wish I could say it was nice to see you, but it wasn't. I feel like I need to go bathe in bleach now. Excuse me." Colton made to move, and Mick threw a hand out. Ace snatched hold of his wrist, twisted his arm, and brought the man to his knees.

"I believe Mr. Connolly made it clear he wanted you to stay away from him." Ace released him, and Mick pushed himself to his feet.

He rubbed his wrist as he spat out at Ace. "You're going to regret that." Mick rushed off, and Colton let out a shaky breath.

Ace immediately turned to him. "Are you okay?"

"Yes. I think I'd like that walk now."

Ace nodded. He pressed his PTT button and spoke into

the mic. "Lucky, I'm on the east side of the property escorting Colton down to the beach. He's going to go for a walk. I'll report back as soon as we get down there."

"Copy that."

They were halfway down the walkway when the sound of boots had Ace turning and instinctively pulling Colton behind him. He relaxed at the sight of suited security officers. One of the officers stepped forward, Mick on his heels.

"This is the man who assaulted me. I want him out of here, and I intend to press charges."

"What?" Colton was all but spitting nails as he tried to get around Ace. "That's absurd and a complete lie. But then why am I not surprised?"

"Colton, stay out of this," Mick hissed.

Ace had to put his arms out at his sides and grip the banisters to keep Colton from rushing Mick and planting one on his face. As much as he would have loved to see that, he'd rather keep Colton away from the asshole. First things first.

"Good evening, gentlemen. I'm going to have Mr. Connolly reach into my jacket pocket and pull out my ID. Is that all right?"

They nodded, and Colton removed the wallet with Ace's identification. He handed it to the officer closest to him. The man's eyes widened, and he smiled widely at Ace.

"Mr. Sharpe. It's an honor to meet you, sir. I'm Jason Miller." He held out his hand, and Ace shook it. "The work Four Kings Security did during that horrible storm last year was an inspiration. You all deserved every bit of praise the governor gave you. Thank you for your service."

"I appreciate that, Jason. Our state needed the support, so we jumped in to help."

LOVE IN SPADES   115

"What are you doing?" Mick asked, indignant. "You're supposed to be arresting him, not fanboying over him."

Jason was clearly not impressed with Mick's attitude, but he was a professional, so he turned to Ace. "May I ask what happened, Mr. Sharpe?"

Ace opened his mouth when Mick cut in.

"Really? You're going to ask *him*? He's just going to lie."

"Jason," Colton said, his smile wide as he held out his hand. "I'd like to thank you and your team for your work here tonight. I'm Colton Connolly."

Jason and the rest of his team were suddenly on high alert. "Mr. Connolly, I'm so sorry for this."

"It's all right, Jason. Mr. Sharpe was doing his job. He and his team are here as my personal security. Mr. Wellington approached me, and I made it very clear that I had no intention of speaking to him. When he approached aggressively and tried to grab me, Ace intervened. I don't want this man anywhere near me, and if he refuses, feel free to escort him from the premises." Colton turned his cold eyes on Mick. "This better be the last I see of you, Mr. Wellington, or I'll be the one pressing charges."

Mick's nostril's flared as he looked from Colton to Ace, then back before he spun on his heels and stormed off. Jason motioned for one of his men to follow Mick before he turned his attention back to them.

"I apologize for the inconvenience, gentlemen," Jason said. "It's a real pleasure meeting you both. If you have any issues or concerns, please come see me or one of my associates."

Ace thanked Jason and waited for them to be out of earshot. He faced Colton, concerned by the heartache on display. "Are you okay? Do you want me to escort you to your room?"

Colton shook his head, his gaze off toward the ocean. "No, I'm fine. Thank you. But I could really use that walk now."

"Of course." He motioned for Colton to go ahead, and when they reached the end of the walk, Colton stopped. He removed his jacket and laid it over the railing before he removed his cufflinks and proceeded to roll up his sleeves to the elbows. His shoes and socks soon followed, tucked behind the stairs that led down to the sand. He rolled his pants up to his knees, unconcerned about the expensive designer slacks. The breeze was blowing off the ocean, making the humidity more bearable. Ace added his socks and shoes to Colton's stash beneath the stairs, but he kept his jacket on since his ID and touchstone were in his inner jacket. He'd faced far worse conditions during his service than beach weather.

Colton strolled closer to the water to walk along the surf's edge, the water splashing against his ankles and the breeze ruffling his soft hair. Ace followed at a distance, scanning the surrounding areas scattered with palm trees, shrubbery, and torches speared into the sand. Colton appeared lost in thought, his hands shoved into his pants pockets and his head lowered. He'd stop on occasion to toe at something in the sand. Ace gave him space, but after several feet, Colton stopped and waited expectantly. Wondering if something was wrong, Ace quickly caught up.

"Everything okay?"

Colton nodded, his smile warm. "Would you.... I'd like you to walk beside me, if you wouldn't mind."

"Sure." Ace joined Colton, and they walked side by side. He remained vigilant and quiet. If Colton wanted to talk, he would. If he needed to be left to his own thoughts, Ace could give him that too. Mick had really upset him, and by what was said, it was obvious the two had been involved. Had Mick cheated on him? What dumbass would cheat on Colton Connolly? Besides being gorgeous, the man was sweet, funny, had an incredibly generous heart, and that was only after being around him a few days. Ace made a mental note to ask King about Mick, though Mick being the one threatening Colton didn't make sense. Not when Mick had obviously been in a relationship with another man, and he didn't seem interested in hiding it. Either way, Ace would look into it.

It was a beautiful evening, the music from the party playing off in the distance as the dinner portion of the evening commenced. Ace mentioned it to Colton, but Colton didn't seem very interested in dinner at the moment. He wanted to walk along the beach, so that's what they did. The sound of the ocean soothed Ace, and the moonlight reflecting on the water seemed to stretch on forever. Ace had always loved the ocean, which was why he lived a mere two blocks away. In the early morning, he'd walk down to the beach and go for a swim before heading to Bibi's Café for breakfast.

Colton stopped and faced the water. "We used to date. Well, I thought we were dating. Little did I know it was all a very elaborate ruse."

"I don't understand," Ace replied quietly, following Colton, who headed for dry sand. Colton dropped down onto it and brought his knees up, then wrapped his arms around them. Ace sat beside him.

"My grandfather, may he rot in hell, was a terrible human being. My father tried to keep me from seeing him, but like I said, the man was vile. Back when my grandfather ran the company, he'd threaten my father with it if he didn't allow my grandfather to see me. My father gave in because

Connolly Maritime would be mine one day. My legacy. My grandfather knew from early on that I was gay." He stared out at the water, tears in his eyes. "He'd call me all kinds of names when I did something he believed wasn't manly. It was his way of trying to make sure I grew up to be a 'real man.' During one visit, I fell and dislocated my shoulder, and he said, 'Don't you dare cry, Colton. Crying is for sissies, and no grandson of mine is going to be a sissy.' I was ten years old."

Colton's grandfather sounded like a real dick, but it wasn't Ace's place to say, so he kept his opinion to himself.

"I met Mick in college. He was everything I thought I wanted. Handsome, smart, fun. He loved to be with me, thought I was the most amazing guy he'd ever met. Whatever I needed, he was there. He was interested in my work, in seeing me succeed, and wanted to know about everything that made me happy. Two years into our relationship, I asked him to move in with me. Our lives were perfect. Or so I thought.

"A year after he moved in, I was ready to propose. I came home early to surprise him. I know what you're thinking. Bastard was cheating on me. Well, he was, but that's not what I caught him doing. He was having a meeting with my grandfather. They were in my office talking about Connolly Maritime and a shipping contract I'd rejected due to the client's shady reputation. I thought it was strange that my grandfather would be discussing contracts with my boyfriend. Then it hit me what was really happening."

The pieces were slowly starting to fit together, and although Ace had an idea of what Colton's grandfather had done, he waited patiently for Colton to tell him.

"My grandfather was instructing Mick on what he needed to say to convince me to take the contract. He said

'Do whatever it takes. He's going to propose. Act surprised, accept it, and use it.' Then Mick replied, 'Marriage will cost you extra.' And they started to negotiate the terms of our marriage. At this point, my grandfather no longer had any say in the company, so he'd lost his leverage with my father, who wouldn't even take his calls, but my grandfather did have shares. He hired Mick to manipulate me."

"What happened then?" Ace asked gently, his heart squeezing at the stray tear that rolled down Colton's cheek.

"I swallowed down all the pain, held my head high, and walked into my office. I told them to get the hell out of my house and that I never wanted to see either of them again. The next time I saw my grandfather was at his funeral. I thought I'd feel remorse for pushing him away, but when I stood there over the open grave as they lowered his casket, I only felt guilt, guilt for not feeling anything. He'd made me feel inadequate and weak since I could remember. I never received any love from him, only disappointment that I wasn't what he wanted me to be."

"I'm sorry, Colton." Ace leaned in and wiped another tear that escaped. Realizing what he'd done, he murmured a quick apology and pulled away, but Colton caught his wrist.

"Thank you. I'm sorry I gave you a hard time. I know you're just doing your job." Something in his tone and the way his eyes searched Ace's had his heart skipping a beat.

"It's my job to protect you, Colton, not to care, but I do. You're a good man, and I will do whatever it takes to make sure you stay safe, but I would never betray your trust."

Colton nodded, his expression softening as he released Ace. He turned his attention back to the ocean, and they sat together in silence for what seemed like forever before Colton spoke up. "It's so peaceful out here. I love the beach at night."

"Me too." Ace looked up at the clear night sky. "When I can't sleep, I walk down to the beach with a blanket and sit there for hours watching the ocean. Sometimes I fall asleep listening to the waves."

"Does that happen often?"

Ace shrugged. "Not as often as it used to. When we came home for good, we were in a pretty bad place. King had us all living with him. The house was big enough for all six of us, but also out of the way so we wouldn't disturb the neighbors."

"Disturb the neighbors?"

"The fighting." Ace closed his eyes, his face tilted toward the sky. It still hurt to remember. "We were all so angry, and with no one around, we took that anger out on each other."

"Angry?"

Ace nodded. He opened his eyes to gaze out at the ocean. "When you watch half your unit—your brothers—get blown to pieces right in front of you because some asshole waited too long to find his balls and make the call that needed to be made, you tend to get a little angry."

"Oh my God, Ace." Colton put his hand on Ace's shoulder, and it felt nice. "I'm so sorry. I had no idea."

"SF is sort of like Fight Club in the sense that you don't talk about it. Anyway, King took us all in, made sure we made our appointments with the doc. Started using our words instead of our fists. He'd been our second-in-command, so we were used to taking orders from him. It was second nature to listen when he spoke."

"And you?"

"I was a weapons sergeant like Lucky. Red was one of our medical sergeants, Jack a communications sergeant, and Joker an engineer sergeant, because of course, the short guy

LOVE IN SPADES   121

with the shortest temper had to be in charge of demolitions." Ace chuckled, shaking his head. His smile fell away, and he sighed. "One day I was on the verge of quitting therapy. It wasn't helping me, or so I believed, and King took us all for a drive. We ended up at Pip's house. He was our other medical sergeant. When his mom saw us, she burst into tears. I was on the verge of having a panic attack right then and there." Ace blinked several times to keep back his own tears. "I was so pissed at King for bringing us there, but I behaved myself for Pip's mom, told her how sorry I was, how proud she should be of him. We told her funny stories about him, and she insisted I take some of his things because he'd always talked to her about me. Apparently the kid had looked up to me. I'd had no clue. Then King took us to Deuce's house, and his wife and little girl were there. After I hugged them both, I excused myself and went out to King's truck. I was still reeling from seeing Pip's mom, and then seeing Deuce's little girl? I snapped. When King caught up to me, I punched him in the face. I was furious. I couldn't understand why he would put us through that. We were barely hanging on, and he was making it worse.

"Then he said, 'We wouldn't have left them behind when they were alive. Are we going to do it now that they're gone? They need us.' And I froze because he was right. I'd been trying so hard not to think about my brothers and what happened to them in the hope of easing my own pain. I didn't think about them, or their families who needed us more than ever." He reached into his jacket pocket and pulled out the pack of cards.

"You had those at the house," Colton said softly.

"They were a gift from Pip's mother. She was always buying him decks of cards. When she spotted these, she knew Pip would have loved the design, so she bought them and gave them to me." He swallowed hard and sniffed, wiping away a tear that escaped and rolled down his cheek. "Pip always had a pack of cards on him. He was good, but we always beat him, and he was determined to win against us one day. King, Red, Lucky, and I have been playing cards all our lives. We played on the base, during training. The rest of the guys would volunteer us for games because they knew we'd win. We had a knack for it, I guess."

"Is that where the nicknames came from?"

Ace smiled. "That was Pip. He was the youngest in our unit, real sweet guy, always so damned optimistic. We were always teasing him about how he shit rainbows. He was a tough son of a bitch but looked like a fluffy bunny. He nicknamed us the Kings because he said something about the four of us together gave off this larger than life, kingly presence. Personally, I thought he was full of shit but couldn't deny that the four of us had formed a bond since we'd met. He nicknamed us, then the rest of the group, and he was so damned excited about it. No one had the heart to tell the kid no. He was the annoying little brother none of us had.

"He picked Ace for me because he was a big dork," Ace said with a chuckle, his heart squeezing at the image of Pip and his wide smile. "Sometimes I'd say something, and he'd put his thumbs up, this big dopey grin on his face, and say 'You're aces.' He was ridiculous. Lucky got his name because he was always boasting about all the men and women he'd gotten lucky with in the clubs back home. He's always been a bit of a player. Red was the king of hearts because he was the sweetheart of the group. Always polite, opening doors for people, thanking them, winning hearts with that charming smile of his. King was our fearless leader, but Pip was always going on about how King was a diamond in the rough, and one day someone was going to

LOVE IN SPADES   123

get through that grumpy exterior to the jewel underneath. Used to drive King crazy. It was amazing. Jack really is a Jack of all trades. Guy's like fucking MacGyver. Give him a paperclip and some bubblegum and he'll build you a rocket launcher. Crazy smart too. Joker, well, the name's self-explanatory, but as you've heard, he can be a little scary." Ace's smile fell away, and he let out a sigh. "I'm grateful to have them in my life, but I miss Pip like hell. I miss all of them."

"I'm so sorry." Colton slipped his arm through Ace's. It was nice, sitting here together, Colton's arm around his, and his warm body pressed to Ace's side from shoulder to knee. Ace allowed himself to lean into Colton, absorbing the comfort he offered. "Thank you."

"For what?" Ace asked quietly as Colton laid his head against Ace's.

"For trusting me."

"You trusted me," Ace reminded him. "I appreciate that, and so you know, it means more to me than you think."

Colton pulled back enough to deliver the sweetest kiss to Ace's cheek before he laid his head back against Ace's. They sat in companionable silence, and Ace was at peace. It had been a long time since he'd sat with someone on the beach watching the waves. He appreciated Colton's quiet support, but it was his willingness to trust Ace that hit him harder than expected. Whatever was happening between them was more than physical, and every minute he spent with Colton was another crack in the wall Ace had created around his heart.

SEVEN

"COLTON?"

The man was beautiful, no doubt about it. Over the last few days, Colton found himself taking his breakfast out on the veranda at the same time every morning. At first he'd told himself he wanted to start his day off with a calming view of the ocean. When Ace jogged down to the beach wearing nothing but sports shorts and sneakers, Colton's libido promptly informed him he wasn't fooling anyone.

Colton sat up in the hopes of getting a better look at the tattoo that ran from his left pectoral muscle over his shoulder and down his arm. It was black lines, very detailed, but Colton couldn't tell what it was of from this distance. He could, however, admire all that tanned skin and sculpted muscle. It was a body forged from grueling military training and harsh conditions. Colton worked hard at keeping himself fit, but he did it from the comfort of his home gym.

Strong broad shoulders tapered down to a trim waist, the sports shorts accentuating that perfectly round ass. Ace had strong legs and firm calves. The man was a sleek powerhouse of physical fitness. He was also incredibly sweet as he played with Ginger, Colton's neighbor's golden retriever. Ginger's person let her out every morning, and as soon as she did her business, she went for a play on the beach. Now she'd found a new playmate, she headed straight for Ace every time, running alongside him as he jogged along the shore. They played tag and fetch and made Colton want one of his own. The dog wouldn't be a bad idea either.

"Maybe I should get a dog."

"I'm sorry?"

Colton turned to face Nadine, who sat across from him on the veranda where they were having breakfast together before getting down to business. She crossed one long leg over the other, looking gorgeous as usual in her designer white pantsuit, the color and cut going beautifully with her dark skin and ample curves

"A dog," Colton said, taking a sip of his coffee. It wasn't even seven in the morning, and the humidity was already fogging up his sunglasses. He moved them to his head. "I think it'd be nice to have someone to come home to."

Nadine eyed him. "Are we still talking about the dog?"

"Yes, we're still talking about the dog," he said with a laugh, throwing his napkin at her.

She put her hands up in surrender. "Just checking. Did you hear anything I said before your brain short circuited and you started daydreaming about... dogs?"

Colton blinked at her. "Um, no."

"Ah, I see." She gazed off into the distance and sighed. "The view *is* pretty spectacular." She shot him a glance and waggled her eyebrows. "The ocean isn't half-bad either."

Colton laughed. "You see? So you can't blame me. God, that's so unprofessional. Perving on your security detail."

LOVE IN SPADES 127

"Not perving," Nadine said with a sniff. "Admiring the man's assets."

"I like the way you think."

"Things have improved I see."

"Why fight it? If having the Kings here will make my father feel better and show him once and for all that he's overreacting, then so be it."

"So things between you and Mr. Guard-My-Body are getting along?"

"Funny." Colton shook his head in amusement. "Yes, we're getting along. He's doing his job. I was being childish and let my emotions get the better of me. It wasn't right for me to take it out on him."

Nadine let out a mock gasp, her hand going to her chest. "You? Being a diva? I don't believe it."

Colton narrowed his eyes. "Remind me why I keep you around again?"

"Because I'm the best executive assistant you will ever have, and because I'm your friend, so I know better than to put up with your bullshit."

"That would also explain all the meddling."

A napkin wacked him in the face, and he fell back in his chair with a cackle. He loved getting a rise out of her. "How's Joshua doing?" he asked, picking up a slice of toast.

"I love that kid. He's a whizz and such a sweetheart. You found us another gem."

"I had a feeling about him. I'm glad he's doing well." He sipped his latte as Nadine removed her tablet from her bag.

"Okay, you said you wanted to go over your schedule."

Colton nodded. "I want to cancel and postpone anything that's not critical."

Nadine blinked at him. "Seriously?"

"Until this mess is over."

"Why?"

Colton tried not to squirm under her piercing hazel eyes. "I'm supposed to be on vacation, remember?"

Nadine scoffed. "You haven't taken a vacation since your last trip to Disney World. You were twelve. Try again."

"Fine. I'm supposed to be on vacation, and I don't want to make the Kings' job harder than it has to be."

"The Kings or one particular King?" Her eyes sparkled with mischief that Colton chose to ignore.

He shrugged casually. "The sooner they figure this mess out, the sooner I get my life back."

"Right."

Colton arched an eyebrow at her. "Is there something you'd like to say?"

"Nope." She tapped away at her tablet with her perfectly manicured nails. "So, what are we keeping?"

"My father's retirement party, obviously, and the Sapphire Sands Charity Masquerade. Send my regrets to the hosts of the other three engagements, and cancel travel arrangements. We'll keep anything that's at least three months out until we see where things are."

"What about the party you promised Laz to celebrate his invite to next year's Fashion Week in Paris? It's tomorrow night, and the venders are scheduled to start coming in from noon onward."

Colton let out a groan. "Shit, I forgot about that. I love Laz, but his friends drive me fucking crazy. My house is going to be overrun by a hoard of slutty models."

"Are you saying all models are slutty?" She narrowed her eyes at him, as if he'd forgotten her short modeling career. Nadine's mother had groomed her since childhood in the hopes of making her the next modeling sensation. Too bad she hadn't asked Nadine what she wanted. Whenever anyone asked her why she left that world, Nadine shrugged and said she enjoyed eating too much. In truth, it had been her mother's dream, not hers. Now she was a stunningly beautiful woman who could walk into any boardroom and hold her own against any corporate suit. Anyone who thought she was just a pretty face or pair of boobs would be annihilated. That's why he paid her ridiculous amounts of money. The woman had no fear.

"No, I don't think all models are sluts," he said, giving her a pointed look. "Only Laz's friends. Or should I say Bryan's friends."

"Gio's had no luck either, huh?" Nadine asked, her hazel eyes filled with sympathy and concern, a concern she shared with Colton and Laz's older brother, Gio, who was a good friend and Colton's old college roommate.

"How can Laz not see what a horrible influence Bryan is? He's managed to alienate all the good people Laz had around him before they met. Bryan's nasty, catty attitude drove Laz's friends away, and he can't see it because Bryan's convinced him that what they have is love. If that's not bad enough, wherever Bryan goes, he's followed by his little entourage of vapid, squawking ostriches."

Nadine gasped. "Colton, that's mean. What have those poor ostriches ever done to you?"

"You're right," Colton said, shaking his head remorsefully. "What was I thinking? I'm sorry." He let out a heavy sigh. "Laz is such a happy-go-lucky guy, always so sweet and cheerful. I worry about him surrounded by all that toxicity, though the drugs are what we're worried about most. Laz swears Bryan doesn't touch the stuff, but there were rumors about a party Bryan was at last year in Milan that got out of control. Laz wasn't there, thank God, but it also meant Bryan could deny everything."

"Is that the party where a model was found dead in the pool?"

Colton nodded somberly. "Overdose. Laz was supposed to have gone with Bryan, but I was able to get him a press pass for Guns N' Roses when they were in Miami. Laz had a huge fight with Bryan over it, but he wasn't going to miss the opportunity to meet his dad's favorite band. It meant too much to him. Gio wants me to have a talk with Laz, but what am I supposed to say to him that his brother hasn't?"

Nadine let out a heavy sigh. "Laz always tries to see the good in people, which is great, but that also leaves him open to getting taken advantage of. Maybe he'll listen this time. The kid's looked up to you since he was in high school. If he's going to listen to anyone, it'll be you."

Colton wasn't so sure, but he'd give it a try, for Gio and for Laz. The two had been through so much already, he couldn't do nothing. At least once a month he tried to have lunch with Laz if he was in the country and not being dragged around the world by his selfish boyfriend.

"The party's still on, then?" Nadine asked to confirm.

"Yes."

"And your lunch meeting with Helen?"

"Give her my sincerest apologies, but we'll have to reschedule."

Nadine nodded as she made notes. They talked some more, gossiped, and he hugged her tight at the front door, promising to keep her informed. Then he headed outside, greeting members of the Kings' security team. They greeted him in return before notifying Ace of his movements. Originally it had annoyed the hell out of him, but now, having Ace know his whereabouts didn't bother him. Knowing Ace was on the other end of that radio made Colton feel... comforted.

Outside, he took the stairs down to the pool area and changed into swim trunks inside the cabana. He grabbed a beach bag, stuffed a couple of towels inside, a bottle of sunscreen, and a bottle of water before he slipped into some flip-flops. He took the huge beach umbrella leaning against the outside of the cabana and headed for the private walkway that led down to the beach. Ace was on his way up. His smile when he caught sight of Colton was breathtaking, and Colton wasn't sure whether it was the bright sun and fierce heat making his skin flush or the sight of Ace heading toward him wearing nothing but wet swim shorts and a dazzling smile.

"Hey," Colton said, his voice breaking. *My God, could he be any more awkward?*

"Hey," Ace replied, his crooked smile making Colton melt. He leaned against the railing. "What time are you planning to head out for your lunch meeting?"

"I've apparently come down with one of those twenty-four-hour bugs." He coughed weakly into his hand, making Ace chuckle.

"Man, that sucks. What's the doc prescribe?"

"A lazy day on the beach, drinking sangria and playing with the neighbor's dog."

"I think maybe I need to switch doctors." Ace motioned to the house. "I should go get dressed."

"Why?"

Ace's lips twitched like he wanted to laugh. "I shouldn't get dressed?"

"I mean, if you're going to be out here with me, why are you going to change? You'll get sand in your boots. Also, I know you're a professional, but an all-black uniform in Florida weather? Really?"

Ace did chuckle then. "Actually, black is the best color

to wear in the sun. Yes, it absorbs the sun, but it also absorbs your body's energy instead of reflecting it out."

"I'll keep that in mind for next time," Colton said with a wink. He motioned to the beach behind Ace. "I'm going to go for a swim."

"Lead the way."

It was still early in the morning on a weekday, so few people were out, mostly a jogger here and there. With it being a residential area rather than a tourist one, the only beachgoers tended to be people who lived in the area. Colton picked a spot near the water but not too close, and Ace reached for the umbrella.

"Here, let me. You sort out your towel."

"Thanks." Colton beamed up at him and removed the huge beach towel from the bag as Ace opened the umbrella and speared it into the sand in one swift move. He angled it back, and Colton thanked him again before handing him one end of the towel. The barely-there breeze wouldn't be enough to move it, but he always kept four of the sandbag weights in his beach tote just in case. All set up, he dropped down onto the towel and started lathering himself up with sunscreen. He'd be back inside before the noon sun came up, but he knew better than to be out here without sunscreen. Even on a stormy, cloudy day, the sun still managed to burn.

"Need help?" Ace asked, and Colton would have loved to be able to see the man's beautiful gold-green eyes, but the mirrored aviators prevented it.

"That would be great. Thank you."

Ace took the bottle from him, and the sand shifted behind Colton when Ace dropped to his knees behind him. He heard the cap open, and he closed his eyes when his mind conjured up images of a different type of bottle being opened. Ace's hands on his back didn't help, and Colton struggled to think unsexy thoughts. He was *not* going to get a hard-on while Ace put sunscreen on him. That was easier said than done with Ace's big strong hands gliding across his skin, massaging his shoulders, and making him feel so damned good. Colton hung his head forward, and a groan slipped out.

"You're tense," Ace said, pressing his fingers into the muscles between Colton's neck and shoulders. Colton hissed at the sudden pain. "Sorry, it'll feel better after. I promise."

Colton nodded. "I trust you."

Ace's hands stopped moving for a heartbeat before he resumed undoing the tension knots in Colton's muscles. What caused the sudden halt? Colton recalled Ace's words regarding Colton's trust meaning more to him than he could know. Had someone betrayed Ace's trust or failed to trust him? It seemed very important to Ace, and Colton couldn't imagine betraying him. Another jolt of pain went through him, and he jerked, throwing his arm back on instinct, and clutching Ace's thigh.

"Sorry. Almost done," Ace said, his voice low and husky.

"It's okay." Colton's words weren't more than a whisper, and he silently cursed himself. The man was trying to help him out, and Colton was having seriously dirty thoughts about him. Ace had made it clear that whatever was happening between them couldn't happen. Colton needed to respect the man's wishes.

Ace's hands slid from his shoulders to his neck, and Colton leaned his head back, gazing up at Ace, who dropped his chin to look down at him. His thumbs caressed Colton's jaw, sending the most delicious shiver through him, and Colton dug his fingers into Ace's thigh, his pulse speeding up.

"Ace...."

Ace cleared his throat, his hands slipping from Colton. "There you go. All done."

"Thanks." Colton smiled, doing his best not to let his disappointment show. If he wasn't careful, he could end up doing something foolish, like losing his heart. He turned his attention to the water. "I went over my schedule with Nadine. We canceled and rescheduled any engagements that weren't a priority. Unfortunately that means tomorrow's pool party is still on."

"Unfortunately?" Ace took a seat beside him on the towel, legs bent and arms resting on his knees. "You don't sound too happy about it. Can't you cancel?"

Colton shook his head. "I'd promised a good friend I would help him celebrate his invite to Fashion Week in Paris next year. Laz is a very talented fashion photographer whose career is finally taking off. I went to college with his older brother, Gio, and Laz was always around. He's a good kid. It's his boyfriend and his boyfriend's friends I'm not a fan of." Colton shared his concerns with Ace.

"I'll make sure the team keeps an eye on them," Ace said, his frown deep. "Thing is, if your friend Laz is crazy about this guy, he's not going to want to hear anything said against him. He needs to see for himself. Have you and Bryan spent time around each other?"

"We've been to some of the same parties. The only reason he tolerates me is because I know a good number of important people in his industry. He might come off like an airhead, but believe me, that's a very clever disguise. The man is dangerous. He's sly and calculating."

"Okay. Thanks for the heads up. I'll be sure to keep you

posted. And thank you for rearranging your schedule. I know how inconvenient that is, and I appreciate it."

"It makes sense. Besides, I'm supposed to be on vacation, right?" Colton winked at him. "King's already vetted the guests, but that doesn't mean someone won't cause trouble. Nadine informed each guest about the added security, and how if anyone shows up not on the list, they're not getting in. Bryan's going to be extra pissy."

"Why's that?"

"He has a habit of turning his plus ones into open invitations, and I'm not having that in my home. It's enough I made an exception for him and his entourage. We've also made it known that anyone who dares to bring drugs into my home will be dealt with."

Ace nodded. "We'll take care of it. Discreetly of course."

"Thank you."

"So, is there going to be anyone at the party that's not a model?"

"The rest are members of the fashion industry in some way or another. A few designers, PR people, fashion magazine editors, a few more photographers, though no one has permission to take pictures. It's part of the agreement they made when they RSVP'd. No photos, no video."

"Not your first rodeo, huh?"

"Oh God, no. I've been working the party circuit since I was a kid. My grandmother would throw the most ridiculously elaborate parties and invite everyone who was anyone. My mom's parties were trendier, but no less pretentious. It was all about status and gossip. What was everyone wearing, who had lunch on who's yacht, who was sleeping with their pool boy, because yes, my life resembled an episode of *The Young and the Restless.*"

Ace laughed, and Colton smiled at the sound.

"Made for fascinating people watching. The parties my parents threw in the eighties are still my favorite. The shoulder pads alone. I'm talking impressive wingspan here. You should have seen them trying to work the room. I still remember one party where my mother turned suddenly to talk to a friend and almost took out a waiter."

Ace threw his head back and laughed, and Colton couldn't help but join in. He put a hand to Ace's shoulder.

"No, really. You know in those old movies when you get the one guy carrying a really long ladder, and he swings around, and the ladder ends up whacking someone and knocking them on their ass? That's what it was like, but with more sequin."

"Stop," Ace laughed, removing his sunglasses to wipe the tears from his eyes. "I can't breathe."

They both laughed like a couple of schoolboys before a bark caught their attention and Ginger came bounding over, kicking up sand when she skidded to a halt beside them, her tail wagging furiously as she launched herself at Ace, licking him all over. Colton had never been so envious in his life. What he wouldn't give to lick Ace all over.

Ace jumped to his feet, and took off with Ginger barking excitedly as she ran circles around him. Damn, but the man was stunning. His tanned skin glistened from the lotion he was wearing and the sun beating down on him. He didn't seem to notice, but Colton imagined Ace had most likely faced far worse conditions. Deciding he wasn't going to let Colton miss out on the fun, Ace waved him over, and Colton got to his feet. He jogged over, laughing when Ginger ran around him. After working up a sweat playing with Ginger, Colton was ready for a swim. He tossed his sunglasses in the sand, and cast Ace a wicked grin.

LOVE IN SPADES   137

"Last one in gets to tell Lucky what happened to his Gucci sandal." Namely Ginger had turned the expensive footwear into an overpriced chew toy.

"Oh hell no."

Colton laughed as he bolted toward the water. He'd been about to dive in when Ace grabbed him around the waist and hauled him off his feet. Determined not to go down without taking Ace with him, he wrapped himself around Ace, and threw his weight into it, bringing them both crashing into the warm water. Colton popped up and wiped the water from his face. He laughed when Ace slowly rose from the water, his expression deadpan. For some reason, that had Colton laughing his ass off.

"You think that's funny?"

Colton nodded. "I do, actually. Especially the way your hair is sticking up," Colton said, putting an index finger to each side of his head. "Looks like you have two little horns."

Ace ran his hands through his hair, his chest and arm muscles flexing with the move, leaving Colton with a slack jaw. The amount of sex appeal was obscene, and Colton quickly closed his mouth, narrowing his eyes when Ace's grin turned smug. He headed for Colton, his movements sleek and powerful as he cut through the water.

"What are you doing?" Colton asked, slowly moving away. "Ace?"

Ace's lips curled into a wicked grin, and he dove under the water. Colton stilled, waiting for Ace to pop, but he didn't. Jesus, the guy could hold his breath for a long time. It was like he'd vanished. Until something grabbed Colton's legs. He released a barrage of curses as he was lifted, his arms flailing in an attempt not to lose his balance as Ace came up under him, and Colton ended up on Ace's shoulders.

"You ass!" Colton hugged Ace's head to keep himself steady as he sat on the man's broad shoulders while Ace laughed himself silly. He held on to Colton's thighs, and started walking. "What are you doing?" Colton squeaked.

"Going for a walk," Ace said as if it were obvious.

"No, you have something devious planned; I know it."

Ace chuckled. "Are you doubting me?"

"Absolutely. Remember the pool?"

"In my defense, *you* were being an ass."

Colton let out a mock gasp. "Are you using inappropriate language toward your client?"

"I'll show you inappropriate." Ace growled deep in his throat, and Colton shivered.

"Ace," Colton moaned. "Please don't make that sound while my crotch is pressed against the back of your head."

Ace stopped moving. Before Colton could ask if he was okay, Ace sank into the water, and disappeared again, leaving Colton standing there wondering what the man was about to do next. One thing was for sure, Ace always kept him on his toes. Hands caressed his legs, and Colton groaned, his eyes closing as Ace slid his hands up Colton's body until he resurfaced, his arms around Colton and front pressed to Colton's back. Colton covered Ace's hands with his and leaned back into him before turning in his arms.

"We should head back," Ace murmured, his eyes on Colton's lips.

"You drive me fucking crazy, you know that?" Colton huffed. He slipped his hands beneath the water and cupped Ace through his shorts, making him groan. "How about you stop teasing me, take control of these gorgeous balls, and bury yourself deep inside me."

Ace cursed under his breath. He opened his mouth to

reply, but Colton put his fingers to Ace's lips and released his hold on him.

"You know where to find me." Colton turned and swam back to the shore. If Ace was determined to drive him out of his mind with his sensual caresses, lingering looks, and sultry voice, then it was only fair Colton return the favor.

Ace was quiet on the way back to the house, and Colton hid his satisfaction. Despite Ace's sunglasses, his frown told Colton he was seriously contemplating his words. It was clear Ace couldn't help himself when it came to being in Colton's personal space. He loved having the man there, but something had to give.

They took turns rinsing off beneath the outside shower, and as they headed for the cabana, Ace stopped him.

"After lunch, meet me in the game room. I want to teach you some self-defense moves."

Colton nodded. "Sure. Do you need me to wear anything in particular?"

"Sneakers and workout clothes will be fine."

"Sure." Colton headed inside, aware of Ace remaining several steps behind. Ace seemed lost in thought as he muttered something to Colton about seeing him in a bit. Colton nodded, holding back a laugh. Once in his room, he quickly undressed and showered. By the time he'd dressed in a loose pair of charcoal-gray workout pants, a black V-neck T-shirt, and running shoes, he was starving. He headed down to the kitchen, where he found Ace sitting at the counter staring off into space as Red scooped what looked like beef and broccoli into a large bowl of white rice. He placed it in front of Ace and smiled wide when he saw Colton.

"Hey. Hungry?"

"Starving." Colton went over to the giant now-half-empty pot on the stove. "God, that smells amazing. You know I did offer to have food brought in for you guys." He took a seat at the counter next to Ace, who nodded a quick greeting before going back to his food. What was this now? Oh, this wouldn't do.

"I'm so sorry, Colton. Have I overstepped? We're kind of used to cooking. We tend to take turns, but Ace is excused, and Lucky's been busy with the team, so I've been doing it. I don't mind."

Colton tilted his head. "Hm, do I mind having a handsome man cook delicious food for me?" He held back a smile when Ace's fork paused halfway to his mouth. "Nope. I have no problem with that at all. But if you find you're not able, please just have food brought in."

Red nodded and placed a bowl in front of him. "Drink?"

"I'll have some of that amazing sweet tea you brewed the other day."

"Sure."

"I'll get it," Ace said, jumping out of his chair.

"It's fine, Ace. You're eating," Red said, but Ace was already up and removing the pitcher of sweet tea from the fridge. He placed it on the counter before plucking a glass from the cabinet and filling it. After returning the tea to the fridge, he placed the glass in front of Colton, a lemon wedge sitting on the rim like Colton preferred. He checked to make sure Red was turned away before leaning in, hissing quietly.

"Handsome?"

Colton shrugged before taking a sip of his tea. He did his best to hide his smile when Ace plopped down beside him and pulled his bowl close, stabbing his food like he was preventing it from attacking first.

LOVE IN SPADES   141

"Mm, que rico. Damn, that smells good." Lucky strolled into the kitchen and joined Red at the stove. "You make the best beef and broccoli. I was thinking tonight I'd make mama's carne asada. What do you think?"

Red moaned. "Yes, please. But you have to make the yuca with the mojo."

Lucky grabbed Red's face and squeezed his cheeks. "For you, bro, anything." He planted a big sloppy kiss on Red's cheek, and Red shoved him away playfully.

Colton chuckled. He loved watching the three Kings interact. He imagined it was how brothers behaved. They argued, laughed, roughhoused like big kids, drove each other crazy, but most importantly, they loved each other. At times Colton wished his parents hadn't stopped at one child.

"What is wrong with your face?" Lucky asked Ace, poking his cheek. Ace smacked his hand away and glared at him.

"Poke me one more time, and I'm gonna break that finger."

Colton winced. From what he'd seen, he got the feeling Lucky didn't respond well to threats, family or not.

"Yeah? Is that so?" Lucky said, lifting a finger and wiggling it in front of Ace. "This finger? This finger here?"

Ace seemed to be in a mood, and fearful for Lucky's life, as well as his furniture, Colton blurted out the first thing that popped into his mind.

"The dog ate your shoe."

Somewhere to his right, Red choked on his food while Ace gaped at Colton. Lucky squinted at him.

"What? What are you talking about?"

"Your, um, your missing Gucci sandal. Ginger ate it.

Well, she didn't eat it, she chewed on it. Repeatedly. It did not survive."

Lucky gasped, his expression one of sheer horror. "My Gucci?"

Ace doubled over and howled with laughter, his hands on his stomach and his face turning bright red. Red joined him, and Colton tried so hard not laugh. So hard.

"I'm sorry," Colton said, his voice breaking from how badly he was trying to control himself.

"Motherfucker!" Lucky turned pained eyes on his cousin. "Do you think King will—how do you say that? ¿Crees que me reembolsará el dinero? It was a work-related incident."

At that, Ace laughed harder. He tried to talk, but when nothing happened, he gave up.

"I'm serious, bro." Lucky folded his arms over his chest and pouted. "I loved those shoes."

"Oh my God, I can't breathe," Ace wheezed. "Please. *Please* ask King to reimburse you for your Gucci sandals. I need to see that."

Lucky flipped him off. "Whatever."

"I'm sorry, Lucky. I'll be more than happy to replace them. Come on, sit down. Have some lunch."

"Thank you, Colton, but they were a limited edition. Very hard to find." Lucky sat next to Ace, mumbling to himself in Spanish. Colton didn't get all of it, but some words in there certainly didn't require translation. Red served him up a bowl, and Lucky grumbled a "thanks." Poor guy. Maybe Colton could have a word with one of his acquaintances in the fashion world and see if someone could track down a pair of those sandals. If not, maybe Colton could surprise him with a little something special to make it up to him.

LOVE IN SPADES   143

Once they'd eaten lunch and helped Red clean up, Ace motioned for Colton to follow him into the game room, which had plenty of space and the carpet would provide a better cushion for the times Colton was sure he'd land on his ass. Ace was back to wearing his black cargo pants, black T-shirt, and combat boots. He stopped in the center of the room and turned to face Colton.

"Do I get a gun?" Colton asked.

"Have you ever fired a gun?"

"No. I'm not really a fan."

"It's amazing how many clients believe we're going to arm them. Even if you were an expert marksman, you wouldn't get a gun. You get a pen."

Wait.... "A pen?"

"Yep. Titanium." Ace handed Colton a silver pen, and Colton hesitantly took it from him. He held it up in front of him and peered at it.

"I'm supposed to fend off an attacker with a pen?" Was it a Bond pen? If he clicked the end or twisted it, would it release a toxic gas or set off an explosive? He clicked the end, and the ink nib popped out. Nope. It was just a pen.

"It's a tactical weapon," Ace assured him. "With the right amount of force in the right place, it can cause some serious damage."

Colton eyed him skeptically. "You're messing with me."

"No."

"What if *they* have a gun?"

"That's a different lesson."

Colton sighed. "Okay, show me."

"Not if you're going to give me attitude."

"I'm not giving you attitude."

Ace held his hand out. "Give me the pen."

"No. It's my pen." Colton clutched it to his chest. "You gave it to me."

"Seriously?"

"Yes. This is the only defense I have. You're not taking it from me."

"Colton, you do realize I could take it from you without you even realizing."

"Oh yeah, Mr. Hot-Shot-Green-Beret? Then do it."

"Colton," Ace warned.

"Come on. I want to see your super-secret moves."

"I don't even know what to say to you right now, other than you're being ridiculous. And I have your pen." Ace held up a silver pen.

"What the hell?" Colton gaped at his empty hands before his head shot up. "How'd you do that?"

"With years of practice. Now, are you going to pay attention?"

"Yes."

"Good."

"Can I have my pen back?"

Ace pressed his lips together like he was trying to keep from laughing. The guy was so fucking sexy. Colton wanted to climb him and do terrible things to his body. Instead he took the pen Ace handed him.

"Thank you."

"Okay, put that in your pocket. First I'm going to demonstrate the moves." Ace pulled his own pen from his pocket."

"Ooh, yours is black. It looks very serious."

"It's the same as yours, but black."

"It camouflages with your clothes."

"Yes."

"Does it come in different colors?"

"You should know that I'm two seconds away from putting you in a sleeper hold."

Colton threw his head back and laughed.

"You shit." Ace punched Colton in the shoulder, making him laugh harder. "You're purposefully trying to get a rise out of me."

"It's so easy. You're easy."

"Not until the second date."

Colton snickered. "I bet."

Ace's gold-green eyes danced with amusement. "Hey, I expect to be wined and dined before I put out."

"Classy lady."

"Damn right." Ace stepped back and held his pen up. "Okay, so I want you to get a firm grip on it."

The words were out of Colton's mouth before he could stop them. "That's what he said."

"Oh Jesus, would you pay attention? I'm trying to show you life-saving techniques here."

"I'm sorry. You're right." Colton was so not sorry.

"Okay, now grab it firmly, and I swear to God if you say 'that's what he said' at any point during this demonstration, I'm going to dropkick you."

"I'm sorry," Colton said with a laugh. He inhaled deeply, then released the breath slowly through his mouth and schooled his expression. "Okay, serious face. This is me being serious."

"I can't with you right now." Ace headed for the door, and Colton ran up to him, grabbing his hand.

"Wait, I'll behave. I promise."

Ace crossed his arms over his chest. "I don't believe you."

"Why?"

"For one, you can't stop laughing."

"This is true." It was like he was drunk, but he wasn't. Scratch that, he was. He was drunk on Ace and how he'd never had this much fun with anyone in his life. No one made him laugh like this without even trying. He could tell Ace wasn't mad, and he'd even go as far as to say the guy might be enjoying himself despite his incredible poker face. Colton held his pen out to Ace. "I'm ready. Show me where to stick it. But be gentle. It's been a while."

Ace groaned and ran a hand over his face. Colton doubled over laughing.

"What's gotten into you?"

"I think maybe Red put something in his delicious beef and broccoli."

"Red? You mean *handsome* Red?"

Colton smiled wickedly. "What? He is handsome. I think it's the freckles. I have a thing for freckles."

Ace arched an eyebrow at him. "I have freckles."

Colton stepped up to him and pretended to inspect his face. "Hm, well, what do you know. You do. They're very faint, but they're there."

"They're in other places too."

Colton hummed. "Is that so?" He lifted a finger to tap Ace's nose when suddenly he found himself with his back pressed to Ace's front, Ace's arm around his neck, and his free hand on Colton's waist.

"Now, how about we get started."

Something told him he was going to enjoy this demonstration.

EIGHT

"COLT!"

Laz came bounding over and threw himself into Colton's open arms, making him groan. Last night's demonstration had left him sore, and not in a fun way. What Colton had hoped would lead into some sexy-times turned into an intense lesson in self-defense. Though being able to throw Ace over his shoulder had been oddly satisfying.

"It feels like I haven't seen you in forever," Laz said, smiling brightly. He might be all grown-up at twenty-eight years old, and a well-known photographer traveling the world with his infamous model boyfriend, but to Colton he was still that scrawny kid who'd show up at their dorm room to play video games and annoy the hell out of his big brother.

"It's so good to see you, Laz." Colton held him out at arm's length, smiling at the übertrendy haircut he was sure hadn't been Laz's idea. He ran his fingers through the long black curly fringe, the sides styled in a high fade. "Nice do."

"Thanks." Laz shrugged. "It was Bryan's idea."

Of course it was. Colton tried not to frown at Laz's too-thin frame. Laz had always been slender, but at just under six feet tall, he looked underweight. Bryan— long-legged, blond, and with cheekbones sharp enough to cut someone— sauntered up to them, blue eyes sweeping over Colton.

"Hey, handsome." Bryan flung an arm over Laz's shoulder, and Laz made to scratch the back of his head, forcing Bryan's arm off his shoulder. *What's this now?* Had something changed since Colton had last seen these two?

"Hi, Bryan." Colton motioned down to Bryan's barely-there white swimsuit—if it could be called that—and the shimmering, sheer white coverup that failed miserably at its only objective. "Ready for the pool, I see. Where are your friends?"

"Outside changing. I don't see why we need to bother with clothes anyway. You don't allow photos, and it's a private party."

"It's still my home," Colton said politely. "And I'd rather not have anyone's bare ass on my furniture." He needed to thank Ace for strategically placing security personnel around the house, including upstairs near the bedrooms. Bryan's friends had the habit of getting drunk and searching out the nearest place to get laid, and that was so not happening in one of his rooms.

Bryan scoffed like a petulant child before something shiny caught his attention. "Ooh, who's that?" Bryan bit down on his lower lip.

Colton rolled his eyes and shook his head before turning to see who Bryan was trying to eye-fuck, despite his boyfriend standing right next to him, and Colton's jaw clenched. He turned back to Bryan, eyes narrowed.

"That's Ace. He's my personal security."

Whereas Laz's expression turned concerned, Bryan's turned interested. *The little shit.*

LOVE IN SPADES 149

Laz put his hand on Colton's arm, giving it a gentle squeeze. "Colt? Is everything okay? Since when do you need personal security?"

"It's a long, boring story. Trust me," Colton said, waving a hand dismissively. Laz didn't look convinced. "Really, Laz, it's no big deal. Dad's overreacting, and I'm letting him be all fatherly. After his heart attack, he's supposed to be taking it easy, so I'm letting this play out."

"Can we meet Mr....?"

"Sure."

Ace turned, as if sensing Colton's eyes on him, and headed in his direction. Colton couldn't fault Bryan for his interest. Ace was even more handsome and imposing than usual in his all-black suit and black shirt, which Colton would guess was his intention. No one could mistake his role at the party. The suit emphasized the breadth of his chest and shoulders. He walked with confidence, exuding power and an air of danger.

"Ace, this is Laz, a good friend, and his boyfriend, Bryan."

Ace took hold of Laz's hand and shook it, his smile wide. "It's nice to meet you, Laz."

Bryan made a show of holding out his hand, as if he expected Ace to kiss it. Colton had to give it to Ace, the man was an expert at schooling his expression. His smile didn't falter, but it didn't reach his eyes. He took hold of Bryan's hand and gave it a squeeze before letting go.

"Good to meet you, Bryan."

"So, you're here to personally protect Colton. Does that mean you go wherever he goes?"

"Correct."

"That must get so boring," Bryan said with a pout.

Colton barely refrained from rolling his eyes. It wasn't

the first time Bryan had proclaimed Colton to be stuffy and boring.

"Not really," Ace said, hands clasped in front of him.

Bryan stepped up to Ace and squeezed his bicep with a giggle. "My God, you're so big."

Laz's eyes went slightly wide, and his lips pressed together in a thin line, but he didn't speak. Colton had seen this act before, and whereas it usually got Bryan the attention he was after, Ace wasn't having any of it. He politely removed Bryan from his person.

"I'm going to have to ask you to keep your distance, Bryan." He smiled then, and Bryan melted under his gaze. "I'm currently on the job and can't afford to be distracted."

The stroke to Bryan's ego did the trick, and Bryan let out a little gasp. "Oh, of course. I'm so sorry." He took a step back and batted his lashes. "I know you're personally assigned to protect Colton, but let's say someone else at the party was in need of your... services. Would you step in to assist?"

"It depends on the situation, but don't worry, my team is here to provide support."

Bryan nodded before someone called him, and he excused himself. Laz stayed behind.

"Everything okay?" Colton asked him.

Laz looked uncertain, and Colton motioned toward the bar outside since everyone was busy having fun in the pool or chatting around it in the lounge chairs. "Have a drink with me."

It was a beautiful day in the high eighties with enough sea breeze to battle the heat and humidity. The event company Nadine hired did a wonderful job with the décor, the tropical theme subtle with its use of color, most of it found in the gorgeous flower arrangements expertly laid out. Bryan and his friends preened, flirted, and flaunted for the crowd as if everyone had come to see them. The group was made up of about a dozen models—young men and women who were beautiful on the outside, but not so much on the inside. The rest of the guests consisted of fashion industry professionals. Colton made sure to greet them on the way to the bar, making polite but short conversation. Many were good people, and Colton enjoyed talking with them, but he was more concerned about Laz right now.

When they reached the bar, they took a seat on the stools and put in their orders with the bartender. Ace stood close to Colton, and Colton was taken aback by how at ease it made him feel. He'd never felt unease in his own home, and with the exception of having to put up with Bryan and the model hoard for a few hours, he didn't feel uneasy now, but having Ace beside him was soothing.

Bryan's friends gathered around the pool, sipping cocktails and cackling loudly, many of them giggling at the various members of the Kings security team surveilling the property, several of whom had been assigned to the pool area. As expected with so many beefy men and women in uniform around, the horny vultures circled, batting their lashes and pouting their lips.

"Are they going to be okay?" Laz asked worriedly.

Ace smiled warmly. "Don't worry, your friends are in safe hands."

"No, I meant your team," Laz said, his frown deep. "Those guys don't know the meaning of personal boundaries."

Ace blinked at him, then smiled. "They'll be fine. They're trained for all kinds of threats, no matter the package they come in."

Laz nodded and thanked the bartender for his cocktail

before turning to Colton, his expression a mixture of sadness and anger. He checked to make sure Bryan wasn't within hearing distance before murmuring to Colton.

"He cheated on me."

"What?" Colton's temper flared. *That no-good little bastard!* "Why haven't you kicked him out on his ass?"

Laz let out a heavy sigh and leaned in, speaking quietly. "He threatened to kill himself if I left him."

"Jesus Christ." Colton took a moment to think about Bryan and everything he'd seen and heard from associates in the fashion industry. Although he wasn't one to listen to gossip and rumors, certainly not enough to form an opinion of someone, he'd been around Bryan enough to know the man. "Can I offer some advice?"

"Of course."

"Bryan is a manipulative, selfish man. He loves his life and his lifestyle, lives on the attention. He knows you're a good man and that you'd never do anything to hurt someone, much less him. He's using that against you. The next time he threatens to harm himself, tell him you're concerned and you're going to make sure to get him the help he needs. His reaction will tell you everything you need to know."

"Thank you, Colton."

"Ace?"

They looked up, and Colton smiled warmly at Red.

"Hey, Red."

"Hi, Colton." Red smiled, a dimple forming on his cheeks and confirming the charm Ace had spoken of. It was hard not to let your guard down around him. The man was taller than Ace by at least a couple of inches, and certainly had more muscle, but he had that boy-next-door kind of face, and despite his build, he gave off a friendly, approachable vibe. He was the guy who helped you change a flat tire and helped old ladies carry their groceries to their car.

"Red," Ace said, patting Red's shoulder, "this is Laz, a good friend of Colton's. Laz, this is Red. He's one of the Kings and basically one of my brothers."

"Hi," Laz said softly, taking Red's outstretched hand. His cheeks flushed, and Colton did a double take. He held back a smile as Red covered Laz's hand with his own.

"It's so nice to meet you, Laz," Red replied, his smile warm.

Colton and Ace exchanged glances before turning their attention to the two men who were still holding hands. As if sensing he'd held on a little longer than necessary, Red pulled away with a timid apology.

"It's okay," Laz said before he started nibbling on his bottom lip, which was adorable, and Colton knew it meant Laz was feeling a little flustered by the rugged king of hearts.

"Everything okay?" Ace asked Red, who turned his attention back to Ace.

"Yeah, um...." He shook his head as if clearing it. "I wanted to let you know that King's arranged a meeting with Frank on Thursday."

Ace nodded. "Thanks, buddy."

"Frank?" Colton asked, curious. He'd spoken to Frank not long after the club incident to apologize for his behavior in the man's club and for not keeping him informed. Frank had been upset with Colton for not confiding in him, but they'd talked things out. It made Colton realize that although he'd seen the threats to himself as nothing to be concerned about, it was wrong of him to believe those who loved him wouldn't be worried for him.

"We're going to have a meeting with him and his team

to discuss security during the masquerade," Ace explained. "Everyone on the guest list is being vetted by King, and Jack's running a risk assessment on the club. Don't worry, we'll have everything covered by the time you walk through the door."

Laz almost choked on his cocktail. He wiped his mouth and turned worriedly to him. "Colton, that doesn't sound like nothing to me. The Sapphire Sands Charity Masquerade has crazy security as it is, yet an entire plan has to be put in place because you're attending?"

Colton sighed. "Laz, some nut's been sending me hate mail. It's nothing new. It's possible the Kings scared this guy away. I haven't received any threats since my father signed the contract with them. It's a precaution. Okay, this is a party. Laz, you hungry?"

"Oh God, I'm starving."

Colton motioned over one of the waiters and asked him to load up a couple of plates from the buffet table and a third plate with finger foods for Ace and Red to pick at if they wanted to while they stood around surveilling. The waiter promptly returned, and they all dug in. Ace grabbed one of the small appetizers and stuffed the whole thing in his mouth, letting out a moan and making Colton laugh. The man really loved his food.

"Jesus, Ace. You can at least pretend to have some manners," Red teased.

"Whatever," Ace said with a grin, picking up an appetizer in each hand. "These bruschetta and prosciutto canapés are amazing."

"Have you tried the mini salmon tartes?" Colton asked. Ace shook his head, and Colton took one from his plate. He held it up for Ace, and Ace bent over and wrapped a hand around his wrist to steady it before biting off half, his eyes practically rolling to the back of his head as he let out a decadent moan.

"Oh my God."

"I know, right?" Colton popped the other half in his mouth before turning to Laz, who was giving him a funny look. "What?"

Laz shrugged, and Colton could tell his friend was trying very hard not to laugh.

"What? Do I have something on my face?" Colton wiped his mouth with his napkin just in case. He had no idea what had Laz giving him such a strange look.

"What?" Ace asked, and Colton looked up to see Red's bemused expression.

Colton was about to question Red, when Bryan appeared.

"Wow, really, Laz? Stuffing your face? You're supposed to be slimming down for Paris."

Laz swallowed and put the other half of his sandwich down, his cheeks flushed with obvious embarrassment.

"Colton, I can't believe all the carbs and sugar you have out here." Bryan huffed, his hands on his hips. His tiny white bathing suit was practically transparent, and Colton did his best to not comment.

Don't be catty. Don't be catty. Fuck it. "There are guests here who do eat, Bryan."

Bryan waved a hand in dismissal. "Whatever. Laz, stop shoveling all those calories into your mouth. No one wants a bloated photographer at Fashion Week, and you still have all that fat to lose."

"Fat?" Red visibly bristled. Oh, he did not look happy. "He's practically skin and bones."

Ace coughed into his hand. "Red."

"What? It's true. He's a gorgeous guy, but he's too

skinny for his height and build. He should be gaining some healthy weight, not losing it."

Laz's cheeks flushed, and a little smile tugged at his lips. He looked shyly at Red. "You think I'm gorgeous?"

Bryan scoffed. "Clearly the sun's in his eyes and he's not seeing right. With those dark circles around your eyes and all those carbs you've been scarfing, you look like a stuffed raccoon right now."

Laz glared at him. "And whose fault is that? You kept me up all night whining about your schedule and how they have you on back-to-back shoots, but then if they give it to someone else, you bitch about how they're trying to replace you. Jesus, Bryan. Do you ever think about anyone but yourself? I need to get away from you right now." Laz stood, but with the pathway congested with partygoers, he went around, edging close to the pool as he made his way toward the house.

"Who the hell do you think you are? You don't get to walk away from me!" Bryan stormed after Laz and grabbed his arm. Everything moved at lightning speed. Colton barely had time to register what the hell was happening when Ace and Red took off. Laz jerked his arm out of Bryan's grip, and Bryan pushed him hard, causing Laz to slip on the wet floor. Colton called out to Laz, horrified when Laz hit his head on the tiles before falling into the deep end of the pool. Screams filled the air, and before anyone could make a move, Red was diving in after Laz.

"Laz!" Colton pushed people out of his way to get to the pool when a pair of strong arms wrapped around him, stopping him.

"Colton, wait," Ace said into his ear. "Red's got him. The floor's slippery. I don't want you falling too. Come on." He carefully led Colton to the pool as Red surfaced with

Laz in his arms. Ace and Colton reached the edge at the same time as Red, and together they lifted Laz out of the pool and laid him on the floor as Red climbed out. Ace rolled Laz onto his side, and Colton breathed a sigh of relief when Laz immediately hacked up water.

"Oh my God." Bryan tried to crowd Laz, but Ace stopped him.

"I'm going to need you to stand back and give him room." Ace motioned for one of his team members to approach. An unspoken exchange happened between him and the tall, elegant Hispanic woman with dark eyes, high ponytail, and no-nonsense expression. She nodded and gently maneuvered Bryan away, all the while murmuring something at him. Bryan didn't look happy, but he did as she instructed. Bryan was smarter than to try and get around the woman. She could probably bench press him without breaking a sweat.

Laz shivered, and when Red kneeled beside him, Laz held on to his wrist and didn't let go.

"Are you okay?" Colton asked gently as Red inspected the cut on Laz's temple with his free hand.

Laz nodded, and Red turned to take the large thick towel Lucky handed him. He gave it to Ace, who wrapped it around Laz, while Lucky draped another towel around Red's shoulders.

"We should get him inside," Red said.

"Don't go," Laz told Red, sounding almost panicked.

Red ran a hand tenderly over Laz's head. "I'm not going anywhere," he replied softly. "I promise."

Laz nodded, and Red helped him to his feet and put an arm around him. Holding Laz against him and using his own towel to cover Laz's head, Red shielded him from the gathering onlookers. The five of them headed inside as Bryan hurried over.

"Laz, baby, wait. I'm coming with you."

Colton spun and threw a hand out to stop Bryan. "You're not going anywhere."

Bryan's icy-blue eyes bore into Colton, and his lips curled into a snarl until he remembered they weren't alone. Colton, however, couldn't care less. This was his home, and Laz was his responsibility. With a performance worthy of an Oscar nomination, Bryan's bottom lip trembled, and his eyes filled with tears. He put a hand to his chest, his voice loud enough for everyone to hear.

"Please, Colton. It was an accident. You know how much I love him. He needs me."

Colton leaned in, his voice menacing. "You're the last thing he needs right now. Either stay here, or I'll have you and your friends escorted from the property."

Bryan's friends crowded him, patting his shoulder, hugging him, fussing over him, and glaring at Colton. One of them called Colton a bitch, but Colton really didn't give a shit. He turned and hurried inside where everyone was waiting for him.

"Upstairs." Colton rushed up the stairs and down the hall to one of the empty guest rooms. "There's a first aid kit in the bathroom," Colton said.

"Okay. I'll take care of him," Red said, his arm still around Laz, who clung to him as he shivered.

Ace patted Red's arm. "You do that. I'll go grab you some clothes."

"Thanks." Red helped Laz into the bathroom, and Ace turned to Lucky.

"Can you check on the guests? Let them know everything's okay. I want you and Grace keeping an eye on Bryan especially. I don't trust that guy."

Lucky nodded. "Got it."

"I'm going to get him some dry clothes." Colton went to his room, grabbed a pair of sweatpants, a T-shirt, and a hoodie, along with a pair of warm socks. With Laz's current weight, Colton's clothes were going to make him look like he was playing dress-up, but he'd send someone out to buy Laz some clothes in the morning. He knew Bryan was a bad influence on Laz. He'd had no idea how bad it really was. No way was he letting Laz out of his sight, especially with Gio in Tokyo on a business trip. It was bad enough Laz had been hurt under his roof.

When Colton returned to the bedroom, Ace arrived with some clothes for Red, who was helping Laz to the bathroom.

Red handed Laz the clothes Colton passed off before gently inspecting Laz's brow. "It's not deep. Let me know when you're done, and I'll get it cleaned up and bandaged, okay?"

Laz nodded and closed the door to change. When Red started undressing, Colton turned to give him some privacy. The man was damned quick. When Laz opened the bathroom door, Red took the wet clothes from him and handed that to Ace along with his own wet clothes. He followed Laz into the bathroom, then checked beneath the sink where he found the first aid kit. Once it was on the sink and open, he went to work.

"I'll drop these off in the laundry room." Ace motioned to the clothes in his hands.

"Thank you," Colton said, turning to watch Red and Laz.

"No problem." Ace hurried out, and by the time he returned, Red had cleaned Laz's wound, and applied a small bandage. He helped Laz get into bed before he took a seat on the mattress beside him. Was Laz aware he'd scooted over to snuggle Red? The big guy didn't think twice. He wrapped an arm around Laz and held him tight against him. Ace reappeared and took a seat on the edge of the bed to look Laz over. Colton had never been more grateful for Ace's presence, and that of his brothers. They gave off a sense of calm and confidence. Like nothing could touch Colton or Laz because they were there, and Colton was certain that was exactly the case. Knowing the Kings were trained for all manner of scenarios helped set Colton's mind at ease.

"No stitches needed?" Ace asked, carefully looking Laz over.

"It wasn't as bad as it looked," Red replied. "I cleaned it up and dressed it, so it should heal with minimal scarring."

"Thanks, guys," Laz said, sounding exhausted.

"Laz," Colton said gently. "When's the last time you had a good full night's sleep?"

"Um...."

The fact it took Laz that long to come up with an answer didn't bode well.

"Right, well, you're going to stay here tonight and get some rest. I—"

"Shit," Ace muttered, looking down at his phone. "Lucky's just texted. He says Bryan is throwing one hell of a fit downstairs about seeing Laz."

"Have Lucky escort him from the property," Colton said, but Laz shook his head.

"Wait, please. Let me just talk to him."

Colton fought the urge to argue with Laz and nodded at Ace, who tapped away at his phone, most likely texting

Lucky. Within seconds a commotion outside caught their attention, but before any of them could investigate, Bryan stormed into the room. "Oh, I see how it is." He glared daggers at Red.

Laz groaned and closed his eyes. "Bryan, please, not now."

"The second my back is turned, you're getting into bed with another guy?"

"What? Are you insane? I almost drowned!"

"My God, it's a scratch. When did you turn into such a whiney little bitch?"

"That's enough," Red growled. "You need to leave."

"No. I'm his boyfriend. *You* need to leave." Bryan turned to Laz and thrust a finger at Red. "Get rid of him."

Laz's eyes turned cold. "No. Red stays. You go."

"What?"

"You have some nerve accusing me of cheating when you're the one who cheated over and over."

Bryan scoffed and folded his arms over his chest. "I already told you, they're rumors. Someone's trying to start shit to mess with my rep."

"The only one ruining your reputation is you. And it's not a rumor when I see it happen."

Bryan's face paled, and his arms dropped away. Not the expression of an innocent man. "What?"

"I saw you in the back room with those two guys! They were fucking your brains out! I kept hoping you'd confess, talk to me, but instead you kept doing it. I'd hear all these rumors of you sleeping with anyone who could get you what you wanted, so I needed to see for myself, and I did. They weren't rumors. You looked me right in the eye, and you lied to me. You've been lying to me for years, and I'm tired of it. I'm done. It's over. *We're* over."

Bryan laughed. "You can't be serious."

"I'm so very serious."

Bryan pouted as he took a step forward, but he stopped in his tracks when Ace took position at the foot of the bed, his deep frown menacing.

"Baby, please. I'm so sorry. I don't know what got into me. I made a mistake. A huge mistake. It'll never happen again. I swear."

The waterworks started again, but Laz was having none of it. Colton was so damned proud of him. It seemed Laz hadn't been as oblivious to Bryan's behavior as they'd all believed.

"Save it."

The tears dried up fast. "Do you really think you're going to get anywhere without me?" Bryan snarled. "You were a nobody when I met you! You couldn't even afford the equipment you needed without big brother and his rich friends to help you. *I* made you, and I can easily break you. When I get through with you, you'll be lucky if you can get a wedding gig!"

"Maybe. Or I could leak the pictures to the press."

The color drained from Bryan's face. "What pictures?" Realization seemed to dawn on him, and he flinched as if he'd been struck. "You didn't."

Laz's gaze turned hard. "Did you really think I'd walk away without insurance? I know you, Bryan. You're petty, vindictive, and mean. I've seen you ruin people's careers on a whim. I wonder what Elena Vicente would do if she saw the pictures of her supposedly straight husband with his dick buried in your ass in the bedroom of the apartment he bought you with *her* money. I bet after she kicked the bastard to the curb, she'd make sure no designer ever

LOVE IN SPADES 163

worked with you again. That clothing line you've been dreaming of? Never going to happen."

"You wouldn't."

"I worked damned hard to make it where I have, and I've made it this far because of *me*, not you. You try to take that away from me, and I swear I will take you down with me."

"Fine." The truly malicious look that came into Bryan's face had Colton bracing himself. "Let's see if your big, strong man still wants you when he finds out what a little whore you are. At least I did it on my terms. You let him use you like a cheap hooker!"

"You son of a bitch! I confided in you!" Laz launched himself out of bed and tackled Bryan to the floor, the two of them thrashing around. Bryan managed to clip Laz in the head before Laz punched him in the face. The guy was going to have one hell of a shiner. Red grabbed Laz, and held him tight against him, as Ace held a kicking and screeching Bryan away from Laz.

"Get him the fuck out of my house," Colton snapped. "I want him and his friends gone."

Ace nodded, speaking quickly and quietly into his microphone. Within seconds, Bryan was being dragged from the room.

"You're going to regret this, Lazarus! I swear you're going to pay for this!"

"Asshole," Laz mumbled, climbing back into bed under the covers Red held up for him.

"Are you okay?" Red asked softly, brushing Laz's hair away from his face.

Laz nodded, his arms wrapped tight around himself. He couldn't seem to meet any of their gazes, especially Red's.

When it was only the four of them again, Colton closed

the door, and Laz burst into tears. He covered his face with his hands, his shoulders shaking hard from his sobs. Red brought him into his arms, and although Laz hesitated at first, he soon gave in and buried his face against Red's chest.

"It's going to be okay," Red said gently, murmuring quiet words Colton couldn't hear but knew were intended to soothe Laz. The big man all but enveloped Laz's smaller frame, and Laz curled up as close to Red as he could possibly get, his knees drawn up.

Colton ran a hand through his hair. What a damned mess. He was considering leaving the two alone since Laz was obviously distressed and felt comfortable with Red, but as he turned for the door, Laz pulled away from Red.

"He's telling the truth. I let someone fuck me to keep my job."

The words speared through Colton's heart. "Laz, you don't—"

Laz shook his head. "It was my first trip to Europe. Bryan asked me to go with him on a shoot in London. He said he was going to introduce me to a big fashion photographer who could show me the ropes. The guy was nice, and he seemed genuinely interested in helping me. He let me shadow him and even let me step in a few times to take some shots. The second day of the shoot, he invited me back to his studio. I thought it was for another shoot, but it was just the two of us." A tear rolled down Laz's cheek, and he brushed it aside.

"He came onto me, and I politely told him I'd rather keep things professional between us. He said he could introduce me to some important people who could help me with my career. I thanked him and was going to leave when he grabbed me. He said everyone had to start somewhere and how that usually meant on their knees. When I told him no, he said if I didn't, I'd never make it. That my career would be over before it started. I'd never been so scared. And alone. I didn't know what to do. When he started kissing me... I let him. I... I let him... fuck me. I confided in Bryan because I thought he loved me and could help me make sense of what I was feeling, but he acted like it was no big deal. Like it was par for the course if I wanted to advance my career. For a while, I believed him, but deep down I knew the truth. Bryan's right. I'm no better than he is. Actually, I'm worse. Bryan *wanted* to sleep with those men. I was a coward. I let someone fuck me so I could keep my job."

"Hey, you're not the one to blame here," Red said gently. "That asshole took advantage of you, threatened you. Just because you didn't fight him, doesn't mean you consented. You were young, vulnerable, and he abused his position to abuse you. I hate to say it, Laz, but you probably weren't the first, or the last."

"Oh God." Laz sobbed against Red's chest, and Colton felt helpless.

"The man should be in jail," Red said, rubbing soothing circles across Laz's back. "You did nothing wrong."

Laz pulled back and gazed at Red with tearful eyes. He looked so damned young and vulnerable, and it killed Colton. Laz had always been strong and more world-weary than any kid his age had a right to be. He hadn't always been the most confident, but he was a survivor, a fighter, and now he looked so... broken. "You really believe that?"

"I do."

Colton was going to crawl out of his skin. He couldn't stand here, and do nothing. "Laz, get some rest. If you need anything, you let me know. We'll talk tomorrow, okay?" Colton turned to Ace, speaking quietly. "Would it be okay for Red to keep Laz company? I don't want to leave him alone, and he clearly feels safe with Red."

Ace nodded. "Yes, of course." He turned to face Red. "Hey, big guy, why don't you take the couch tonight," he said motioning to the pullout couch on the other end of the room. "If that's okay with you, Laz."

"Yes. Please," Laz said, sniffing. "I'd really like him to stay."

Colton pointed to the smaller of the doors in the room. "There's extra pillows and bedding in there. If either of you need anything, please ask." He left the room with Ace, who closed the door behind them. Colton quickly made his way down the hall to his room, then stopped beside his bedroom door. He leaned against the wall with a heavy gasp.

"Colton? Are you okay?"

Colton shook his head as Laz's words replayed in his head. "I knew something was wrong." He ran a hand over his face and let his back hit the wall. "Fuck. I was there. I was in London, and.... Oh God." He ran his fingers through his hair as he paced when Ace blocked his path and took hold of his face.

"Hey, it's okay. Breathe. Just breathe."

Colton shook his head, tears welling in his eyes. "I was there, Ace. We were in the same damn city, and I had no idea he was—" He closed his eyes, his chest constricting.

"Exactly. You had no idea. How could you know? You can't blame yourself for not knowing, Colton. Look at me."

Colton forced his eyes open and took hold of Ace's arms, needing to feel his solid, steady strength. "I knew something was off. I knew it. I couldn't pinpoint it. We had lunch one afternoon, and he was so... distant." He started to shake involuntarily, and Ace pulled him into his arms. Colton held on tight, his face pressed to Ace's shoulder, allowing the man's warmth to seep into him and spread through his body, pushing out the cold that threatened to cripple him. Some asshole had taken advantage of Laz, and he couldn't do a damned thing about it. Fuck, this would shatter Gio. He'd been taking care of his little brother since their dad passed away. He'd sacrificed so much to give Laz the best life he could, and together the two had weathered one storm after another, but they'd made it through. Colton admired them, and he hated that his friend would blame himself. A thought occurred to him, and he pulled back.

"Can the Kings find out who the photographer is?"

"Colton, you need to talk to Laz about this. He's the only one who can bring charges against this man. From what I've seen, you need to understand that Laz may not want to. That could change, but right now he's hurting."

"The man took advantage of him," Colton growled. "He should be arrested. He's probably out there hurting more people!"

"I know, and I agree, but it's not your decision to make. All you can do is offer Laz help. He feels ashamed of what happened, and he blames himself. Your priority right now is helping him heal. Until Laz understands he's not to blame and that his going through with the act doesn't mean he consented or excuse what happened to him, he's not going to want to seek justice. It's frustrating and heartbreaking, but sometimes all we can do is offer our support."

"You've seen this before."

Ace nodded, his gold-green eyes darkening. "The thing about our line of work is that we're usually invisible to most people, and that's often the goal, but there are times when people forget we can see and hear everything. Not everyone who does what we do shares our moral code. There are companies with personnel who are paid to look the other

168 CHARLIE COCHET

way, to side with their clients no matter what. Our clients come first, but we won't deal with clients who expect us to break the law, ignore it, or be passive to illicit activities. That's not who we are. We won't stand by and allow a client to assault someone in any way. We're not without sin, but we won't be a part of someone else's."

Colton released a heavy sigh. Ace was right. Laz was what was most important, and Colton would do everything in his power to help his friend. When, and if, he was ready to seek justice against that predator, Colton would be ready. He still felt miserable about it. "What do I do now?"

Ace went thoughtful. "Let me talk to King and see what he says. I won't mention Laz. That's between us. If there's a route we can take that doesn't involve Laz, maybe we can do something to help. Right now, you're going to tell me if you want us to send people home. We can smooth things over with the guests. Then we're going to go for a walk on the beach."

"How did you know?" For Colton, the beach had always been more than fun in the sun. The ocean soothed him, comforted him, gave him peace.

"We're not so different in that respect," Ace said quietly, and Colton remembered what Ace had told him about walking down to the beach when he had nightmares. "What do you think?"

Colton smiled, touched by Ace's intuitiveness. "I'd like that."

"I'll meet you out there in ten minutes, okay?"

"Okay."

Ace turned to go, but Colton grabbed his arm, and Ace gave him a questioning smile.

"Thank you, Ace. For everything. It really means a lot."

"You're welcome." Ace's smile squeezed at Colton's

heart. He was such a handsome man, but as they stood there, the seconds ticking by as they gazed at each other, it became clear how much more Ace was. He dropped his gaze to those lips, unable to stop himself from wondering what they tasted like. Would they be soft and warm against his? When he moved his eyes back to Ace's, he inhaled sharply at the fire in those gorgeous eyes.

"Ace...."

"I better go," Ace said, tenderly pulling out of Colton's grip. "Ten minutes."

Colton didn't reply, simply watched him walk down the hall until he'd disappeared downstairs. He snapped out of it and ran a hand through his hair. *Shit.* Once he was in his room, he closed the door and leaned against it. His heart was beating so fast he was afraid it would burst from his chest. This couldn't be happening. He was *not* falling in love. It was ridiculous. Being with Ace day in and day out at all hours was messing with his head, giving him a sense they were more.

"You're overreacting." Not surprising, since it seemed to run in the family. He put it down to his feeling vulnerable and exhausted from today's events. He'd needed someone, and Ace had been there for him, which he appreciated to no end, but that didn't mean he was falling in love with the guy. They were only having some fun, right? If anything, they were friends. Now if he could only get himself to believe that.

NINE

ONCE THE GUESTS WERE GONE, and Ace had checked in with the team, he picked Colton up outside his bedroom door. They'd both changed into more comfortable clothes. Colton looked handsome as always, in a deep blue short-sleeved button-down shirt, and a pair of white linen shorts. He had on flip-flops that matched his shirt, and although he looked tired, his smile when he saw Ace had Ace's pulse picking up.

Ace had gone with one of his charcoal-gray T-shirts and a pair of loose black workout shorts. He put on his running shoes, just in case.

"Ready?"

Colton nodded but paused to look off toward the room Laz was in, concern etched all over his handsome face.

"He's in good hands," Ace promised, placing a hand to his lower back. "Red was our medical sergeant, remember? There's no one better to be at his side right now. He's the gentlest guy there is."

"Unless someone tries to hurt someone he cares about I'm guessing."

"Oh, then he's fucking terrifying," Ace assured him, leading him toward the stairs. "That's the thing about nice guys. You don't want to mess with them. Red's a big teddy bear until there's a threat." They headed downstairs, through the living room to the glass doors at the back of the house.

"I have a feeling the same could be said of all the Kings."

Ace winked at him. "You're not wrong. Except for the nice guy part." The air outside was muggy, but the breeze coming in from the ocean was nice. The skies were clear, and the beach was empty, with a few torches lined up in the sand across Colton's property.

"You don't think you're a nice guy?"

Colton's question caught him off guard, and Ace smirked. "Maybe you're not remembering the first few days of our meeting."

"You were reacting to *my* being an asshole."

"Okay, we were both being assholes."

Colton laughed, and Ace once again made note of how much he liked the sound. He turned his attention to their surroundings, greeting members of his team as they made their way to the private walkway that led down to the beach. The darkness made it feel later than it was.

Together they headed for firmer sand, and they walked in companionable silence along the beach, Ace far enough from the water not to get his sneakers wet, and Colton ankle-deep in the waves, a contented smile on his face. He stopped and looked down into the water, his hands shoved into his pockets. With an almost bashful smile, he looked up at Ace.

"Join me?"

Why not? Ace toed off his sneakers and tossed them in

the sand so the rising tide wouldn't get to them, and then he joined Colton in the shallow water, the tepid water feeling good against his skin. Man, he loved the ocean. Loved how infinite it felt, how small it made him feel in the grand scheme of things when he looked out at the horizon, all that water stretching on for miles and miles. During the day it glittered beneath the sun, and at night the moon's reflection danced in the water.

"I'm glad you're here, Ace."

Ace returned Colton's smile. "I'm glad we could help."

"The threats seemed to have stopped. Maybe they got scared off."

"Maybe."

Colton stopped walking and turned to face him. "You don't sound so sure."

"Whoever sent you those letters and that disturbing package went through a lot of trouble to scare you. Our being here is a double-edged sword. We're here to protect you against a very real threat, but it also shows them that their intimidation worked. They're not going to give up. My concern is that our being here has forced whoever it is to change things up. So far, King's investigations haven't raised any red flags. We need to keep our eyes peeled until they make another move."

Colton sighed heavily but nodded. "Okay." He jumped suddenly and spun around. "What the hell was that?"

"What?" Ace asked, looking around Colton, who jumped again.

"There's something in the water. Something big. It brushed against me."

"I'm sure it's—" Ace didn't have time to finish his sentence before Colton cursed up a storm and jumped on Ace. "Colton!" Ace scrambled to catch him, wrapping his arms around Colton, but the man was so damned tall, and his weight unexpected, that their legs got tangled. They went hurtling down onto the wet sand, a wave crashing into them and soaking them from head to toe. Ace coughed and wiped the water from his face. He laughed at Colton, who lay on top of him, his hair plastered over his face.

"I think it was a shark," Colton sputtered.

The waves crashed against the shore, and a huge mass of seaweed washed up beside them. They both looked at it before looking at each other. Ace schooled his expression.

"That your shark?"

Colton narrowed his eyes. "Big help you are. Aren't you supposed to protect me?"

"Do you want me to shoot it?"

"Yes, Ace. I want you to shoot the seaweed."

"I could, but then someone would hear it and call the cops, and then I'd have to explain to them *and* to King how I drew my gun on a bunch of algae, and I don't know, that seems like an awful lot of paperwork. I don't like paperwork. I can call it in if you want. Get Lucky out here to take care of it. Or ask it out on a date."

Colton let out a bark of laughter, his entire body shaking with the force of it. He was so beautiful. "You're such an ass."

"And this surprises you?" Ace couldn't help but run his fingers through Colton's hair, moving it away from his brow. "You're a very beautiful man, you know that?"

Colton's smile stole Ace's breath away, and he knew he was treading on very dangerous ground. He needed to put a stop to this before it got any more out of his control. He opened his mouth to ask Colton to get off him, and Colton kissed him. Desire flared through Ace, and he parted his lips, opening up for Colton's tongue as he deepened their kiss. It seemed to set something off in Colton, and he kissed Ace like he was trying to steal the breath from his body.

Ace had spent several nights trying not to think about what Colton might taste like, and now that he knew, he wanted more. He wanted more of his lips, his tongue, the heat of his mouth. He wanted to feel more of his firm, lean body against him, of his smooth skin. Ace spread his legs, bringing his knees up so Colton could lie comfortably on him as they explored each other's mouth, hands roaming, fingers caressing.

When they were forced to come up for air, Colton pulled back enough to meet Ace's gaze. As if realizing what he'd done, Colton's beautiful blue-gray eyes widened. "I'm sorry, I shouldn't have—"

"Don't," Ace said, cutting off the rest of Colton's words with his kiss. He moved fast, turning them and rolling onto Colton, reversing their positions. They ignored the waves crashing against them and the sand getting into places it should never be in. The more he tasted Colton, the greedier he became. The alarm bells went off in his head, but he couldn't bring himself to stop. He didn't want to. His body was on fire despite the cool water, and he was surprised steam wasn't rising from the water surrounding their bodies.

Colton writhed beneath Ace, his tongue and lips as greedy as Ace's as they each fought for more. Need like he'd never known spread through him, and his painfully hard cock rubbed against Colton's own erection, the thin fabric of their shorts making it feel as if they were almost naked, the friction sending delicious shivers through Ace. Colton thrust up against him, and Ace groaned.

"Oh God, Ace." Colton wrapped his legs around Ace's ass, his fingers digging into Ace's back as he rutted against him. "You feel so damned good."

Ace thrust his hips, a deep guttural moan escaping him when Colton grabbed hold of his asscheeks and begged him for more. Colton's kiss-swollen lips parted in the most erotic way, the moonlight above them making it possible for Ace to see his beautiful face and his flushed cheeks, his eyes filled with heat and desire.

"Ace, please. I need you to make me come. Please."

Fuck. How the hell was he supposed to deny Colton anything? Their rutting turned frantic, and they gripped each other tight as if they might fall away otherwise, their lips locked in a ravenous kiss that left Ace feeling as if he were about to lose his mind. He needed to feel Colton's skin. Frantically he reached between them, pushing down their shorts enough to grab hold of both their cocks.

"Oh, yes. *Yes.* Make me come, baby."

"Fuck. Colton. Oh fuck." They thrust hard into Ace's tight grip, their hips losing all rhythm while they nipped, bit, and sucked on the other's lips, tongue, and skin, their panting breaths mingling in the humid air.

"Ace, I'm going to come," Colton cried out as Ace's muscles stiffened, his orgasm slamming through him. He shut his eyes tight, his own hoarse cry drowned out by the ocean, and the waves washing away evidence of their intimate moment. Colton trembled beneath him, and slipped his arms around Ace's neck, keeping him close.

Ace let his brow rest against Colton's as their breathing steadied. He smiled at the feel of Colton brushing his lips against his own. Then the reality of what they'd done sank in. *Shit.*

"What the hell did we just do?" Ace whispered.

"Can we not overthink this yet?" Colton pleaded. "I don't regret it. Please, Ace."

Ace nodded, he smiled and kissed Colton again, this

time slowly, sweetly. He nipped at his lips, and Colton hummed softly. The way he responded to Ace was unlike anything he'd ever experienced. Their bodies fit like two pieces of a puzzle.

"You taste even better than I imagined," Colton confessed quietly.

"You thought about this, huh?"

Colton nodded.

"I didn't," Ace said, straight-faced. "Not at all. Not for a second."

"You're so full of shit," Colton said with a laugh.

"Okay, maybe a little. Like once, but then I got distracted by a pastry."

Colton chuckled and shook his head. "You know, for a cardsharp, you have a lousy poker face." He stole another kiss, and Ace retaliated, kissing Colton soundly until it was time to bring this night to an end, no matter how badly he didn't want to.

"We should head back before Lucky hunts us down."

"Do we have to?"

Ace laughed softly. "Yes, we have to."

"Fine. You're right." Colton grimaced. "Also I have sand in my ass. Can we make a note that sexy make-out sessions on the shore leave you with sand in unfortunate places?"

Ace barked out a laugh. "Duly noted." He made to get up, but Colton took hold of his face, his intense gaze holding Ace's.

"Please tell me this won't be the last time you kiss me."

"Colton, I—"

"Please. We can talk about it as much as you want later, and we'll go from there, but don't tell me this is the last time."

Ace could have lied. He could have said yes, but he'd

fucked-up royally. The thing was, he wanted to kiss Colton again. Wanted to kiss him all night, and more. He wanted to feel Colton's naked body beneath him, writhing against him with a need only Ace could fill. Right now, he needed to get himself together, and he couldn't do that with Colton's body under him and those gorgeous blue-eyes pleading with him. "No promises."

"I'll take that."

Ace nodded and stood before helping Colton to his feet. "Come on."

They headed back in the direction they'd come in so Ace could pick up his shoes. They were a mess—their hair and clothes plastered to them, sand everywhere. Thankfully Colton's white shorts were lined, because as it was, they left nothing to the imagination, and Ace made sure to get an eyeful of that beautiful bubble butt before they reached the property. The man had an exquisite body.

Outside they rinsed off at the shower by the pool, managing to get most of the sand off. The water was cold as fuck, and they were both shivering by the time they got out from under it. Colton grabbed them each a warm, large thick towel from the pool towel valet, and they dried off as much as they could, then tossed the towels in the hamper below the shelves before grabbing another couple of towels to wrap themselves in. The air-conditioning inside the house had them shivering again, and Ace hoped to get to his room without incident, but of course Lucky emerged from the kitchen. He gaped at them.

"What the hell happened to you two?"

"Colton got attacked by a shark," Ace said somberly. "I saved his life. Something else I can add to my resume."

"What happened to operating under complete discretion, Mr. Sharpe?" Colton asked, heading into the kitchen and opening the fridge to grab two bottles of water.

"Oh, I'm sorry. Was I supposed to keep my heroics to myself? That sounds very unlike me."

Lucky was hysterically confused. "A shark? Qué?"

Ace couldn't help breaking into laughter. Colton's uninspired expression didn't help either.

"It was dark, okay? Something big moved under the water, and when it touched my leg, I may have overreacted."

Lucky arched an eyebrow at Ace, who waggled his eyebrows.

"It was seaweed."

Lucky shook his head and let out a snort of laughter.

Ace joined Colton in the kitchen and grabbed the bottle of water Colton held out for him.

"Smartass," Colton grumbled, shoving Ace away playfully and making him chuckle.

"Ouch, why are you beating me up? I saved your life."

"Yes, that seaweed was so incredibly lethal." Colton took a swig of his water before leaving the kitchen. "I'm going to go shower and change."

"Watch out for the sharks," Ace teased, cackling when Colton flipped him off. As soon as Colton was gone, Lucky was in his space, his big brown eyes filled with concern.

"What are you doing?"

"What?"

Lucky planted his hands on his hips and averted his gaze. It wasn't like his cousin to mince words. He usually said whatever he had to and the rest be damned. It was one of the things Ace admired most about him. Of course, sometimes that meant he came across as crass or rude, but Lucky didn't see the sense in beating around the bush.

180 CHARLIE COCHET

"Say what you have to say, Lucky."

Seeming to come to some kind of conclusion, Lucky nodded, then met his gaze. When he spoke, his voice was quiet. "I'm afraid you're getting too close, you know?"

"What? Because we're having a little fun?" The problem with working with family was that sometimes they knew you better than you knew yourself, and they could call you out on your bullshit.

Lucky peered at him. "Don't try to play a player."

"I'm not playing."

"Which is even more dangerous. Do you know the level of shit that will come down on you if you get involved with him? And I'm not talking about King, who will, by the way, kick your ass."

"I'm not getting involved."

Lucky ignored that. "What are you always telling me?"

Man, sometimes he hated that his cousin actually listened to him. "Keep your head in the game and don't get distracted. You think I'm distracted?" Did Lucky really think he wouldn't be able to do his job if he was emotionally invested in Colton?

"I think you like him."

"He's a nice guy."

"¡Ay carajo!" Lucky threw up his arms in frustration. "You know that is *not* what I mean! The way you two are together? There is something there, Ace. Anyone can see it. At the party? It was all over your face and his. The way you stand so close to him? How he smiles at you? I mean, come on."

Ace knew exactly what Lucky was referring to, but he played dumb and shrugged.

"Bro, please be careful." Lucky put a hand to his heart. "Tú eres como mi hermano. I love you. I don't want to see you get in over your head. You worked too damn hard to be where you are. Please, just think about it."

Ace nodded. "Okay."

Lucky moved in to hug him, then realized he was still wet. He wrinkled his nose and backed away. "You need to shower. Apestas."

"What, you don't want to hug me?" Ace held out his arms and took a step toward him, laughing when Lucky jumped back.

"Fuck no. You got sand and shit all over you. This shirt is Armani."

"Aw, you're hurting my feelings." Ace darted forward, arms wide, and Lucky took off around the counter.

"No, Ace. Fuck you. Don't touch me," Lucky growled, staying as far away as possible.

"Let me hug you!" Ace ran after him, and Lucky took off outside. He stopped on the other side of the glass wall and flipped Ace off, making Ace double over laughing. Having aggravated his cousin enough for one night, Ace headed upstairs to his bedroom. He paused outside and stared at Colton's closed door. If he knew what was good for him, he'd pretend like tonight never happened. It would be the best course of action for both of them. With a sigh, he walked into his room and closed the door behind him. He came to a halt when he heard his shower running. *What the hell?*

Hurrying into the bathroom, he froze at the sight of a completely naked Colton washing himself. *Oh damn.* Ace stood mesmerized by the vision before him. Water sluiced over every dip and curve of that gorgeous body, over sculpted muscles and smooth skin. Long fingers massaged his scalp as he rinsed his hair. Stepping out from beneath the showerhead, Colton wiped water from his face and smiled ruefully at Ace from over his shoulder.

"I hope you don't mind my using your shower. I had a problem with mine."

Ace fought a smile. "That so?"

"Yes." Colton's expression was sinful as he turned to face Ace. "You weren't in it."

Ace groaned and undressed in record time. He joined Colton in the huge shower, pushing him up against the tiled wall and making a meal out of his mouth. He slid his fingers down Colton's body, palming Colton's hard shaft and drawing a decadent moan from him.

Getting to his knees, Ace swallowed that delicious cock, and Colton bucked his hips, his fingers on Ace's head.

"Oh God, Ace. Your mouth feels so good."

Ace worked his tongue over Colton on a mission to drive the man out of his mind. He sucked, licked, and nipped at Colton's thick hard cock. He pressed his tongue into the slit before swallowing Colton down again, loving the way Colton bucked his hips and held on to Ace for dear life. The glass around them fogged up, giving the illusion they were hidden away from the world. It wouldn't last long, but Ace would take advantage of it while he could. He slipped his hands around to Colton's ass, his nose buried deep in the fair-haired curls of Colton's groin. He hollowed his mouth and sucked hard, urged on by Colton's quiet begging for more.

Ace slipped one finger in between Colton's asscheeks and searched out his hole, groaning when Colton's body trembled. He pressed a finger inside Colton and doubled his efforts. Colton held on to Ace's head, thrusting in deep, and thanks to Ace's lack of gag reflex, he stilled and let Colton fuck his mouth.

"Oh yes. Jesus, Ace. Your mouth is so fucking hot." Colton's movements turned frantic, and he let out a strangled sound as he bent over Ace, hot come squirting inside his mouth. Ace swallowed down the salty thick come, and once Colton had emptied himself, Ace pulled off and stood, then wrapped his arms around Colton and kissed him so he could taste himself. Colton moaned, and their tongues tangled with the taste of his release.

Colton led Ace under the shower, and Ace allowed himself to be taken care of, get soaped up and washed, not an inch of his body missed. After lowering to his knees, Colton ran his hands reverently up Ace's body, stopping to trace the lines of Ace's tattoo.

"I've been dying to get a good look at this."

"Couldn't you see it from your balcony?"

Colton laughed and swatted his ass.

"Ooh, kinky. Yeah, do that again. I've been a very bad boy."

"I'll bet you have." Colton continued to trace the lion portion of his ink down over his shoulder to his pec. "Why a lion?"

"All the Kings have a lion tattoo somewhere. Different style and design. Our commander used to say we fought like lions in battle and no matter how deep in shit we were, we had each other to make sure we never lost our honor or courage. When it came time to brand the company, we thought of him. The lion became part of our crest, and his words turned into our motto. We each got a lion tattoo so we'd never forget what we were to each other, and we'd never forget the man who believed in us."

Colton laid his hand over Ace's heart. "I can't imagine anyone not believing in you."

Ace was thankful for the water he stood under. It meant

the tears in his eyes were washed away before Colton could tell they were there. He blinked away the wetness and let Colton lead him away from the shower. He turned off the water, and they stepped out onto the plush bathroom rug. Colton nipped at Ace's bottom lip before leaning in to whisper in his ear.

"I'd really like you to fuck me now."

Ace's cock twitched, and they wasted no time in drying each other off before their lips were locked together again, towels on the floor. They stumbled into the bedroom toward the bed, and Ace pulled away long enough to lock the door before he rushed back to Colton. He turned Colton and walked him to the bed until the back of Colton's legs hit the mattress and he fell back onto it. With a wicked grin, Colton scooted up the bed, one arm behind his head, his free hand palming his cock between his spread knees. Ace climbed onto the bed and stalked forward, feeling like a predator ready to pounce on the mouthwatering flesh on offer.

Colton shook his head, his expression one of awe. "You're really something special to look at, Ace."

"Too bad you can't see what I do," Ace said, raking his gaze over Colton.

"What—" Colton's question broke off into a groan when Ace hooked his arms around Colton's thighs and speared his hole with his tongue. "Holy fuck," Colton gasped, throwing his hands out to snag fistfuls of the covers as Ace fucked Colton with his tongue. Tasting Colton was quickly becoming his new addiction.

"Please tell me you have supplies," Colton said, breath hitching when Ace nipped at the sensitive skin around his puckered entrance.

"I'll get it." Ace left Colton, loving the whimper he let

out when Ace moved away. He crawled over Colton, and reached over to open the drawer, laughing when Colton wrapped his arms around his neck, kissing him and nipping whatever part of Ace he could reach while Ace rummaged blindly in the drawer. Finally after nabbing the bottle of lube and a condom, he closed the drawer and pulled away to sit back on his heels.

"How do you want it?" Ace asked.

Colton palmed his leaking cock, his knees spread wide, and his body on display for Ace. "Hard. I want to feel you for days."

"Shit, Colton—"

"You asked, and I answered. I want you to fuck me into the mattress, Ace. I want to wake up tomorrow and feel like you're still buried balls-deep in my ass. Make me feel it."

Ace didn't need to be told twice. He moved in to plunge his tongue inside Colton's mouth, their kiss wet and sloppy as Ace popped the cap on the lube bottle. After pouring a small amount onto his fingers, he took over pumping Colton's cock while he pushed two fingers inside of him, the gasp he let out at the intrusion sending a heavenly shiver through Ace. Colton might want it hard, but Ace wouldn't hurt him. He started slow and gentle, scissoring his fingers and stretching Colton until he was all but ready to fall apart beneath Ace.

"Ace, please."

Ace pulled his fingers out so he could get the condom on and lube himself up. He lined himself with Colton's hole, and carefully pushed in, groaning at how tight Colton was. Colton hissed, capturing Ace's attention, and he took hold of Colton's cock again, flicking his thumbnail over his slit, making him arch his back, his hands fisting the covers. Colton sat up, and cupped the back of Ace's neck, tugging him forward to bring their mouths together. He sucked Ace's bottom lip into his mouth before nipping at his chin. Then he bit down on Ace's shoulder, and Ace plunged the rest of the way in. Colton stifled his cry against Ace's neck before flopping onto his back, and Ace began moving. He winced at how tight Colton was.

"It's been a while," Colton admitted, and for some reason that made Ace even harder, if that was possible. He pumped himself inside of Colton, and it quickly became apparent Colton was a screamer. Ace stopped and threw a hand over Colton's mouth.

"As much as I love making you scream, Colt, you gotta keep it down."

Colton nodded, and Ace moved his hand away, receiving a wicked smile. "Sounds like a challenge to me."

"Oh, okay," Ace laughed. "You're on. You best be ready for this, because I'm going to fuck you senseless." Ace thrust into Colton, and Colton bit down on his bottom lip to keep himself from crying out. Leaning forward, Ace braced one arm on each side of Colton's shoulders, his eyes meeting those pools of blue-gray. He pounded into Colton, his balls slapping against Colton's ass. "Is this what you meant? How's that feel?"

"It feels so good, Ace. Fuck yes, like that. Fuck my hole."

"God, I love when you talk dirty. All those filthy words coming from that sweet mouth."

"Yeah?" Colton sucked Ace's earlobe into his mouth before tugging on it, his fingers grabbing fistfuls of Ace's hair. "You like it dirty, don't you, Ace? You like shoving that monster cock up my tight, greedy hole. I love the way you stretch me, fuck me, make it burn."

Ace rolled him over onto his stomach, an arm around his shoulders to keep him in place as he thrust deep and hard over and over, pulling out and slamming back inside as deep as he could each time. He thrust frantically, chasing the orgasm that was whirling and rolling through him like thunder, the room filled with the sounds of their panting.

"That's it," Colton urged. "Fuck me, Ace. Oh God, oh fuck, yes."

Ace lifted up, his hands on Colton's shoulders, his weight pushing Colton down into the bed. He spread Colton's legs wider with his knees, and plunged in deep, making Colton cry out into the pillow. The bed shook beneath them with his animalistic pounding. Colton's body went rigid, before he jerked, and holy fuck, Colton came without being touched. Ace lost it, thrusting in deep once, twice, and then coming so hard on the third that his vision went white, and he emptied himself in the condom as he continued to fuck Colton until it was too painful. His arms trembled, and he winced as he eased out of Colton. He rolled off, falling to his side.

"Fuck," Colton said, breathless.

"Are you okay?"

Colton nodded. "That was... incredible."

"I gotta say, you surprised me." Ace removed the condom, tied it off, and chucked it in the small wastebasket by the bed.

"You bring it out of me."

"Is that a good thing?"

"That you drive me so fucking wild with need that I surprise myself? Yes. That's a good thing."

Ace couldn't help his dopey smile. They lay beside each other in satiated silence as they caught their breaths. As his body cooled, his worries surfaced, but before they could grab hold of him, Colton cuddled up to him, his arm around Ace, and his head against Ace's chest, one leg over Ace's, making him smile. The man was most certainly a cuddler. Colton clearly had no intention of going anywhere just yet. Instead he caressed Ace's skin with feathery touches. Ace closed his eyes and ran his fingers absently through Colton's hair. When Colton's breathing evened out, and his palm lay still on Ace's chest, he knew Colton was asleep. He took Colton's hand in his and brought it to his lips for a soft kiss before laying it back on his chest. Fuck. He was in so much deep shit that he didn't even know where to start.

Colton released a contented sigh in his sleep, and Ace knew this was more than a one-night stand. Somehow, he'd known the minute he'd returned Colton's kiss. He couldn't have just one night with Colton. As he ran his fingers through Colton's soft hair, he accepted how well and truly fucked he was. He cared about Colton, wanted more, but the odds were not in his favor. This was where he'd fold, but how could he? How could he walk away from Colton now? Simple.

He couldn't.

TEN

COLTON WOKE up aching in the most delicious way. He smiled at Ace's sleeping form. Damn, the man was beautiful. His long lashes lay against his cheeks, tiny freckles strewn across his nose. His dark eyebrows were thick, his top lip as full as the bottom, and his square jaw filled with stubble. His muscles were well-defined, his hands strong, and although a few inches shorter than Colton, he was wider. Ace's hipbone peeking out from the blanket stirred things down south. Gingerly, Colton reached down to take hold of that deliciously long, thick cock. It was hard and pointing up toward Ace's flat stomach. Ace moaned, and Colton brushed his lips over Ace's right nipple before poking a tongue out to flick it.

"Mm, that's almost better than coffee," Ace grumbled, his voice laced with sleep, the deep rumble sending a shiver through Colton.

Colton gasped, poking Ace playfully and loving his laugh. "Almost? I must not be doing a good enough job." He used the precome on the head of Ace's cock to help with the friction as he slowly worked Ace's hard length. Ace rolled onto his back, his eyes still closed, and Colton moved the blanket away and planted kisses down Ace's stomach as he continued to bring Ace pleasure. Ace arched his back, his fingers finding Colton's hair. With a little smile, Colton took Ace down to the root, and Ace threw a hand over his mouth to muffle his cry. Loving his effect on the gorgeous man, Colton doubled his efforts, sucking hard, his head bobbing up and down as he sucked, licked, and laved to drive Ace wild. He stuck a finger in his mouth along with Ace's cock, getting it good and wet before slipping it out. Sensing his intent, Ace spread his legs wider, and Colton groaned around Ace's cock before placing his finger against Ace's entrance and pressing gently in.

Ace jerked beneath him, spilling himself inside Colton's mouth, and Colton swallowed every drop. He wiped his mouth, and moved up to kiss Ace, making him hum, his fingers absently running through Colton's hair. Needing to come up for air, Colton slid down and laid his head against Ace's chest. They lay together, quietly breathing. Colton could easily get used to this, to waking up in Ace's strong arms, making love to the sounds of the ocean outside their window while the sun's rays filtered through the gossamer curtains.

"Lucky suspects something."

Colton bolted upright. "What? How?"

"He may be a pain in the ass, but he doesn't miss much. He saw when you fed me."

"It was one tart."

Ace sighed and sat up. He ran a hand through his hair. "It was an intimate gesture."

"Really?" Colton hadn't thought about that. He

supposed he could see how Lucky would think it might be more than it was, but it wasn't like friends didn't share food off their plates. Then again, he supposed Ace wasn't supposed to be a friend either.

"Had it been anyone else, I wouldn't have let them feed it to me," Ace added, wrapping an arm around Colton and dragging him closer. He pulled the blanket up over his lap, and Colton turned, lying on his back and placing his head on Ace's thigh. He smiled as Ace absently ran his fingers through his hair.

"But that's such a little thing."

Ace's face flushed, and he looked away. "Not for me. I, um, I don't like people feeding me. It's a thing."

Colton blinked up at him. "Oh. I'm sorry. I didn't know. I hope I didn't make you feel uncomfortable."

"You don't get it, Colton." Ace dropped his gaze to meet Colton's, his expression a mixture of uncertainty and nervousness. "I let you because I like you. Want you. I could touch you and get close to you in a way that had nothing to do with my job."

"Oh." Colton smiled wide, his heart skipping a beat at the admission. The worry that filled Ace's sparkling eyes had Colton's smile slipping away. He placed a hand to Ace's jaw, rubbing his thumb over the rough stubble. "I've put you in a difficult position, haven't I?"

Ace shook his head before laying his hand over Colton's and leaning into the touch. "It would have happened eventually. I want you, Colton. I shouldn't, but I think we have a chance at something here."

Colton sat up, and Ace wrapped an arm around him. "What happens if King finds out?" He braced himself, knowing whatever the answer was, it wouldn't be good.

"If it gets back to King, he'll pull me off the case and someone else will be assigned to protect you. He'll hand my ass over to me like never before and put me on paid leave. The worst part will be my guilt at having disappointed him and the guys, but him especially. If your dad finds out, I don't know, but it won't be good. We'll most likely lose the contract between Four Kings Security and Connolly Maritime."

"No, you won't. I won't let that happen. This is going to be my company. The Kings are the best fit for us. Whatever happens between us, Ace, I promise you, you're getting that contract."

Ace smiled sadly and kissed Colton passionately. "That's really sweet, Colt, but if it gets out that one of the Kings slept with a client, we're done. Our whole company was founded on trust, and if that goes...."

"I hadn't considered that." Colton swallowed hard. When he'd kissed Ace, he'd only been thinking of himself and what he wanted. The reality of what was at risk made his chest hurt. He'd not only put Ace's reputation at risk, but the rest of the Kings. He could potentially ruin the careers of good men. Pushing down his heartache, Colton climbed out of bed. "I should go."

Ace quickly followed and took hold of Colton's arm, stopping him from moving away. "Wait, what's happening right now?"

"I know you said this isn't on me, but I initiated it, and although I want you, Ace, it would be incredibly selfish of me to put you in a position where you and your brothers could lose so much. I won't be responsible for that kind of pain."

"Hey, hold on a minute." Ace cupped his face and kissed him tenderly. "We need to be cautious and vigilant until the threat is over and the case is closed. Then we can talk to King. He'll help us go from there. If that's what you want. Am I the only one who feels like this could be the start of something special?" Ace dropped his hands to his sides, and Colton already missed his touch.

Colton swallowed hard and laced his fingers with Ace's. "You're not the only one who feels that."

Ace's smile left Colton breathless, and he moved in for a kiss, but a knock on the door startled them both.

"Ace? You going for a run, bro, or what?"

Shit. It was Lucky.

Colton kissed Ace before running for the balcony doors as Ace scrambled for clothes, calling out toward the door.

"Coming. Looking for my second pair of sneakers since the other ones are still wet."

"I'll help you," Lucky said, and Colton slipped outside and closed the door in time to hear Lucky opening Ace's bedroom door.

Colton crouched down and dashed to his room, making sure he wasn't spotted by anyone patrolling the property. He pressed his finger to the lock on his balcony doors, then slipped inside. A knock on his door had him rushing to mess up his bed and make it look slept in before dashing into the bathroom to grab his robe. Tying the sash around his waist, he headed for the door and opened it with a yawn.

"Good morning, Lucky. What can I do for you?"

Lucky peered at him. "Good morning, Colton. Do you have a pair of old sneakers you can lend Ace? You're both the same size shoes."

"Oh, um, sure. Hold on." He made to close the door, but Lucky stopped him.

"Everything okay?"

Colton blinked at him. "Of course. Why?" He put a

hand to his chest and did his best to look concerned. "Did something happen? Should I be worried?"

Seeming to realize he might have unduly alarmed Colton, Lucky waved a hand, his face turning red. "No, no. Everything's okay. I'm sorry. I didn't mean to scare you."

Colton let out a sigh of relief. "Oh, good. One second, let me go grab those sneakers for you." He headed for his walk-in closet, aware of Lucky opening the door wide, despite not passing the threshold.

"Oversleep?" Lucky asked, loud enough for Colton to hear from inside his closet.

He grabbed a pair of running shoes and walked back out, smiling at Lucky. "Yes. Guess I was worn out."

"Ace too." Lucky smiled wide as he took the sneakers from Colton. "Thanks. It's weird, you know? It usually takes a lot to wear him out."

"Well, yesterday was a pretty eventful day."

Lucky nodded. "Right, yes, it was. Oh, eh, Red made breakfast if you're hungry."

"Wonderful. I'm starving."

"Claro que sí," Lucky said with another grin, though his eyes made it clear he had his suspicions about why that was. "Thanks again, I'll make sure he brings these back to you. See you downstairs."

Colton held up a hand. "No rush." He waited for Lucky to disappear into Ace's room before closing the door and leaning against it. Holy shit, that had been intense. He never would have imagined years of schooling his expressions for boardrooms would come in handy against a Green Beret. If Lucky already had his suspicions, then keeping things between him and Ace would be even more challenging than he expected, but when he thought of Ace, his smile, the way he kissed Colton... it was worth it. He hadn't been this fired up about someone in... ever.

From the moment Colton laid eyes on Ace, he'd been attracted to him, and after finding out who he was, or rather who he worked for, Colton had done everything in his power to fight that attraction. It turned out to be more difficult than expected. Ace was funny, smart, sweet, and incredibly loyal. He spoke his mind yet listened to what others had to say. His interaction with Lily showed Colton a whole other side to him, a gentle side.

Waking up to Ace this morning had felt so right, and he missed having that intimacy with someone who cared about him. Thanks to Mick, Colton had closed himself off to relationships, lived in fear of being taken advantage of and having his heart broken, but with Ace, Colton was willing to put aside that fear.

Pushing those thoughts aside for the time being, he went to his closet and picked out a charcoal gray polo shirt and a pair of cargo shorts. He dressed casually, and headed downstairs, where the delicious aroma of bacon assaulted him. His stomach rumbled in need of the crunchy, salty goodness. When he neared the kitchen, he paused long enough to notice Laz staring dreamily at Red. It looked like Ace wasn't the only King who'd managed to make an impression. Red stood in an apron at the stove frying bacon, his back to Laz as he talked about protein while Laz sat in the T-shirt and pajama pants Colton had lent him, elbows on the counter, face in his hands, and a sappy smile on his face as he all but floated away. He was completely oblivious to everything except Red.

"Good morning," Colton announced cheerfully, snapping Laz out of his trance. Laz quickly sat back, cheeks flushed as he mumbled a quick greeting before reaching for his glass of orange juice.

"Good morning," Red replied, smiling wide. "Take a seat. I'll make you a plate."

"Thanks." Colton went about making his morning latte, grateful the Kings were as serious about coffee as he was. Every morning a fresh, piping-hot pot of gourmet coffee waited for him. Soon as he finished, he carried his mug over to the counter and took a seat beside Laz. "How did you sleep?"

"I can't remember the last time I slept through the night like that."

"I'm glad to hear it."

Red placed a plate loaded with scrambled eggs, potatoes, bacon, and toast in front of Laz. "There you go."

Laz beamed up at him. "Thanks, Red."

"You're welcome. Now eat up. You promised you'd take better care of yourself." Red turned back to the stove, and Laz's smile couldn't get any wider.

"I know. And I will."

Colton was glad someone had finally gotten through to Laz. Funny that it turned out to be Red. Then again, Red had a way about him. He was a very handsome man whose muscles had muscles, yet despite his size and obvious strength, he had a kind face, a trusting face. He was the quieter of the Kings, but by no means the least fierce. He'd been part of Ace's unit. As a medical sergeant, Colton could only imagine how much blood and horror the man had dealt with. Had he ever had to patch Ace, or one of his brothers up? Colton had noticed several scars around Ace's body but didn't feel it was his place to ask.

Red set a plate in front of Colton, and he beamed up at Red. "Don't tell, Ace, but you're my new favorite."

"I heard that." Ace walked into the kitchen, eyebrow arched at Colton, making Red chuckle.

"That's what you get for skulking around corners," Colton said, moving his eyes back to his coffee and not to Ace, who'd showered and changed into running shorts and a T-shirt. He probably smelled amazing. Colton found himself stifling a groan at the thought of Ace naked in the shower, water running over every curve and dip. *Really? At breakfast?* Because now was a perfectly appropriate time to get an erection.

"Who's skulking? I wasn't skulking. I happen to have impeccable timing."

"Oh, sorry, you're right. Lucky's the one who's skulking."

Lucky rounded the corner and peered at Colton. "How did you know I was there?"

"The house was too quiet," Colton teased.

Lucky stared at him, and his fellow Kings burst into laughter. "Screw you guys," Lucky grumbled before studying Colton. "No, really. How did you know?"

"It was a *lucky* guess."

Lucky rolled his eyes and went to grab a cup of coffee, ignoring the snickers and snorts from Ace and Red. Ace took a seat at the counter next to Colton, and while everyone was focused on Lucky and his grumping, Ace slipped his hand over Colton's thigh and gave it a squeeze. Colton almost choked on his coffee.

"You okay, Colton?" Ace asked, patting him on the back.

Colton coughed into his fist, his glare aimed at Ace. "Fine."

As Ace, Lucky, and Red teased each other, Colton ate his breakfast. Ever since the Kings had arrived, his house had been filled with laughter. They were very serious about what they did, but they approached each contract based on the client's needs. Since Colton's contract required around-the-clock protection with several members of Four Kings Security staying on his property, it allowed the Kings to conduct themselves in a more casual manner when inside Colton's home. Because of this, the original feeling of having his personal space invaded by strangers had turned into a feeling of comfort. The Kings were approachable and easy to talk to. They were charismatic, charming, and genuinely good men with an insurmountable expanse of knowledge and experience beneath their belts, making it easy for Colton to put his trust in them.

Lucky's boisterous laughter filled the kitchen while Ace recounted a story about Joker accidently setting fire to King's baseball cap while he was wearing it. Red joined in the laughter, and Laz was in tears. It struck Colton how much he'd miss this. He'd never expected to care for any of these men, and now all he could think about was how quiet his home would be once they were gone.

The laughter ebbed once Ace started eating, and Lucky turned to teasing his cousin about the amount of food he consumed. Ace shrugged, stating, around a mouthful of bacon and scrambled eggs, that he loved food. Red told Lucky he needed to eat more fiber, and the conversation turned to something Colton did not want to know about. He turned his attention to Laz.

"What are your plans?"

Laz shrugged and twisted the napkin in his hands. "I don't know. I was supposed to be on a plane to Milan with Bryan to watch him bitch at people for not treating him like the god he thinks he is." He grimaced, then let out a heavy sigh. "My next job isn't until next month, and Gio won't be back from his trip until the week after."

"Why don't you hang around here for a while?"

Laz blinked at him. "Really?"

Colton nodded. He loved having Laz around. It had been too long since they'd spent any significant time together. "Hey, Dad's retirement party is tomorrow night in South Beach. It's going to be huge, and the venue is stunning. We hired a photographer to document the event, but we want some artistic shots to get printed for the meeting rooms. Would you be interested in working the event and approaching it from a design angle? The lighting is going to be spectacular."

Laz's eyes looked like they were going to pop out of his head, and he jumped from his chair. "Oh my God, for real?"

"Of course. Send the bill to Nadine. She'll take care of it."

Laz shook his head. "Oh, I couldn't charge you, Colton."

"I'm not asking you for a favor, Laz. I'm hiring you for a job."

Laz's smile couldn't get any wider. "Thank you."

"We're going to be there until Sunday morning, so I'll have Nadine book you a suite." Colton held up his hand to stop Laz's protest before removing his phone from his pocket. "It's a work expense, so it's taken care of. You can ride with us to the hotel."

Laz nodded. "I'll need to run home to pack."

"Take Red with you." Ace's eyes darted to Colton, and they were filled with something Colton couldn't make out before he turned his attention to Red, who nodded.

"I don't want to inconvenience anyone," Laz said bashfully.

"You're not." Ace walked by Colton, his fingers discreetly brushing Colton's neck, and sending a shiver through him. Did Ace really believe he could torture Colton and not face the consequences?

"I should probably go pack," Colton said. "How are we getting to the hotel? Please don't say anything that flies."

"We have a specially equipped limo that's also been designed with luxury in mind for clients who want to show up to an event in something a little more stylish than an SUV. Jack will be driving us. Your father asked King to provide some additional security, since the firm hired was before we became involved. Red will stay close to Laz in an unofficial capacity, I'll be with you, and Lucky will oversee the team we're bringing in. King will be there to offer support." Ace went pensive for a moment, and Colton could tell he was hesitant to voice the rest.

"What is it?"

"King always does his own risk assessment. He doesn't care who's already been hired. If his client and team are going to be onsite, he does his own. He wasn't satisfied with the outcome. Now keep in mind that the results meet with most companies' standards, but Four Kings is not most companies."

"Do you think Colton's at risk?" Laz asked worriedly.

"I think King plans to have certain areas covered, and we may have to limit which of those areas you go to," Ace told Colton.

"Whatever you think is best."

"Ace, I'll meet you by the pool. I'm going to check in with Jack before we go for our run," Lucky said. "I think he said Joker was going to be in the area. If he's not in the middle of something, he should join us."

"See you there."

Laz slipped off his chair and joined Red by the sink. "I'll help you clean up before we go."

Red nodded, and they both got to work cleaning.

Colton headed for his bedroom, with Ace quietly trailing behind him. Was he thinking about the party or something else? Colton dared to peek over his shoulder and held back a laugh at Ace's lack of subtlety. The man was focused on Colton's ass, his bottom lip caught between his teeth.

"Enjoying the view?" Colton asked, laughing when Ace's gaze shot up, his face flushed. He looked around, and finding the coast clear, he closed the distance between them, wrapped an arm around Colton's chest, his free hand going to Colton's asscheek and giving it a squeeze.

"Baby, I'm doing more than viewing. I'm thinking about all the ways I can take you."

Colton groaned, his erection straining against his pants. He turned and pushed Ace away from him.

"You're a terrible influence," Colton teased.

Ace waggled his eyebrows, and Colton made a dash for his room knowing Ace was right behind him. Inside, he closed and locked the bedroom door. When he turned, he was pushed up against it, Ace's lips all over his, his knee shoved between Colton's legs, pressing up into his painfully hard cock, and their fingers laced together. Colton groaned, thrusting his hips against Ace's as Ace pinned Colton with his hard body. Gasping for air, Colton let his head fall back against the door, rubbing himself shamelessly against Ace, needing more and more friction.

Grabbing Colton's thighs, Ace lifted Colton off his feet.

"Oh fuck!" Colton wrapped his legs around Ace's waist, muffling Ace's laugh with his mouth. He loved kissing Ace, loved the softness of his lips, and the taste of him. Every touch, every caress left him wanting more.

Ace carried Colton over to the bed and dropped him down onto it, then climbed up over him, his lips once again on Colton.

"Fuck, I want inside you so bad, Colton."

Colton whimpered, his body trembling with need. He slipped his hands between them to rub at the hard bulge in Ace's pants. "Yes, please. *Please,* fuck me." A knock startled him.

"Colton, is Ace in there?"

Although he knew Lucky would never enter without permission unless he believed Colton to be in danger, he panicked, and pushed Ace harder than he meant. He cringed when Ace flailed, and fell off the bed with a hard thud, followed by an onslaught of curses in several languages. Colton scrambled off the bed, smoothed out the comforter, and darted into his walk-in closet, hearing Ace behind him.

"What do you want?"

"Why are you snarling at me, bro? I texted you, but you didn't answer. You were supposed to meet me by the pool, remember?"

"Shit, sorry. I was, um, helping Colton try to find his luggage and didn't hear it. Slipped my mind."

Silence.

Colton quickly fixed his clothes and hair, before grabbing his suitcase from the top shelf. "Found it," he said, walking out into the bedroom with the suitcase in hand. He smiled at Lucky. "Oh, hey. Everything okay?"

Lucky narrowed his eyes at Ace before smiling sweetly at Colton. "Buenisimo. Great. I need to borrow him for a minute. News from King. Nothing to worry about."

Colton nodded. "Sure. I'm going to get started on my packing." He placed the suitcase on his bed, aware of the cousins staring each other down before Lucky sighed heavily and motioned toward the door. Ace marched out, and Lucky followed and closed the door behind him, but not completely. Colton considered not eavesdropping, but that lasted about as long as it took him to get over to the door. He inched silently behind it, wondering if Lucky was aware he'd left the door cracked open.

"¿Crees que soy un idiota?"

"No, I don't think you're an idiot. Lucky—"

"No. When King said get close to him, to make him trust you and find out what the hell happened between him and his grandfather, this is not what he meant."

Colton straightened. What the hell was Lucky talking about? Ace had been instructed to get close to him? To earn his trust? What the hell did his grandfather have to do with them? *No.* Colton backed away from the door, the quiet argument no longer within hearing range. Had Ace been using him? His heart squeezed in his chest, and he shook his head, feeling breathless. *No.* This couldn't be happening to him, not again.

The door opened, and Colton spun away needing to get himself together.

"Colton?"

Ace's concerned tone sent anger flaring through him, and he turned, marched up to Ace, and growled at him. "Get the fuck out of my room!"

"What?" Ace stared at him. He snapped himself out of it and put his hands up. "Colton, sweetheart—"

"Don't you *dare*," Colton hissed. "You don't get to call me that. How could you?"

"How could I what? Goddamn it, Colton, talk to me. Why the hell are you so angry?"

Tears welled in his eyes, and he couldn't believe what a sucker he'd been, falling for it twice now. He couldn't even stand to look at Ace. He turned and ran for the stairs, then took them up to his second floor.

"Leave, Ace," Colton snapped as he jerked open his balcony door and rushed out in the fresh breeze. He inhaled deep and closed his eyes against the tears. When he spoke, his voice sounded small and broken. "Please leave."

"I'm not going anywhere until you tell me what's wrong. What's changed?"

Colton rounded on him, angrier at himself than anything. "I *trusted* you. *That's* what's wrong."

"I don't—" Realization seemed to dawn, and he cursed under his breath. "You heard us."

"Yes. I heard. Heard Lucky tell you how you were supposed to earn my trust, get close to me. Did that include fucking me, Ace? Pretending to give a shit about me?" He let out a humorless laugh. "God, I'm such a fucking idiot."

"You are an idiot."

Colton spun to face Ace, ready to tell him to go to hell when the hurt and anger in his eyes made him pause. Before he could utter a word, Ace spoke up.

"Did you bother to hear the rest of it? Or were you too busy jumping to conclusions and thinking the worst of me?"

Colton opened his mouth, but when no words were forthcoming, he quickly closed it.

"I didn't think so. Yes, King asked me to get close to you, to earn your trust in the hopes you would cooperate with us. It's the same with every client. Without trust, how can we do what needs to be done? At the time, I didn't know about what your grandfather had done, only that it seemed to be the reason you were so against cooperating. When King asked me to find out what it was, I told him I'd do what I could but that I wouldn't do anything to jeopardize what trust you had in me."

Ace stepped closer, and Colton forced himself to remain still, especially when Ace cupped his face.

"All King wanted was a way to help you. When you confided in me about what happened, I kept it to myself. *That's* what Lucky was pissed off about. King brought Mick in for questioning, and the guy spilled everything. When King asked me if I'd known, I wasn't going to lie. I told him I knew, but that submitting that information would have been a breach of trust, and I wouldn't do that to you. King understood. Lucky came to confront me about it. He's afraid I'm getting in too deep. What he doesn't know is that it's too late."

Colton dropped his gaze, mortified and ashamed for judging Ace so quickly, and so harshly. Instead of giving Ace the benefit of the doubt, he'd allowed his fear to get the better of him. What had gotten into him? He wasn't usually so impulsive. Hotheaded at times, perhaps, but not reckless, certainly not with his sentiments. "I'm so sorry." The reality of what he'd done hit him hard, and he inhaled sharply. "Oh God, Ace. I'm sorry. I was stupid, rash, and—"

"Easy now. Breathe. I know Mick really hurt you, Colt. But I'm not him. If you ever doubt how much I care, please, talk to me. I will *always* be honest with you."

"You're right." Colton wrapped his hands around Ace's wrists, sighing when Ace brought their heads together. "I loved Mick, and when he betrayed me, it broke my heart, but the thought of you betraying me.... I can't, Ace. I don't think I could survive it."

"So dramatic," Ace teased softly, brushing his lips over

Colton's. "That's what I love most about you. Your passion. That fire inside you." He caressed Colton's cheek with his thumb.

"I'm so sorry I hurt you, Ace."

"I understand why you thought what you did, but if this is going to work between us, there needs to be trust."

Colton nodded, feeling like an idiot. "I do trust you. Please forgive me." He smiled when Ace kissed the tip of his nose.

"You're forgiven. Now come on. We should get inside before someone sees us." Ace took Colton's hand and led him inside, then stopped by the banister at the top of the stairs to kiss Colton who melted in Ace's embrace.

"What is it about you that makes me feel so turned around that I don't know which way is up anymore?"

"I could say the same about you," Ace replied, his voice low and husky as he slipped his fingers beneath Colton's shirt to caress his skin.

"Don't forget, I've arranged for early check-in tomorrow, and I don't have to be anywhere until dinner." Colton nipped at Ace's jaw, loving the groan Ace released. "Make sure you pack appropriately."

"Good idea. I should go. Now."

"Oh?"

"Because if I don't, you're going to end up bent over this banister, and 'broken during a good hard fuck' is not an expense King will appreciate."

"Understood." Colton reluctantly left Ace and headed downstairs into his bedroom, his heart swelling when Ace darted over to plant a big sloppy kiss on his lips. Colton laughed at the man's goofiness.

"Miss me," Ace instructed, pointing at him as he walked backward toward the door.

Colton saluted. "Yes, sir." His stomach flipped when Ace winked at him. Then the man was gone. Jeez, what the hell was wrong with him? Like he'd never been with an attractive man before. Yet when he thought about tomorrow, being with Ace alone for a few hours in a luxury hotel room where they could spend time together, uninterrupted, sexing each other up, holding each other, ordering room service, and bathing together in the private pool, Colton found himself almost giddy with excitement. He was in so much trouble.

ELEVEN

THE LUXURY HOTEL off Collins Avenue in South Beach was stunning, and the view of the ocean from Colton's penthouse suite breathtaking. It was hardly Ace's first time surrounded by such luxury. He dealt with high-profile executives, A-list celebrities, award-winning musicians, and CEOs from multibillion-dollar companies all the time, but the amount of wealth never phased him. He'd once had an actress ask him if he ever envied his clients, and he'd answered honestly. In his line of work, he'd learned that having the amount of wealth most of his clients had meant living with a target painted on your back. For all the freedom wealth afforded, it also made them prisoners. Ace couldn't imagine having to live his life constantly escorted by armed security, having to look over his shoulder wherever he went, fearing for his safety or that of his family. No, he didn't envy them. He had a family who loved him, a successful company he'd helped build, and a career he was proud of. What else could he need?

"Over there, please."

Ace smiled at the sound of Colton's voice. Okay, maybe he needed one other thing. The irony was not lost on him. Colton might not be as high profile as some of his previous clients, but he'd come to mean a great deal to Ace, which meant his safety would always be at the forefront of Ace's thoughts. The bellman thanked Colton, and soon it was just them.

The suite slept four, but Colton was a private person. He didn't share his room with anyone, not friends or family. He'd insisted on sharing with Ace. None of the Kings questioned it as it wouldn't be the first time one of them stayed with a client in a penthouse. Otherwise they'd have to be on a different floor, since some penthouse suites took up an entire floor of a hotel, or they'd be too far for their liking. This room had a pullout queen bed, which he'd assumed he'd be sleeping on had Colton not had the bellman leave all the bags in the bedroom, claiming he'd sort it out later.

Everything was planned for tomorrow's party. Dinner would be in the great room, followed by cocktails out by the cabanas, and a night of entertainment around the pool, the center of which housed a colorfully lit stage where a classy cabaret group was booked to perform for the many guests. His priority wasn't the party. It was Colton. Strong arms wrapped around him from behind, and Ace smiled, placing his hand over Colton's.

"Beautiful," Colton said, and Ace nodded.

"Yeah, it's something else."

"I meant you."

Ace turned in his arms and arched an eyebrow at him. "That so, huh? You trying to seduce me, Mr. Connolly?"

"Maybe." Colton slid his hands down Ace's chest, then to his sides, and his fingers gripped Ace tight. "I hear these walls are pretty thick."

"That's not the only thing that's thick around here," Ace growled, punching his hips forward.

Colton laughed, his beautiful blue-gray eyes alight with amusement. "Oh my God. You did not just say that."

"What? It's true." Ace led Colton's hand to his groin and the hard erection straining against his pants. The man hadn't even done anything, and Ace was already aching for him.

Colton groaned and massaged Ace through his pants. "Mm, what will it take to feel this monster cock inside my tight hole?"

"Are you kidding? I'm seriously considering investing in some tearaway clothes. That way I can just Magic Mike out of my pants." How he loved the sound of Colton's laugh. When he laughed, his face lit up with pure joy. He was breathtaking.

"In the meantime," Colton said, his voice low and sultry as he reached for Ace's belt. "Why don't I help you out of these?"

Ace drew him close and nibbled at his smooth jawline while Colton unbuckled his belt. "I like that plan. Then how about you ride me until we're both sticky, out of breath, and aching oh so good."

"By the way...." Colton pulled his phone out of his pocket, tapped away at the screen, and scrolled through something before handing it to Ace.

"What's this?" It looked like some kind of test result, and—*oh*. Ace's head shot up, his smile splitting his face. "Yeah?"

Colton nodded, and Ace pulled out his phone. It was company policy to get tested every four months. He showed Colton, who glanced at it, grabbed the phone from his hand, and tossed it onto the armchair by the window before pressing his fingers to Ace's chest and pushing. He was being instructed, and Ace trembled with the idea of Colton being in charge. Trusting Colton, he took a step back, then another until his legs hit the love seat. He dropped down onto the cushions, his hands to his sides as he sat motionless. Steadying his breathing, his pulse slowed, his heart rate dropping as he forced himself to calm. If he didn't, this would be over way too soon, and he couldn't have that.

Ace sat mesmerized as Colton strolled over to the nightstand. He fiddled with something, and the sensual beat of "Black Velvet" by Alannah Myles floated through the room. Ace shifted in his seat, adjusting himself. Fuck, Colton was amazing. After returning with the bottle of lube, he tossed it on the love seat beside Ace, then leisurely unbuttoned his shirt, his intense gaze locked on Ace's as he tortured Ace by exposing a little more skin with every button. When his shirt fell open, Ace groaned and pressed down on his aching cock.

Colton *tsked*. "Hands on the couch, hotshot."

Ace did as he was told, his hands balled into fists on the couch to his sides. He didn't trust himself to speak, so he remained silent, his eyes never leaving Colton. His body ached to touch, his cock pushing against the constraint of his pants. Colton slipped out of his shirt and dropped it onto the armchair before toeing off his shoes. He pulled off his socks and flung them onto the chair, then unbuckled his belt, and Ace's breath hitched. Colton let his dress slacks drop to the carpet. He stepped out of them, those snug designer boxer-briefs doing nothing to hide the very stiff cock leaking precome.

Colton approached, and Ace spread his knees, stifling a groan when Colton lowered himself onto the floor between his open legs. He lost himself in Colton's smoky gaze as Colton undid the laces of Ace's boots. He pulled one off, then the other, followed by his socks, his eyes never leaving Ace's. It was taking everything Ace had not to give in, grab Colton, throw him onto the couch, and pound his ass. *Patience.*

"Take off your shirt," Colton commanded.

Ace leaned forward, reached up and behind him, then pulled his shirt off and dropped it to the floor.

Colton moaned, his hand disappearing down in front of him as he stroked himself. "Do you have any idea how gorgeous you are?"

Ace shrugged, a small smile tugging at his lips. He had his family's genetics to thank for his looks. He had his father's green eyes, square jaw, and height, but his mother's golden skin tone and thick, dark hair. His body was a result of years of military physical training, of being pushed beyond his limits. He worked hard to keep himself in shape, but he did it because he needed to be at his best to do what he did. The fact Colton couldn't seem to keep his hands off Ace did silly things to his ego and his heart.

Colton ran his hands up the inside of Ace's thighs, and Ace widened his stance, his breath hitching when Colton's fingers reached his skin. He traced the muscles on Ace's abdomen, his eyes dark with lust.

"Don't move."

Ace nodded, his entire body humming with anticipation. One thing he'd learned about Colton was that he possessed a flirty, unpredictable naughty side to him. Ace loved it. He loved that Colton kept him on his toes, made him laugh, didn't put up with any bullshit. Ace sat perfectly still, his breathing controlled until Colton pushed himself up and placed a searing kiss to Ace's abdomen. Ace jerked, closing his eyes and flexing his fingers, his cock painfully hard, and his skin feeling as if he were baking out in the Florida noon sun. Colton alternated between trailing kisses up his torso, and using his tongue.

"Open your eyes."

Swallowing hard, Ace did, sucking in a breath when Colton flicked his tongue over Ace's nipple.

"Fuck," Ace breathed, his body trembling.

"You're shaking." Colton sucked on the pebbled nub, then nipped at his skin before using the tip of his tongue to reduce Ace into a writhing, needy mess.

"You do that to me," Ace said, his voice husky. "Colton, please."

"Not yet." Colton moved to lavish attention on his other nipple, and Ace thrust his hips up, his nails clawing into the couch cushions. If he didn't get to touch Colton soon, he'd lose it. Self-control and patience were ingrained in him, skills he'd mastered years ago, and yet sweat formed on his brow, his muscles tensed, and it took every ounce of willpower he possessed to do as Colton asked. He'd been taking orders most of his adult life, and although he loved the idea of submitting to Colton, his body was fighting him every step of the way. He wanted Colton in every way, wanted to bury himself deep inside him, claim him, leave his mark. He'd never experienced this before. Never felt the feral desire clawing at his insides.

Colton nibbled at his jaw, and Ace growled, making Colton chuckle. It was low and throaty.

"I love that I've reduced you to nothing but grunts and groans."

Ace grumbled, making Colton laugh. He pulled away, but not before brushing his lips over Ace's, his tongue darting out to tease him. With a soft sigh, Colton pulled away. He stepped back and turned, then bent at the waist to push his underwear down, revealing his delectable ass. All Ace had to do was lean forward and he could squeeze those perfectly round globes. With a smoldering look over his shoulder, Colton pushed his underwear to his ankles. He straightened, stepped out of them, then turned, his long cock bobbing up against his stomach.

"Colt," Ace ground out through his teeth.

"I'm sorry. Why don't I make it all better?" Colton dropped down onto the floor between Ace's knees and reached for his belt, his lust-filled eyes on Ace's as he undid the buckle, and slowly lowered the zipper. "Lift."

Ace lifted his hips, and Colton dragged his pants and underwear down, his rock-hard cock dribbling precome on his stomach. Once his pants were removed and he was completely naked, Colton tortured him some more by kissing up the inside of Ace's leg, nipping at the skin of Ace's inner thigh and making him suck in a sharp breath. *Fuck this.*

Ace grabbed Colton, and dragged him up, bringing Colton onto his lap. Colton straddled him, his arms wrapping around Ace's neck.

"So impatient," Colton teased.

"You're driving me fucking crazy." Ace gripped Colton's asscheeks, his fingers digging into the flesh as Ace thrust his hips up, the friction of their cocks rubbing together sending the most delicious shiver through him. Their eyes met, and they came together in a ravishing frenzy of lips, tongues, and teeth. "I need to be inside you."

Colton nodded, pulling away long enough to grab the lube and shove it at Ace before his lips were back on Ace's, sucking, licking, tongue exploring every crevice of Ace's mouth. Ace flipped open the cap and poured some on his fingers. He pressed one finger to Colton's hole, gently pushing in and loving the deep, sinful moan Colton released. Ace worked Colton's entrance, soon adding a second finger, scissoring him, pushing in deep, fucking Colton with his fingers, loving the way Colton writhed on top of him.

"Yes, oh God, Ace. Please."

"Oh, now you want to hurry?" Ace teased. He handed Colton the bottle of lube. "Get my cock ready for that greedy hole."

Colton whimpered, snatched the bottle from him, and poured a generous amount on his hand before palming Ace's erection, making Ace hiss. Colton twisted his hand, sliding it up and down the length of his cock.

"Put my cock inside you," Ace's voice was hoarse. He needed to feel Colton's tight heat around him like he needed air in his lungs. Thankfully, Colton didn't waste any time. He was beyond teasing. Colton lifted up and lined Ace up with his hole, and Ace shut his eyes tight as the head of his cock slowly breached Colton's entrance. "Oh fuck, yeah, Colton. That's it, baby. Fuck. You're so damn beautiful. I wish I could see how your ass swallows up my dick."

The noises Colton made were decadent, and as soon as Colton was seated against him, Ace grabbed hold of his hips.

"Baby, I'm going to need you to set the pace here because otherwise I'm going to town on your ass."

Colton tweaked his nipples, hard. "Don't make promises you don't intend to follow through on." He pulled himself up, then impaled himself on Ace's cock, making them both cry out. Sweat beaded Ace's brow, and he dug his fingers into Colton's flushed skin. He grinned wickedly.

"Challenge accepted." Ace brought their lips together in a scorching kiss as he plunged into Colton over and over, forcing his cock up into Colton as deep as he could, loving the sound of Colton screaming out his name. The more Colton fell apart in his arms, the faster and harder Ace pounded his ass. He parted Colton's cheeks so he could piston up inside that tight hole, the sound of skin slapping skin joining the music filling the room.

"Tell me we can make this work," Colton breathed. "Please, when this is over, tell me you'll come back to me."

"I will. I promise, Colt. I need you. I need you more than you know." The thunderstorm of want and need that rolled through him was unlike anything he'd ever experienced. Ace had spent so long avoiding relationships, afraid of being hurt again, afraid of losing someone who meant something to him, that he'd forgotten how good it could be. When he became involved with Mason, he'd been hopeful, but when he failed to get through Mason's walls time and time again, Ace began to hold parts of himself back. Falling in love with Mason would have been easy, but they'd been on the path to heartache from the beginning, so Ace left. Colton was different. Yes, risks were involved, but his entire life had been filled with risks. Unlike Mason, Colton trusted Ace with his life, and his heart.

"Don't do this with anyone else," Colton growled, and Ace couldn't help his huge smile. Colton wanted him, all of him, just the way he was. It was in his eyes, in his furrowed brow, the worry lines on his beautiful face, and the way he clutched to Ace as if he never wanted to let go.

Ace kissed Colton. "Only you."

"Oh God, yes. Fuck me. Ace, I can't.... I'm gonna come."

"Yes, come for me, sweetheart. I want you to come all over me."

Colton's hand moved frantically, matching Ace's rhythm as he repeatedly drove himself into Colton, bringing him down against him hard as he pounded Colton's ass. Thank fuck for thick walls, because it became his mission to make Colton scream, and man, did he scream when his orgasm exploded out of him, come shooting onto Ace's stomach and reaching his chin. Colton trembled, but he leaned forward to run his fingers through the sticky ribbons on his chest and put them to Ace's lips. Ace sucked his fingers clean, and when Colton ran another finger down Ace's chest and then put the sticky digit in his mouth, Ace's orgasm barreled through him and he came with a roar, his hips losing control as he chased his release until he was shaking.

Ace let his head fall forward against Colton's chest, and he smiled softly when Colton wrapped his arms protectively around his head, his fingers slipping into Ace's hair as he stroked him ever so tenderly. Ace slipped out of him and enfolded Colton's quivering body in his embrace, wondering when it had happened. When had he exposed his heart and allowed Colton in? What was it about Colton that made him feel *everything*? They hadn't known each other long, but it felt as if they had. Ace had spent every day and night around him, saw him at his best and at his most frustrating. In that time, Colton had become so much more than a client. Ace was aware of every detail. Of the way his hair often fell over his brow, how Colton always looked put-together whether he was in pajamas or a designer suit. How he had more shoes than any one man needed. How he preferred vodka to whiskey, sweet tea with lemon, and had a weakness for freshly baked bread.

"I can't feel my legs," Colton murmured.

Ace laughed and ran a soothing hand down Colton's

back to his crease. He leaned away enough to meet Colton's gaze. "Did I hurt you?"

"Nothing I couldn't handle. It's like you were made for me."

Damn, but he hoped so. "I think you're going to have some bruises." Ace brushed his fingers up Colton's sides, his body feeling heavy and satiated.

Colton shrugged. "I wanted to feel you all day tomorrow."

They kissed languidly, absently caressing and mapping each other's body.

"We should probably get up and shower," Ace murmured, not moving.

"Or...." Colton got up and sauntered off toward the living room, winking at him over his shoulder. "I could go for a swim in the pool. Care to join me?"

"Don't you need your swimsuit?"

The smile Colton gave him, filled with sin and promise, would have made Ace go weak in the knees if he weren't already feeling boneless.

"You coming?"

Ace jumped to his feet, ran into the living room, and hopped over the back of the couch to land on it with a bounce. Colton laughed, and Ace stood, drinking in Colton's toned body. He slipped outside to the balcony where the private pool was, and Ace stood mesmerized as Colton crooked a finger at him.

Ace hurried over to Colton, who playfully slipped out of his grasp. "Where do you think you're going?"

He stalked Colton, admiring the way his sleek body moved. Each flex of muscle, every inch of exposed skin called to Ace. His need to run his hands and tongue over those mouthwatering curves had Ace growing hard again.

Colton entered the pool like some sensual mythical creature, and Ace followed as if under his spell. The water was cool against his skin, but the heat and humidity of the early afternoon made it feel so good. The solid walls on each side of the balcony offered them privacy from any surrounding properties. In front of them was nothing but miles and miles of glittering blue ocean.

Colton swam backward toward the deep end of the pool, his blue-gray eyes clouding with hunger, and it threatened to set Ace on fire despite the cool water he was submerged in. Colton ran his tongue along his bottom lip, his expression the most erotic look Ace ever had the pleasure of being on the receiving end of. He waded over, then stopped in front of Colton, one arm on the pool's edge to each side of Colton's shoulders.

"Hey."

Colton's smile stole his breath away. "Hey."

"You know, I've lived in Florida all my life and I've never had pool sex."

Colton wrapped his arms around Ace's neck, and Ace pressed him up against the side of the pool. He slid his hands down Colton's torso, taking hold of his hips.

"We should remedy that," Colton purred before pressing his lips to Ace's, fueling the fire already inside him into a raging inferno. Ace attacked Colton's mouth, like he needed Colton to supply the breath in his body. Colton wrapped himself around Ace and proceeded to show him what he'd been missing out on, but then he suspected that sex with Colton would be pretty spectacular no matter where they were. Colton couldn't seem to keep his hands off Ace, and Ace was loving every minute of it. Not that it was any easier with Colton. If the man was in the same room, Ace wanted to touch him, kiss him, bury himself inside him.

Once they'd finished messing around in the pool, they took a shower together, giving each other blow jobs. The only reason they didn't have sex when they fell into bed afterward was because they were both too sore and exhausted.

"I need a nap," Colton said through a yawn as he snuggled up to Ace's side.

"We have time," Ace reminded him. "You don't have to be downstairs to meet Laz for dinner until seven." The temperature in the room was perfect, leaving them under a thin blanket. The bed was a California king with lush feather pillows and a memory-foam mattress. Across from it the glass wall allowed for a spectacular view of the beach. The palm trees swayed in the breeze, the sun shining bright in the cloudless sky. Colton absently ran his fingers over Ace's abdomen.

"Tell me about your family. I know you and Lucky are cousins, but your name is Anston, and you don't have the same accent he does."

"That's because I was born and raised here. My mother's Cuban, but my father was American. Anston was his middle name. Although Lucky's mom and my mom are sisters from the same small fishing village east of Havana, my mom was sent over from Cuba back in the sixties during Operation Pedro Pan. Like thousands of parents, my grandparents were afraid of what would happen to their child under the new regime. She was just a kid.

"Her parents had wanted to send Lucky's mom as well, but she was having health issues and was too ill to travel. My mom was one of the lucky kids. Instead of being sent to a foster home or orphanage when she arrived in the US, she was sent to her aunt, who was living in Miami at the time, so my mother was raised by her. By the time her parents came over, Lucky's mom was married and had Lucky. The threat of getting caught leaving the country terrified Lucky's dad. Over the years, the majority of my mother's family migrated over, many in 1980 during El Mariel. When I was in high school, my parents brought Lucky and his parents over."

"And your dad?"

Ace swallowed hard. "He passed away when I was in high school. Heart attack."

"I'm so sorry," Colton said softly, placing a kiss to Ace's jaw.

"I miss him. He was a good man. His family sort of gave him the cold shoulder when he married my mom."

"Why?"

Ace shrugged. "It was a different time. My dad's family comes from old money. They wanted him to marry the daughter of one of their friends, some socialite. He was their only son, so they had his life all planned out by the time he started college. When his parents found out he'd fallen in love with the Cuban girl who made the beds, they lost their shit. They gave him an ultimatum. Leave my mom or be cut off. My father walked away from them and never looked back. His family tried to bribe my mother to leave him, threatened to have her deported when she turned them down, and then did everything they could to make her life miserable."

"That's horrible! What a bunch of assholes." Colton seethed, and Ace smiled at his sweet man's indignation for his family.

"Yeah, but don't worry. My mom might be small, but she's got bite. Between her and my father, they put a stop to that nonsense real quick because by then, they'd married and had me. If Dad's parents wanted to see their only grandkid, they were going to stop their bullshit. My mother might have forgiven them, but she never forgot. When my father died, his parents tried to step in and take over, wanting me to move to Massachusetts so I could go to Harvard and study law." Ace snorted. "Me? A lawyer? They were out of their damn minds." He sighed, thinking about what a mess his life had been at the time. "Then I came out, and the fighting got worse. They blamed my mother. Saying her bad parenting turned me gay. It was ridiculous. I couldn't stand the fighting, the way they were hurting my mother. I needed to get away, to figure myself out and what *I* wanted. So I joined the military."

Colton yawned, and Ace laughed softly. He kissed the top of Colton's head and closed his eyes. "Go to sleep."

"But I want to hear more about your family and your time in the military," Colton huffed. He was adorable.

"We've got time," Ace promised. "Get some rest, because when we get back tonight, you're not going to be getting much sleep."

Colton hummed and settled against Ace. "Well, when you put it that way." His breathing steadied, and Ace soon followed, a smile on his face.

It was a good thing Ace had set his alarm earlier than needed, otherwise instead of being a few minutes late, they'd have been very late, thanks to Colton and his new favorite way of waking Ace up. Not that he was complaining. Of course, when they had somewhere to be, it made getting there on time more of a challenge. Add to that the fact Colton traveled with a substantial amount of clothing and shoes.

"Sorry we're late," Colton said, taking a seat at the table across from Laz. "I was having wardrobe trouble."

Ace sat beside him, across from Red. "That's what happens when you bring a month's supply of wardrobe for a two-night stay."

"I like to be prepared," Colton said with a sniff as he picked up the wine menu. "They have your favorite beer."

Ace snatched the menu from him. "Prepared for what? An impromptu fashion show face-off? Who needs that many shoes?" They did have his favorite imported beer. Excellent.

Colton rolled his eyes and took the menu back. "Whatever. Just for that, you can wait until I'm done with the menu."

Ace looked around the chic restaurant owned by some fancy chef. It was elegant, with its white-and-black décor, an electric blue strip of carpet running beneath the center aisle of tables, and a huge gold-and-crystal chandelier hanging from the ceiling. "What? This place can't afford more than one menu?" Laz broke into laughter, and they turned to stare at him. "What?"

"Oh my God," Laz said, struggling to breathe from laughing so hard. "You two are hilarious! It's like you're married." He wiped away at his tears, his huge grin aimed at Colton as he pointed to Ace. "He's a keeper."

"Funny guy," Ace muttered, shaking his head. He met Red's gaze and ignored the look of concern in his friend's hazel eyes. Clearing his throat, he thanked the waiter who filled his glass with water.

Colton and Laz chatted away, always including Ace and Red in the conversation. Ace noted how Laz never missed an opportunity to lean over and touch Red. The kid was totally smitten, and by the stupidly sweet smile on

LOVE IN SPADES 225

Red's face, Ace figured his friend wasn't all that immune to the kid's charm.

The restaurant was packed, the drinks delicious, though after one beer both he and Red had water. They were still on the job, despite the intimate dinner they'd been instructed to be a part of. Sometimes their dinner expenses were outrageous, but if their client wanted them to join in, it made their job easier. In situations like this, it was important to blend in rather than stand guard to one side of the dining area, making people uncomfortable. Usually they'd sit at a table beside their client's table, but that hadn't been necessary with Colton even before they'd started secretly seeing each other.

The food arrived, and suddenly Ace was ravenous. He'd ordered the pork with sweet potato, and Colton ordered the duck with steamed pancakes and plum sauce. It was beautifully presented, and Ace had to admit, it was delicious. They talked while salsa music filled the air. Ace was having a great time, and he had to remind himself more than once that he wasn't out on a dinner date with Colton. He was here on a job, which meant reining himself in. Colton was trying, but they'd slipped up twice. Once, when Colton leaned over with a forkful of duck and plum sauce for Ace to try.

Quickly realizing, he smiled at Ace. "Doesn't that look amazing?"

Ace nodded, shoving a big bite of pork into his mouth before Colton ate the duck meant for Ace. The second time was on Ace, who'd wiped some plum sauce off the corner of Colton's mouth. Thankfully he'd used his napkin and not his thumb like he'd wanted to. Red kept sneaking glances at him, and although he wouldn't give Ace an earful like Lucky would, Ace hated not being honest with Red. They never kept anything from each other. As soon as this was over, he'd talk to his friends and hope they understood. Colton was a client, but Ace had never felt anything like this. King and the others had to know that. He might be a pain in the ass, but he'd never taken such a risk. That had to mean something, didn't it?

TWELVE

"MY FATHER'S going to be so drunk by the end of this," Colton said with a laugh as he turned to Ace. He inhaled deeply, loving Ace's scent, a mixture of subtle cologne and woodsy shower gel. He was utterly delectable in his black suit and shirt, the top two buttons undone, and his skin calling for Colton to kiss. He shouldn't stand so close to Ace, but it was difficult not to when his body craved Ace's presence. Several women and men had stopped to admire Ace when he'd made an appearance at Colton's side. He couldn't blame them. How could anyone not be captivated by Ace—the chiseled jaw, stunning green eyes, and lush mouth, or his broad shoulders and tapered waist. When he walked, he exuded confidence and strength.

Ace's rumble of a chuckle did terrible things to Colton's groin. "We'll keep an eye on him."

Colton hummed as he turned away before anyone could see how desperately he wanted to jump Ace's bones. "As long as you don't forget about me."

"You kidding? I'm having trouble keeping my eyes off you." Ace's voice was low and throaty, and he discreetly brushed Colton's fingers with his own. "Not to mention my hands. You look incredible, by the way."

"Thank you." Colton knew he looked sharp in his blue Armani slim-fit suit with the mauve tie and pocket square, but having Ace comment on how good he looked, his eyes darkening with lust, was everything. "I fail to see how your inability to keep your eyes off me is a bad thing."

"When I'm supposed to be vigilant of my surroundings? Yes, it's a bad thing."

"You have a small army here, including several officers standing guard at the doors making sure whoever comes in and out is on the guest list. I think we're covered."

The turnout for his father's retirement was impressive. Everyone who'd been invited and RSVP'd was in attendance. Laz had been practically vibrating with excitement as he flitted about the place taking photos. Everyone was enchanted by him, and from the few guests Colton had spoken to, several were interested in hiring Laz for exclusive shoots. Every now and then, Colton would spot Laz setting up a shot, and it made Colton smile because not long after he'd spot Laz, he'd see Red.

The venue was stunning, and the event company Nadine had hired did a fantastic job. The outside pool area was lit up by neon pink, purple, and teal, the bright colors reflecting across the water, and in the center a cabaret troupe performed in spectacular costumes adorned with huge feathers and glittering diamonds. Behind them, one of the top local Latino bands, dressed elegantly in white linen suits with Panama Cuenca hats, played a pulse-pounding salsa beat, while the handsome young man in the center sang about falling in love. The guests danced, others clapped and moved to the music where they stood. The energy was infectious, and even those who weren't carried away by the music were chatting, drinking cocktails, and having a good time. For those who wanted a more private place to chat, several cabanas were situated around the pool, with soft lighting and comfortable seating.

"Colton!"

The happy squeal had Colton turning, and he smiled widely at Annie. She was exquisite in a pale blue beaded-bodice evening gown with a deep V-neck, her dark hair combed to one side and draped over her shoulder.

"You look stunning," Colton said as he gently hugged her and kissed her cheek.

"Thank you. You look gorgeous, like always." She glanced behind Colton and did a double take, making Colton chuckle. "Ace, it's so good to see you again." She held her hand out to him, which he kissed, and she swooned a little.

"It's good to see you too, Annie. How's Lily?"

Annie beamed, and it was clear she was a little smitten with Ace, but then who didn't fall under the man's spell when they talked to him? Maybe it was his easy smile, his sense of humor, or the way he managed to make everyone around him feel at ease.

"Full of mischief. She still brings up the magic trick you did for her. You made quite the impression on her."

"She's adorable," Ace said, smiling wide. "Can I get you both a drink? The bar's right there."

"Thank you." Colton gave Ace his drink order, and Annie did the same. The bar was only a few feet away, and even when Ace reached it, he could easily see and get to Colton.

"Oh my God, Colt." Annie squeezed his arm. "How do you get anything done with that man around? I'd be walking into walls." She waggled her eyebrows at him. "Is he single?"

"Why? Are you interested?" Colton teased. She slapped his arm. "Ow, why are you assaulting me?"

"Colton, the man is gorgeous."

"He's also off-limits. I'm his client."

"And when you stop being his client?" She stared at him intently. The woman was far too perceptive for her own good. "And don't even think about lying to me, Colton. I've known you way too long."

"Is he still pretending he's not interested in the hot supersoldier?" Nadine asked, stepping up to Annie and giving her a hug. "So good to see you."

"Nice to see you too." Annie returned her embrace before focusing her attention back on Colton. "He's being evasive."

"And you're both meddling," Colton said with a sniff. "Nadine, you look stunning. Even if you are sticking your nose in my business." The long deep-scarlet gown was striking against her dark complexion, and it molded to her curves like a second skin. He was surprised the men gawking at her when she sauntered by hadn't walked straight into the pool. Considering their less-than-subtle ogling, he'd secretly hoped one or two might have fallen in. Shame.

Nadine laughed, the delightful sound causing more than a few heads to turn in her direction. "You call it meddling; I call it nudging you in the right direction. Ooh, here he comes."

"Nadine," Ace said cheerfully. "Good to see you. You look beautiful." He handed Annie and Colton their cocktails. "Can I get you a drink?"

LOVE IN SPADES   231

"Thank you, Ace. It's a pleasure to see you again. I'd love whatever Annie's having. Thank you."

Ace nodded and went back to the bar, both women's eyes following his every move and making Colton laugh. "Oh my God, stop eyeballing the man's ass."

Nadine moved her eyes to Colton, her expression very serious. "When this is over, if you don't say something to that man along the lines of 'I'd like you in my bed,' I'm going to question your life choices."

"You're both ridiculous."

Nadine narrowed her eyes, and Annie gasped, her voice low when she spoke. "Oh my God, you two already played hide the sausage!"

Colton choked on his drink. "What the hell, Annie? You're a mother!"

"And? What, I can't have a sex drive because I've had a child?" She arched an eyebrow at him, and he wiped his mouth on the cocktail napkin. These two were trying to kill him.

"You did," Nadine squeaked happily. She was so damn giddy Colton thought she might hurt something. "Was he amazing? Of course he was amazing."

"Who said we did anything?" Colton did his best to appear nonchalant. If he could evade Lucky, he could elude these two.

"Some dude is hitting on your man," Nadine said, pointing behind him.

Colton turned, his frown deep when Peter from accounting laughed at something Ace said. Like Ace had told the funniest joke in the world. He slapped Ace's arm playfully, then kept his hand around Ace's bicep. He leaned in close to say something, and Ace chuckled, shaking his head at whatever Peter was saying.

"You're right," Annie said. "He's totally hitting on Ace. Did he actually lick his lips? Way to be subtle, Pete."

"Bitch needs to be put in her place," Nadine said with a hum. "Just saying."

Colton took a deep breath and turned back to them with a smile. "Ace is a grown man. He can handle himself."

"Peter wrote something on a napkin," Annie whispered conspiratorially, "and stuck it in Ace's front jacket pocket."

"Oh, hussy's bold." Nadine shook her head, her narrowed gaze on Peter. "Seriously, you need to stop being so handsy, Pete. Yes, the man has exquisite bone structure, but he doesn't need you pawing at him."

"Would you two stop it," Colton hissed.

"Oh, Ace is coming back." Nadine straightened, and Annie took a sip of her drink as he approached.

"Here you go." Ace handed Nadine her drink, and she beamed at him.

"Thank you. I see you met Peter."

Ace nodded. "Yeah, friendly guy."

"A little *too* friendly, if you ask me," Colton muttered before taking a sip of his cocktail.

"Are you referring to this?" Ace held the napkin up between his index finger and middle finger, his eyes filled with mischief.

"What does that say?" Colton plucked the napkin from him, squinted at it, then dropped it in his martini glass. He let out a gasp. "Oh, my goodness. How clumsy of me. I'm so sorry, Ace."

"I think it's salvageable," Ace said, laughing when Colton stabbed it with his finger and swirled it around until it was in pieces.

"No, don't think it is." Colton sighed. "Such a shame."

LOVE IN SPADES 233

The girls broke into laughter, and Ace playfully nudged Colton with his elbow. "Jealous?"

Colton scoffed. "Of course not. It's simply unprofessional to hit on someone who's clearly here to do a very important job."

"Right," Ace said, sounding amused. "So, if Peter were to give me his number again...."

"Then I can't be held responsible for whatever fate befalls that napkin. Lot of water around here." *Wait a second. Shit.* Colton's eyes widened, and he quickly cleared his throat. "Um, not that it's any of my business. I mean, you're, uh, single." His cringe at the word *single* wasn't going to win him any Oscars. He worried his bottom lip as he turned to Ace. "I'm so sorry."

Ace smiled warmly at him, easing Colton's mind. "Relax. They clearly know. Peter isn't the only one lacking in subtlety around here." He gave them all a pointed look.

Colton turned to his friends. "You can't breathe a word to anyone. This could really hurt Ace's career. We're waiting until this is all over."

Annie made a zipping motion across her lips, and Nadine snorted oh so delicately.

"If I didn't know you were saying it because of how crazy about him you are, I'd be offended. When have I ever talked about your business to anyone?"

This was true. Nadine was one of his closest confidants, not only at work, but as a friend.

"You're right. I'm sorry." Colton took hold of her hand and kissed it. "Do you forgive me?"

"I do. Only because I love you and want you to be happy." She smiled sheepishly at him. "Also, I submitted a request for vacation time."

"And I would never tell anyone," Annie promised, her

eyes growing glassy. "After everything you did for Lily, for me? How could I ever do anything to jeopardize our friendship, Colton?"

Colton hugged Annie tight, promising he wasn't mad. How could he be? They wanted him to be happy, and after all these years of thinking he'd never find the right person for him, Ace had found him.

"This looks like all kinds of trouble right here." Nolan stepped up to them, and Annie hugged him tight, making him chuckle.

"Hi, Dad."

"Hey, kiddo."

"I'll have you know that the only troublemaker here is Colton," Nadine said, winking at Colton.

"I don't know what you're talking about. I'm a paragon of class and sophistication."

Ace snorted, and Colton slowly turned to him, an eyebrow arched. Everyone burst into laughter, and Ace coughed into his fist.

"Sorry, had something in my throat," he said, pretending to wheeze. "Probably pollen or something."

"Or something all right," Colton muttered, handing Ace his martini glass with the disintegrated napkin. "Just for that, you can get me a new drink."

Ace chuckled. "Sure."

"While you do that, I'll go use the restroom."

"I'll escort you," Ace said with a frown. "I'll grab your drink when we get back."

"Ace! There you are." Jeremy, Annie's husband, appeared behind them and patted Ace on the shoulder. "I wanted to ask you a couple of questions."

"Sure, but first I need to escort Colton—"

LOVE IN SPADES   235

"Ace, it's fine. The bathroom is right there." Colton pointed to the door near the hotel entrance.

"I'm coming with you, or at least let me grab someone else."

"Dude, it's right there," Jeremy said, earning himself a scowl from Ace. "He's a big boy. He'll be fine."

"Ace, I really need to go. It's fine."

"I need to visit the ladies room," Annie said. "I'll go with him. If I see or hear anything, I'll get you right away."

"It's not a big deal, Ace," Colton assured him. There were a lot of guests here tonight, but plenty of security, and no one could get in without being on the list. It wasn't like he was leaving the pool area.

"Okay, but I'm sending someone to check on you."

Colton nodded and left with Annie at his side. He'd only had a few drinks, but he was desperate, and being stopped every few steps by people thanking him for the party, offering him congratulations, and wanting to chat was appreciated and valued, but not the best time for it. The ladies' restroom was just next door.

"I'll meet you out here," Annie said before disappearing inside.

Colton reached for the door but noticed the small plaque. "Out of order?" Colton cursed under his breath. He was pretty sure he'd seen another bathroom inside. Ace was talking to Jeremy, and whatever it was, looked important. Jeremy mentioned wanting to hire Ace for a job, so Colton didn't want to interrupt. Plus, he was about to pee himself. He hurried toward the glass doors leading into the hotel, and one of the guards standing by.

"Excuse me. If Ace comes looking for me, can you let him know I'm in that bathroom there? The other one is out of order."

The man nodded, and Colton could hear him putting a call out to Ace.

Hurrying inside the men's room, Colton dashed over to the urinal. "Oh my God." It was so good. He'd have to have a talk with the hotel. There had been no mention of a restroom being out of order, and it was terribly inconvenient for their guests. He supposed it could have happened tonight. The elegant bathroom he stood in was empty, and once Colton finished his business, he washed his hands and dried them. He checked himself over quickly in the mirror, then headed for the door.

The door opened, and Colton moved out of the way so he wouldn't run into the poor guy. "I'm so sorry. Excuse me."

"Colton, how good to see you," the man said, his smile wide and friendly.

"Oh, hello. I'm sorry, I don't think we've met." Colton was meeting several of the guests for the first time. They were mostly his dad's golf buddies, or friends from his yacht club.

"Your father and I spend a lot of time at the yacht club. He's been interested in buying my Regulator 34."

"Ah, yes! I remember now." A few weeks ago, his father had been rambling on about a thirty-nine-foot yacht one of his club buddies was selling. Colton held his hand out to shake. "Mr. Wells, right?"

The man beamed at him. "That's right." He shook Colton's hand before laughing. "Sorry, this is a very strange place to do this. How about we have a drink at the bar?"

"Sure, I just need to return to the party and let my friend know."

Wells shrugged. "Call them from the bar."

LOVE IN SPADES   237

Colton plastered a smile on his face. "It won't take a minute. I can do that while you finish up here. Excuse me."

The smile disappeared from Wells's face, replaced by a cold, dark stare. Colton quickly moved back when three other men in suits entered the bathroom, blocking the door behind them. Colton retreated toward the stalls, his eyes widening when Wells—or whoever the fuck he was—pulled a syringe from his jacket pocket.

"It looks like you've had a little too much to drink, Mr. Connolly. Why don't I help you?"

"Stay the hell away from me," Colton warned, scanning the bathroom for a way out. With no windows and only one door, which was currently blocked, he was trapped. Colton reached into his pocket as one of the men pulled a gun on him.

"Hands where I can see them," Wells said. He approached Colton, and Colton waited.

Wells charged, throwing out an arm to grab him, which Colton snatched hold of, ducked under, and twisted behind the man, then shoved him face-first into the bathroom wall, the needle dropping to the floor. Remembering everything Ace had taught him, Colton kicked the side of the man's knee, putting all his force behind the kick, and a crunching sound was quickly followed by a scream. If they were planning on drugging him, it meant they wanted him alive. Otherwise, they would have shot him already.

The other men charged, but the door slammed open, and Ace thundered in like the god of war himself had been unleashed. The three men launched an attack on Ace, who used his skills to fend off their assault, making sure to disarm them. He thrust his palm up into one man's nose, then dropped to one knee and punched the guy on the side of the knee before spinning and jumping to his feet. Colton took a step forward, terrified by the look in Ace's eyes. He'd never seen them so dark, so cold. An arm wrapped around Colton's neck, jerking him back into a hard body, and knocking them both into the wall.

Wells attempted to jam the needle into Colton, who managed to grab his wrist. He reached into his pocket, pulled out his pen, and doing as Ace had taught him, stabbed the pen into the flesh of Wells's thigh. The man let out a snarl, losing his grip on Colton's neck and allowing him to get out from under the guy's hold. Colton snatched the syringe, flipped off the cap, and stuck it into the man's arm, then shoved the plunger down. Wells crumpled to the floor, and Colton turned, his heart beating in his ears. The men were all on the floor unconscious, and Ace stood over them, chest heaving, blood on his lip, his knuckles bloodied and bruised.

"Ace?" The word came out as a whisper, and Colton started to shake.

Seeming to snap out of it, Ace darted over, took hold of his arms, and followed him down to the floor as Colton's knees gave out from under him.

"Baby, are you okay? Are you hurt?"

"I'm okay." Colton nodded, his breathing heavy and his hands shaking.

"Oh God, I was so scared I'd get here and find out I was too late. I don't know what the hell I would have done if—"

"Shsh, it's okay, Ace. I'm okay." Colton cupped his face and kissed him, needing to feel him close. Ace returned his kiss, but a sharp bellow startled them both.

"What the hell is going on?"

Oh fuck.

"Dad."

THIRTEEN

THIS COULDN'T BE HAPPENING.

Colton got ahold of himself, letting Ace help him to his feet but not pushing him away. Instead he leaned into Ace's embrace as his father marched over and took hold of Colton's arm. Ace released him, and Paxton looked Colton over, a mixture of fear and anger in his eyes.

"Colton, are you all right?"

"Yes, I'm fine."

"You're bleeding."

Colton followed his father's gaze to his right hand stained with blood. He shook his head. It was Wells's, from when Colton had stabbed him with the pen. "It's not mine." Before he could utter another word, his father had Ace by the collar, shoving him against the wall.

"You were supposed to protect my son!"

"Dad, stop!" Colton pushed himself between his father and Ace. He'd never seen his father this furious, and he understood how freaked-out his dad must be, but Colton wasn't going to let him take his anger out on Ace.

240   CHARLIE COCHET

Paxton thrust a finger at Ace. "I paid you to keep him safe, not sleep with him!"

"Dad, that's enough!"

King came running in with Lucky and Red close behind him. "What's going on?"

Paxton rounded on them with a snarl. "Is that how you run your company, King? Your men sleep with their clients?"

King held up his hands in front of him, his tone calm and soothing. "Mr. Paxton, I can assure you—"

"You can forget about that contract with Connolly Maritime," Paxton growled. "What's more, you're done in this business!"

"Mr. Paxton, let's discuss this."

"You're done," Paxton snapped, thrusting a finger at King. "Four Kings Security is done. Get my son to the hospitality suite. You'll get paid, and then I want you all out of our lives for good." Paxton stormed out, and Ace took a step toward King.

"King, I'm sorry. I—"

"Is it true?" King asked, his voice exuding nothing but calm. "Did you get involved with Colton?"

Ace met King's gaze. "It's true, but, King—"

"No," King stated firmly, a finger held up to quash any argument. "I'm going to try and fix this." He shook his head, his blue eyes filled with hurt when he met Ace's gaze. "You've really disappointed me, Ace. We'll discuss this later. Get this mess cleaned up."

Colton flinched along with Ace, his heart splintering for him when King walked out. Ace tried to go after him, but Red stopped him, his voice rough with emotion when he spoke.

LOVE IN SPADES 241

"Let him go, Ace. It's not a good idea to talk to him right now."

Tears filled Ace's eyes, his gaze on the door King had walked out of, but then Lucky exploded, shoving Ace.

"You son of a bitch!"

"I'm sorry," Ace said softly. "I'm so sorry, Lucky."

"How could you? We're family!"

Ace closed his eyes. "I know."

"Do you? Because you don't act like it sometimes. It's bad enough you get involved with a client, but you lied to me, to my face! I knew something was going on, but I was like, no, Ace wouldn't lie to me. We've never lied to each other. You're a fucking asshole." Lucky shoved Ace one more time before disappearing, not bothering to give Ace a chance to explain further.

Ace gripped the edge of the granite counter, his head hanging down and his eyes shut. Colton kept his distance, which was a good thing, because after several heartbeats in complete silence, Ace let out a fierce cry and punched the mirror in front of him. The heartbreaking sound and the force behind Ace's fist startled Colton, but he wasn't scared of Ace.

Colton's heart squeezed as he slowly approached. He placed a hand on Ace's shoulder, and for a split second, he worried Ace might shrug him off and walk away, but he didn't. Ace turned to Colton, wrapped his arms around him, and pulled him close so he could bury his face in Colton's neck. Colton held him tight, his cheek to Ace's hair as he offered what comfort he could.

"I'm so sorry," Colton whispered, running his fingers through Ace's hair. "I don't seem to be having much luck with public bathrooms these days."

242 CHARLIE COCHET

A hint of a smile tugged at Ace's lips when he pulled back. "You should go. Red will take you to your father."

"What happens next. With us?"

Ace brushed his fingers down Colton's cheek. "Whatever happens, it won't change how I feel about you, Colton."

"That's all I needed to know." He kissed Ace. It was passionate but brief. Reluctantly he left Ace in the bathroom and followed Red down the hall to the elevator.

By the time they reached the hospitality suite, Colton was seething.

"I'll be outside if you need me," Red said, and Colton thanked him before entering the room. His father was inside by the wall of windows that looked out onto the ocean. It was a starless night, no clouds, just darkness.

"I need to talk to you."

"Not now. Unbelievable. I put my trust in them." Paxton reached into his suit jacket and pulled out his cellphone.

"What are you doing?"

"Calling my lawyer."

Colton snatched the cell phone out of his father's hand. "You're not doing anything of the kind. What's more, you're going to apologize to King for threatening him, and we're going through with the contract with the Kings for Connolly Maritime."

"Colton, you're not thinking clearly. You were attacked, and that son of a bitch took advantage of you!"

Colton prided himself on never losing his temper. This was not one of those times. "Don't you dare! I know what taking advantage of feels like, so don't even try it!"

Paxton flinched, but Colton refused to back down.

"Mick took advantage of me. He used me, betrayed me, planned to marry me so he and your father could control my

LOVE IN SPADES 243

life and my legacy. I am *done*. This is *my* life, and I'll be damned if I'm going to let anyone tell me how to live it."

"You—"

"Love him, Dad."

Paxton stared at him. "What?"

Colton couldn't help the small smile that tugged on his lips. "I'm in love with him."

"Don't be ridiculous," Paxton scoffed.

Colton narrowed his eyes. *Oh hell no.* "Now you listen to me. I love you, but I'm a grown man, and *no one* tells me how I feel, who I get to love, how long that should take, or how to live my goddamn life. I was the one who started things with Ace. He was reluctant because he feared this exact thing would happen. Anston Sharpe is a damned good man who put up with all our bullshit to keep me safe. From the moment we met, there was something between us, and because of me, because I believed it would all work out, he took a chance on me. We were going to wait until this was all over to tell you and King, but those assholes took that from us. I want this. I want *him*."

"Colton—"

"No," Colton snapped. "It's over." Colton tapped at his phone, then put it to his ear. "King? Please come to the hospitality suite. My father has something he wants to discuss with you."

"You really love him?"

Colton released a heavy sigh as he leaned against the back of the couch. "I know it seems fast, but sometimes you know. I was with Mick for years, and it turned out I didn't know him as well as I thought I had. With Ace, it took me days to see the kind of man he is. He's an open book, Dad."

"Colton, the man is ex-Special Forces. He had a whole other life before you."

Colton shrugged. "Ace's time in the military is no one's business but his and those who served with him. If, and when, he wants to share that part of himself with me, then I'll be there to listen." Colton handed his father's cellphone back to him. "I know this whole thing has been about you protecting me, and I'm sure part of that is down to wanting to atone for what your father did, but it's not necessary. All I want from you is your trust."

Paxton sighed and nodded. "You're right." His frown deepened. "Our family does have a habit of being a tad emotional."

"And they call *me* a drama queen."

His father chuckled, and then a knock on the door drew their attention.

"Come in," Colton said, glad to see King. The man was impressive, no doubt about it. He had a presence about him. Despite being Colton's height and not as muscular as Red, he was larger than life. He carried himself tall, his dirty-blond hair and bright blue eyes a stark contrast against his tanned skin. His eyebrows were thick, his stubbled jaw chiseled, and when he stood at attention, chin lifted high, it was clear that inside Ward Kingston beat the heart of a warrior. This was the man who'd helped piece his broken brothers back together.

Paxton cleared his throat and took a step forward. "King, I owe you and your men an apology. I let my emotions get the better of me. Seeing Colton in the same room as those men who'd come to hurt him... I was beside myself. It was wrong of me to threaten you in the manner I did. The contract between Connolly Maritime and Four Kings Security is safe. Ace's involvement with my son won't be leaving this room. I'll even make sure it becomes part of the confidentiality agreement in the new contract. Do you forgive me for my behavior?"

"There's nothing to forgive, Mr. Connolly. You had every right to be upset. I can assure you this is an isolated incident. No one in our employ has ever crossed that line with a client, and Ace will face the consequences of his actions."

"What does that mean?" Colton asked, pushing away from the couch.

"When Ace became emotionally involved, he compromised himself, you, and our firm. He should have taken himself off the case, but he didn't. Trust is everything in our business, Colton, and Ace broke that trust. We're very fortunate that you and your father are good men and can forgive this indiscretion. Had it been anyone else, we may not have been so lucky. I can't sweep this under the rug, and Ace knows that."

With the matter resolved with his father, Colton turned to Paxton. "Dad, can we have the room please?"

Paxton nodded. He walked to King and put his hand on the man's shoulder. "You're an honorable man, King. You and all your men." He patted King's shoulder. "Don't be too hard on Ace, son. Love makes smart men do stupid things."

King's eyebrows shot near his hairline, but he simply nodded.

As soon as Paxton closed the door behind him, Colton spoke up. "What are you going to do to Ace?"

"It hasn't been decided. I might call the shots in most cases, but the four of us are equal partners. As much as I would love to say he won't receive special treatment, he's our brother and co-owner. However, that doesn't excuse his actions, and he knows that. We all do. The four of us will have a meeting and discuss how to move forward."

Colton nodded his understanding. "How you handle things in your company is none of my business, but like I told my father, I was the one who initiated things between us. Ace was reluctant."

"Yet he proceeded nonetheless."

"Do you know what scared him most?"

King tilted his head, studying him. "What's that?"

"Disappointing you. He loves you, King. You're his family. I mean, you all are, but you.... The way he talks about you. You're his hero."

The only sign that showed King was upset was the way his jaw muscles tightened before he answered. "Then he shouldn't have betrayed me or his brothers the way he did."

Colton marched up to King, indignant. "It's not about you! It's about us and what we mean to each other. I love him."

"What?" For the first time since entering the room, King looked stunned.

"I love him. I don't know when it happened, but it did."

It seemed to take a minute to sink in before King turned and ran his fingers through his hair. "Jesus." He rubbed at his stubbled jaw before turning back to Colton. "You really love him?"

"Do you think Ace would have risked hurting you for a fling? A one-night stand?"

King shook his head and let out a heavy sigh. "No."

"I want to be with him. Make him happy. After everything you've all suffered, doesn't he deserve to be happy? To be loved? You all deserve that, King."

"He told you?"

It wasn't said as an accusation. King sounded more curious than anything.

"About what happened to your unit? Yes. About coming

home and how you helped him and the rest of your brothers find their way. The way he lights up when he talks about you and his brothers—you're his world."

"He should have come to me," King said quietly.

"He was going to. After this was over, he was going to ask for your advice on how we should proceed in public. Not once did he stop thinking about you or the others. We both fucked up royally, I know that, but it's not every day you find someone worth risking so much for."

King nodded. "Thank you for the insight." His phone buzzed, and he removed it from his inner suit pocket, looked at it, sent a speedy text, and returned it to his pocket. "The police have arrived. They're taking Ace's statement, so I need to go. I'll let you know when it's time to give yours. In the meantime, please stay here. Red will take over Ace's duties. I'll notify you when it's safe to contact him."

"Okay." Colton hated that he couldn't talk to Ace, but he didn't want to make things worse for him. As badly as he wanted to be in the man's arms, he'd wait. Someone knocked, and King called out on his way over.

"Yes?"

"It's me," Red replied from the other side.

King let Red in and spoke quietly with him before he turned and excused himself. Red locked the door behind him.

"Hey." Colton went straight for the minibar. He desperately needed something strong. After fixing himself a whiskey on the rocks, he carried his glass over to the couch and sank into the plush cushions. Red took a seat beside him, his expression filled with concern.

"How are you doing?"

"Miserable. But I'm alive, so that's something. How's Ace?"

Red sighed. "Not good, but he'll get through this. Whatever happens, he knows he's still family."

Colton took a sip of his whiskey. "I've really fucked things up for him, haven't I?"

"Do you care about him?" Red asked, his hazel eyes intense.

"I love him." Colton frowned down into his glass. "That's three people I've told, and none of them have been Ace."

Red placed a hand on Colton's shoulder. "You'll be able to tell him soon. I promise. In the meantime, you need to stop blaming yourself. Ace knew what he was getting himself into, but you obviously mean a lot to him. It'll work out."

"Thank you."

A knock on the door had Red on his feet. "Yes?"

"It's me. Nolan."

Colton nodded for Red to let him in. Red opened the door, and Nolan ran in, practically shaking with worry. Colton stood and came around the couch to meet Nolan, who hurried over and checked him for injuries.

"Oh my God, Colton, are you okay? Paxton said you were here. He told me what happened, and I came right away. Is it true a group of men attacked you? Here?"

"Yes, but Ace took care of them. I'm okay."

Red chuckled. "Don't sell yourself short, Colton. You did pretty damn good yourself."

"Thanks to Ace and the self-defense techniques he taught me. I'll never underestimate a writing utensil ever again."

"I can't believe this." Nolan ran a hand through his hair. "Goddamn, Jeremy. I swear the man is a jinx. If he'd let Ace go with you and stopped being so selfish, this might not have happened."

"Hey, Nolan. It's okay. I'm fine. How about a drink?"

Nolan nodded. "I think that would be a good idea. I swear my son-in-law has been nothing but a pain in the ass since I met him. Ace should have gone with you. This shouldn't have happened."

Colton poured Nolan a drink and turned as Nolan removed a gun with silencer from his jacket and pulled the trigger, shooting Red twice.

"No!"

Red dropped to his knees, his hands pressed to his stomach, blood seeping through his fingers as he gasped for breath.

Oh God, no!

"Red!" Colton dropped the glass and ran for him, but Nolan blocked his path.

"What the hell did you do?"

"I'm sorry. I'm so sorry. I'm going to need you to come with me, Colton."

"Please, Nolan. We need to get him some help. Oh God." This had to be a horrible nightmare. It couldn't be happening. "Red, please hold on."

"Colton, if you don't come with me right now, the next bullet I fire will be into his skull."

"Jesus. Okay." Colton put his hands up, and Nolan motioned him toward the door. "What do you want from me?"

"If you don't shut up and get us out of here without incident," Nolan warned, "I can promise you someone else you care about won't be making it out of this hotel. Think about your father."

"Okay." Colton nodded. "I'll cooperate. Just don't hurt anyone else."

"Then move."

"Hey."

Ace took another swig of his beer before answering King, who grabbed a seat on the stool beside him at the bar. "Hey."

The police had Ace's statement and were in the process of interviewing anyone and everyone who might have seen anything. They'd taken the men away and would be looking into who they were. Colton was safe with Red, waiting for his turn to give his statement. It was a clusterfuck. And yet Ace could only think of Colton. How he should be with his man, holding him, reassuring him. Colton was most likely blaming himself, and Ace needed him to understand he shouldn't be. The severity of what could have happened probably hadn't even hit Colton yet.

"I'm prepared to face the consequences," Ace said, taking another sip of his beer. His skin felt too tight for his body, and his muscles tensed with the need to be doing something, anything.

"Are you?"

LOVE IN SPADES 251

"I fucked up, King." Ace nodded, tears welling in his eyes, and he couldn't help his choked sob. "I'm so sorry I disappointed you."

"Asshole. Come here." King brought Ace in for a hug, and Ace clutched him fiercely.

Ace had a huge family, with aunts, uncles, cousins, second cousins, grandparents, but not one sibling. As an only child, he'd often imagined what it would be like to have a sibling. Lucky had filled that role from the moment they'd met back in high school when Lucky came over. Ace had helped tutor him in English while Lucky taught him how to get into mischief without getting caught. When Ace said he was joining the Army, Lucky didn't hesitate. Wherever Ace went, Lucky was at his side, and then they'd found brothers in King and Red.

With a sniff, Ace moved away. "I think I'm in love with him."

"You *think* you're in love?"

Ace let out a soft laugh. "Okay, I *am* in love with him."

"When?"

"I don't know. I guess it was building up since we met. I kept trying to push it down, ignore it, walk away, but when he kissed me, I knew I couldn't. Then I saw those assholes in there trying to hurt him, and the realization almost knocked me on my ass. I know I should have told you. I should have taken myself off the case, but I needed to be the one to protect him, King."

King arched an eyebrow at him. "Why? Lucky not capable? Red?"

"Thing about Colton is, he's a little stubborn."

King wrinkled his nose. "No shit. Looks like you found your perfect match."

"I'm really sorry."

"Stop apologizing."

"I'll talk to Paxton. He might punch me in the face, but I swear I'll do everything I can to make this right." He made to get up, but King stopped him.

"No need."

"What do you mean?"

"Your boyfriend went to bat for you, and let me tell you, he went in swinging and laid that shit down."

Ace stared at him. "Really?"

"Oh yeah. First with his dad and then with me."

"With *you*?" Ace's jaw dropped, and he couldn't help the bark of laughter that came out.

"Yep. I was impressed. We didn't lose the contract, and Paxton's even willing to add a clause to the confidentiality agreement. No one will know what happened outside the six of us. I'm still going to have to bench you for a while."

Ace nodded his understanding. "Of course." He cringed. "Anything else?"

"You're going to have to make peace with your cousin. He's real hurt over this, and you know how serious he takes his moping."

"I know," Ace said with a soft laugh. "I'll make it right with him." It would take a lot of groveling. So, so much groveling. But eventually, Lucky would forgive him. "I think Red's got a soft spot for Colton's friend Laz."

The exasperated sigh King released as he let his head hang was epic. "You guys are killing me here."

"He's not a client, though."

"Well, thank fuck for small miracles." King squinted at him. "Has he done anything about it?"

"No. Laz broke up with his asshole boyfriend, and he's got... things to sort out. It's obvious he's got a little crush going on, but you know Red. He's got his own demons to battle."

King nodded sadly. "I know."

"When's the last time you got laid?" Ace sipped his beer, ignoring the full force of King's glare.

"Keep it up and you'll be protecting teen pop stars from here until you retire."

Ace shuddered at the thought. "Duly noted." King went pensive, and Ace turned his attention to him. "I can hear the wheels turning in that scary brain of yours."

"This was never about Colton's sexuality."

Ace agreed. "These men were professionals."

"The hate mail was to redirect suspicion." King stood, and Ace followed, tossing some bills by his empty bottle before walking with King through the bar toward the nearest elevator.

"We need to talk to Colton," King said. "This puts Connolly Maritime back on our radar."

"But we looked into everyone. No suspicious activity in their finances, contracts, associations."

"Doesn't mean someone isn't hiding something. My guess is that whoever's behind this is going to regroup and try again. We need to investigate everyone on the guest list. Someone on that list let those guys in here." His phone buzzed, and King pressed the button. He placed it to his ear as the doors opened and they stepped inside. "Hello?" King straightened, his face draining of color. "*What?* Stay with him. We're on our way."

"What's going on?"

"That was Jack. Red's been shot."

Ace's heart lurched to a halt, or so it felt. When the doors opened, they bolted from the elevator and ran down the hall just as paramedics rushed into the hospitality suite.

Images of Pip flashed through his mind, and Ace felt sick to his stomach. When he reached the room, Ace almost lost his dinner. It was like the world had gone silent. Jack was holding Red, his bloodied hand pressing down on Red's wounds, shouting at him to stay with them.

"Ace!"

All Ace could see was himself, shaking and crying as he held Pip's lifeless body, explosions going off around him, dirt and debris raining down on him, King screaming for him to move.

"Ace!" King's voice brought him out of the past, and Ace gulped a lungful of air. "Wait outside."

Ace shook his head. He pushed by King and dropped to his knees beside Red as the paramedics worked on him furiously. His eyes were closed, his face ashen. Ace looked up into Jack's tearful gaze.

"Is he...?"

Jack shook his head.

"Oh God. Red!"

Shit. Ace jumped to his feet, grabbed Laz before he could reach Red, and started dragging him toward the door.

"No! Red! Let me go." Laz fought him, but he was no match for Ace. Tears streamed down his face as Ace picked him up and off his feet. "Red!"

They lifted the gurney with Red strapped onto it.

"I'm going with him," Laz spat out.

"Laz—"

"I'm not leaving him."

"Ace," Jack called, and Ace turned. Red was awake and fighting the paramedics. He tugged the oxygen mask off.

"Ace," Red croaked, and Ace released Laz and ran to Red's side. "You have to... you...."

LOVE IN SPADES   255

"It's okay, buddy. Take it easy." Ace ran a hand over Red's hair, trying to soothe him.

"Colton. He took Colton," Red said through a gasp for air. "Nolan took Colton."

What the fuck? "Was he the one who shot you?"

Red nodded.

"Get him out of here," Ace told the medics, and they were off, Laz following, holding Red's hand.

"Laz, take care of him. We'll meet you there," King called out. Laz nodded fervently, then turned his attention back to Red as they disappeared.

Ace spun to face King. "We need to find Colton. We need to get him back and make that son of a bitch, Nolan, pay for what he did to Red. If he doesn't make it, I swear to God...." His voice broke, and King took hold of his shoulder, giving it a squeeze.

"Hey, Red's made of stronger stuff, you know that. He's going to make it through this." He turned to Jack who was just standing there, staring down at his bloodied hands. "Jack?"

Jack's head shot up, his eyes glassy.

"Go get cleaned up, buddy."

Jack nodded before hurrying out of the room.

"Where's Colton?" Paxton demanded, running into the room. "I was told someone was shot."

"Nolan's kidnapped your son."

Paxton shook his head. "That's not possible."

"He shot Red!" Ace snarled. "Which means it was someone close to Colton, someone we'd cleared. The only people who could have given the authorization to let those men in was someone inside the company. I'm sorry to say this, Paxton, but Nolan has been behind this whole thing.

The threats were bullshit. It was part of something bigger. It's connected to the company. It has to be."

"It makes no sense."

"Do you know where Nolan might have taken him?"

Paxton wiped a shaky hand over his face. "They could have gone anywhere." He looked like he was about to be sick. "Why would he do this? Nolan is family."

"I don't know, but I sure as hell am going to find out," Ace replied.

Paxton met Ace's gaze, the heartbreak written all over his face. "Please bring my son back."

"I'm going to find him, even if I have to burn this whole fucking city to the ground."

King stepped in front of Ace. "You need to calm down."

"Fuck, calm! I've lost enough people I love, King. I can't lose Colton too."

King nodded his understanding before turning to Lucky, who'd just rushed into the room with Joker at his side. "We need to figure out where Nolan might have taken Colton, and we're going to need the truck."

"Miami's a fucking bigass city," Lucky said somberly.

"Joker, I want you to reach out to your contacts on the streets. We need to find out who's in town that might want Colton Connolly. I would look into anything connected to shipping."

"I'm on it." Joker set up his tablet on the coffee table across from Jack, who'd finished cleaning up and returned with his laptop.

King paced, his eyes closed as he pinched the bridge of his nose. "We need to look at this from a new angle. Colton had plans to overhaul Connolly Maritime's security." King turned to Jack. "I need you to get into Connolly Maritime's system and find out if any clients were found in breach of

LOVE IN SPADES 257

contract or recently terminated. Get someone onto the security company that was about to lose their contract."

"I've got something," Joker called out, hurrying over. "I sent an alert out to all our people, and Bernadette was the first to red-flag her reply. She's on a job in the high-rise next door to a luxury condo still under construction on Biscayne Blvd and NE 10th St. She spotted lights and movement coming from one of the top floors about half an hour ago. It could be nothing, but construction crew has gone home for the day, and it's the first time she's spotted anyone there after dark."

"That's almost a straight shot down Venetian Way," Lucky said. "We can get there in less than twenty minutes."

"You know what else is real close?" Ace said, his gut twisting. "Dodge Island."

"Oh God." Paxton leaned one arm on the back of the couch for support. "PortMiami. We have a contract with one of the cargo terminal operators there. Security is tight, but anyone with an ID from Connolly Maritime has access. We have cargo coming in and out all the time, as well as several storage containers on site."

Ace turned to Jack. "Are there any shipments scheduled to leave anytime soon?"

Jack typed away at his laptop. "Shit. There's a freighter loaded and ready to ship out in the morning from bay 110, wharf 2. It's heading for the Port of Barranquilla, Colombia."

"They're not going to wait until morning." King's eyes filled with a fire Ace knew all too well. He'd seen that look many times, right before an op. "We're looking at a search-and-rescue mission here, fellas. Ace, Lucky, Jack, Joker, you're with me. Joker, call in the cavalry. I also want a team heading to the construction site in case they're still there.

My guess is they're going to want to move Colton out as soon as possible. Jack, reach out to our contacts at the Seaport Operations Bureau. Give them a heads up that we're on our way, but make sure they don't make a move until we arrive. I don't want the kidnappers to know we're onto them."

Everyone packed up at lightning speed. As they headed out the door, they assured Paxton they'd keep in communication with him. When they arrived at the hotel parking lot, the Knight XV was waiting for them. The luxury armored SUV with military engineering was top-of-the-line, and sexy as fuck. Hand-built in Canada as an armored law enforcement vehicle, a limited number had been produced, and the Kings had been the first in the United States to get their hands on one. It boasted a built-in oxygen survival kit, black box, reinforced steel doors, optimum surveillance, including night-vision cameras, and a protection system for under-vehicle blasts. If a King was riding out to battle, it made sense to have a Knight at his side.

They'd spared no expense. If they were going to protect their high-risk clients, they were going to do it right. Colton might not be a visiting foreign dignitary or high-profile celebrity, but Ace would do whatever it took to get him back. He climbed into the back and grabbed one of the tactical vests and thigh rig.

Time to do what they did best.

FOURTEEN

CALM. He had to remain calm.

"Nolan, please. Let's talk about this."

A sharp jab against his lower back had Colton moving forward again. He couldn't believe this was happening. How could someone he'd known for so long, someone his family trusted, betray them like this? He needed to know why. Nolan was a good man. What could have pushed him to this? Jesus, he'd *shot* Red.

The breeze from the ocean swept through Colton's hair, and he tried his hardest to fight the dread threatening to consume him. The island was quiet tonight with no cruise ships waiting to depart and only a couple of shipping liners docked. Even if there had been cruise ships in port, the likelihood of anyone seeing Colton was slim to none, not with them being at the far end of Terminal One near the south ship channel of the Fisherman's Channel. The light surrounding the cranes and the lampposts scattered around the island weren't enough to illuminate the pitch-black water that stretched on for miles. In the distance, the twinkling lights of Miami and Fisher Island reminded him of how isolated he was. His thoughts went back to Fisher Island, and Ace.

Ace....

Hope flared through him, and he straightened with a renewed sense of purpose. All he had to do was buy himself enough time until Ace came for him, and Ace *would* come for him. Colton believed that with every fiber of his being. As they walked through the yard, flanked by shipping containers stacked high, Colton tugged at his wrists. Not that he expected anything to give. The hinged handcuffs Nolan had used were a far cry from the zip ties Ace had taught him to escape from.

"Nolan, talk to me." Colton was struggling to wrap his head around all this. Nolan had watched Colton grow up. He and his family had joined Colton and his parents at parties and events. They'd had barbecues and pool parties. Nolan had been with Paxton when he'd had his heart attack. His quick thinking helped save his life. Why would he do this?

"I'm sorry, Colton. I'm so sorry, but I have to hand you over to them."

Good. If he could get Nolan talking, then maybe he could.... *I don't know, do something other than get killed.*

"Them? Who's them?"

"The men I owe Lily's life to."

Colton almost stumbled to a halt. He turned to stare at Nolan. "What are you taking about?"

With a sigh, Nolan's shoulders slumped, a pained look coming into his eyes. He kept the gun aimed at Colton, making sure to keep his distance. "Lily was going to die, Colton. A heart was never going to become available in time. Then one night, I got a call from a man who asked me what I would do for Annie's little girl. I said I'd do anything.

LOVE IN SPADES   261

He said he had the means to get her a heart. I thought maybe he was trying to get some money out of me, but I was desperate. I asked him how much, and he said he didn't need my money. He needed my connections with Connolly Maritime. More specifically, a means to import whatever he needed to get into the country."

Colton couldn't help the gasp that escaped him. "Nolan, what did you do?"

"I signed a new client."

"The only new client you signed around that time was...." *No. It couldn't be.* Colton's eyes widened. "Jeremy? Is Jeremy behind this?"

Nolan scoffed. "Jeremy is a pompous ass. He could never pull off something like this. I needed a client and container with product I could manipulate."

"How?"

Nolan waved the gun at him, motioning for him to keep moving. "A specified weight is needed each time, so I make sure an equal amount of produce is removed."

"How do you account for the discrepancies when the produce arrives?"

"It's written off as a loss so by the time it reaches the warehouse, the numbers match up. Jeremy's always moaning about how much he loses in the transport but how inevitable it is, considering it's fresh produce."

"You used your own son-in-law?"

"Please. Jeremy is an ass."

"He's still Annie's husband and Lily's father."

"They deserve better," Nolan snapped, and Colton couldn't disagree, but still.

"What does any of this have to do with me?" They were nearing the last rows of containers.

"Think about it, Colton."

The answer was obvious. "The new security system I want to implement. The regular audits and inspections."

"You're very thorough, Colton, and far more hands-on than Paxton. With his health issues, and how close he was coming to retirement, he was leaving more and more up to the people around him he trusted."

"Like you." Colton understood why Nolan had done what he'd done, but that didn't mean he was about to forgive Nolan for his betrayal.

"With you taking over, wanting to implement these changes, bringing in the Kings? We couldn't have you inspecting Jeremy's shipments. At first they wanted to kill you, but I didn't want that; you have to believe me. I told them what they were doing wasn't long-term. If you didn't stumble across the truth, someone else eventually would, and killing you wasn't a guarantee that Paxton or the board wouldn't go through with your plans or hiring the Kings. I suggested they take you instead. Paxton would do and pay whatever they asked of him to keep you alive."

"And the threats?"

"A distraction for when you disappeared. The police and everyone else would be searching locally for someone who doesn't exist. Eventually they'd assume you'd been killed, giving my associates time to prepare."

Colton stopped and turned, his heart broken. "Why would you do this?"

"If I didn't cooperate, they'd kill my family. They'd kill Annie and Lily. What was I supposed to do?"

"Did you send those men at the hotel after me?"

Nolan shook his head. "They needed some information about you. Where you lived, worked, the clubs you frequented. It was supposed to be easy. They were going to make it look like someone had broken into your home

LOVE IN SPADES 263

and taken you, but your house turned into a damned fortress."

"That must have really pissed off your guys."

"Hard to make it look like a crazy stalker when no one could get near you. I never expected you to change your schedule, but you did. They were getting agitated, making threats."

"You got desperate."

"The only way to get to you was through me. I got them into the hotel, into the party. When I was informed they'd failed, I was given different orders. I had to bring you in myself. You'd trust me."

"Now what?" They were at the end of the line, and Colton followed Nolan's gaze behind him to the huge vessel stacked with Connolly containers. *Oh God.* They were going to move him out of the country. He'd heard enough horror stories from his father's friends, of heirs or high-profile executives being kidnapped. What were the chances of him making it back alive after leaving US waters?

"As long as Paxton cooperates, they'll keep you alive."

Colton shook his head, pleading. "Nolan, you can't."

"I'm so sorry. I don't have a choice."

"For fuck's sake, are you planning on talking him to death? Why the hell have you kept me waiting?" A large, muscular man dressed in camouflage pants, a tan shirt, and boots removed the assault rifle slung over his shoulder to aim it at Colton. Several more men joined him, and Colton took a step back. "You're stalling, Nolan. You think I don't know stalling when I see it?"

"I'm not," Nolan assured him. "This isn't easy. He's my friend's son."

"We had a deal," the man snarled. "Get him on that ship, or I call the men sitting outside your daughter's house.

All that's standing between them and your granddaughter is the babysitter. They can snap her neck without breaking a sweat."

"Oh God." Nolan's hands shook, his gun still aimed at Colton. "I will, but please, Mr. Ferris. Don't hurt him."

"Then move," Ferris barked when Nolan hesitated.

"I'll go," Colton said, hands up in front of him. "Don't hurt his family."

Ferris let out a snort of disgust. "Even the hostage has more balls than you do, Nolan. Everyone, on the ship." Ferris shoved Colton toward the huge liner docked beneath the enormous steel crane used to load the shipping containers. A group of armed men followed them to a yellow metal set of stairs that led to the ship's deck. Colton paused, and the muzzle of Ferris's assault rifle pushed into his back. "Don't even think of doing anything stupid. Start climbing."

Colton did as he was told, sneaking a glance at Nolan, who was being ushered toward the stairs as well. Was Nolan coming with them, or did they not trust him enough to leave him on his own? The climb was slow, but about halfway up, he could see out across the island. Nothing looked out of the ordinary, and a few faraway lights twinkled on the water from small boats. How would Ace find him? Even if Red managed to live and tell the others what happened, how would they know where to look?

"Move," Ferris snarled. "No one's coming for you. I have men stationed around the island. The moment they spot any movement, they'll inform me. There's no one here."

Colton remained silent. Just because the Kings couldn't be seen, didn't mean they weren't nearby. If anyone could infiltrate the island without being spotted, it was a group of ex-Special Forces soldiers. Colton had every faith in the

LOVE IN SPADES   265

Kings. In Ace. He had to believe they were coming for him because he couldn't stand the thought of anything else. He continued up the stairs, and when he reached the last few, he made the most of his long legs, taking the final steps three at a time.

Confident they wouldn't shoot him dead, he ignored Ferris's threats and jumped onto the ship, then bolted for the riveted wrought-iron platform the containers sat on, and ducked beneath it, using the beams to shield himself should Ferris decide to shoot his leg out from under him or wing him.

"Colton, what did I say about doing something stupid?"

Colton used the darkness of the platform to help remain hidden as he swiftly moved from one pillar to another. A shot rang out, and he froze.

"The next bullet I fire will go into Nolan's head."

Damn it. He closed his eyes and did his best to push down the panic threatening to overtake him. He had to remain calm. "I'm coming," Colton called out, cursing under his breath. That was why they'd brought Nolan up here. To make sure Colton cooperated.

Hurrying across to the other side of the ship, he rounded the platform and remained near the edge of the deck. Unlike a regular ship, the cargo freighter was built to carry shipping containers, leaving the sides open for easy loading and unloading. No high walls, no railings, nothing but platform and the deep blue sea.

"I'm over here," Colton shouted, waiting. He swallowed hard as Ferris marched over to him, grabbed a fistful of Colton's hair, and jerked him forward.

"Now you listen to me, you shit. You try anything, and I will kill Nolan and every member of his family. Do you understand me?"

Colton clenched his jaw and nodded only to receive a backhanded slap so harsh it made him stumble sideways, his bottom lip split and his cheek pulsing from the blow. He glared at Ferris, straightening to his full height.

"Don't get fucking bold, Colton." Ferris turned to face his men. "Hidalgo, you and— Where the fuck is Yanni?" Everyone looked around, some shrugging. Ferris pointed to one of his men. "Tanner, find out where the fuck he went."

Ferris grabbed Colton's arm, and gunfire erupted from somewhere beneath the platform. Chaos broke out as Ferris's men scrambled, ducking for cover behind containers as Ferris shouted orders and his men fired into the darkness. He grabbed Nolan and shoved him at Colton, and Colton took the opportunity to grab Ferris's rifle.

"Nolan, run!"

Nolan didn't hesitate. He bolted across the ship while Colton wrestled with Ferris, his handcuffed wrists making it awkward. All he needed was for Nolan to make it to the stairs. With Ferris keeping a death grip on the rifle, Colton used it to his advantage, twisting to get Ferris onto his back, then flipping him over his shoulder. Ferris fell, but tugged hard on the rifle, bringing Colton down with him. They thrashed around on the floor, each trying to get the upper hand, but then Ferris pulled back a fist and punched Colton in the ribs, knocking the wind out of him. After scrambling to his feet, Colton took off running as fast as he could. Shots pinged off the iron beams, sparks flying. He skidded when he reached a gap between platforms and hurried up the narrow metal steps to the platform, a wall of shipping containers to each side of the darkened space.

Colton did his best to maneuver in the darkness, the only light coming from the moon high above him. If only he didn't have these damned cuffs on. He moved swiftly but silently, remembering what Ace had taught him about steadying his breathing. Ferris was quiet, and it would have been easy to become complacent and believe the man had given up, but Colton doubted it. Gunfire filled the air, along with sirens, and Colton wished he could somehow let the Kings know where he was, but then he'd also be giving away his position to Ferris.

Slipping out from between two rows of containers, Colton headed for what he knew was the bow of the ship. He wasn't entirely sure what he would do when he arrived, but he couldn't stand here and wait for Ferris or one of Ferris's men to find him. With his back to one of the containers, he edged toward the end and peeked out. Nothing.

Carefully he continued forward, away from the commotion happening far off toward the stern of the ship. When he reached the end of the platform, he peeked out, and again didn't see anyone. No shadows moving, no footsteps. On the other side of the smaller platform, a walkway with a set of stairs on each end led down to the bottom deck. He made a dash for it, but a bullet hitting the container ahead of him and to the left brought him to a halt.

"Don't fucking move," Ferris snarled.

A shadow swept over Ferris, and he looked up in time to get knocked to the floor, Ace landing on top of him. Ferris quickly recovered, pushing Ace off him and regaining his footing. Colton watched as they battled in hand-to-hand combat the likes of which Colton had never seen. It appeared Ferris had some kind of training as he held his own against Ace, blocking his punches and kicks. Ferris retaliated, throwing a right hook that Ace ducked under, each man trying to reach the assault rifle. They struggled to get the upper hand, punching the shit out of each other. The rifle went skidding across the deck and over the edge onto the deck below. Colton took off after it, the sound of scuffling, grunts, and fists coming into contact with body filling the air. He hurried down the stairs and bolted for the rifle, but he was tackled to the ground, the air rushing out of his lungs when he hit the floor, his head cracking against the hard metal and momentarily stunning him.

A shot rang through the air, and Ferris's man fell to his knees before slumping over. In the distance, Lucky and King sped toward him. Colton pushed to his feet, swaying as a wave of dizziness hit him. He stumbled back but spun on his heels regardless to look for the rifle just as Ferris snapped it up with a painful grunt. Ferris was holding on to his side, a huge military-grade knife plunged into his flesh, as blood flowed over his fingers and trickled from the side of his mouth.

Colton shuffled back near the edge of the deck as Ferris aimed the rifle at his chest. A shot rang out, and Ferris stared at Colton, stunned.

"Colton!" Ace came running, and Colton smiled as suddenly a heavy weight slammed into him, and the boat slipped away from beneath his feet. He gasped for breath, the world spinning off its axis as he tumbled along with Ace and Ferris. It took Colton a heartbeat to realize Ferris had barreled into him, and Ace had tried to stop it, sending them all hurtling over the edge. Colton hit the boat's hull with his shoulder, and he cried out at the pain, another *thunk* resonating seconds later. Then he was swallowing saltwater, darkness surrounding him as he kicked his legs and tried to find the water's surface.

Colton's lungs burned, his muscles ached, and panic threatened to drown him. A strong arm wrapped around

LOVE IN SPADES   269

him and dragged him. He broke the surface, coughing and sputtering ocean water.

"Lucky," Colton gasped, clutching on to him.

"Are you okay?" Lucky asked, wiping water from his face before swimming with Colton toward the emergency rope ladder someone had tossed over the side of the boat.

Colton nodded. "Yes," he wheezed, reaching the ladder. "I can't climb with these." He showed Lucky the cuffs, and Lucky nodded.

"Throw your arms around my neck and wrap your legs around me. I'll take you up."

Colton did as instructed, holding on tight as Lucky climbed. "Where's Ace?" The ladder shook, and Colton glanced down over his shoulder, his blood going cold. "Ace!"

King gripped the ladder with one hand, the other holding Ace, who was slumped over his shoulder.

"Colton, you need to stop moving, or you're going to knock us both down," Lucky ordered.

"Sorry." Colton closed his eyes, wishing he could do more than hang on to Lucky. At least Lucky didn't seem too bothered by Colton's weight. They reached the top fairly quickly, where Joker and Jack pulled Colton onto the deck. Lucky climbed up, and then the three of them helped grab Ace and drag him onto his side before assisting King.

"Ace!" Colton shoved his wrists at Joker. "Get these off me."

"Colton—" Joker tried to calm him, but Colton was terrified. Ace wasn't moving. "Get these off me!"

Jack hurried over and unlocked the cuffs, and Colton darted to Ace and dropped to his knees beside him. King had rolled Ace onto his back to swiftly and efficiently check him over.

"He's not breathing."

"Does he have any injuries?" Colton asked, not seeing blood anywhere, but it was hard to tell since Ace was wearing all black.

"I think he hit his head on the way down." King tipped Ace's head back, pinched his nose, and proceeded to give Ace mouth to mouth. Colton shivered, the chill going through him having nothing to do with his wet clothes. Even with it being late in the evening, the heat and humidity kept the cold away, but Colton couldn't stop shaking.

Ace spasmed and King jolted as Ace sputtered and threw up water. King rolled him forward, patting his back gently as Ace coughed and wheezed. Police sirens filled the night, but the best sounds were coming from Ace as he hacked up water.

"He's okay," King said, falling back onto his ass in relief. "He's okay."

"Ace." Tears blurred Colton's vision as Ace sat up. He wiped at his mouth before turning that beautiful smile on Colton.

"Hi, baby." Ace's voice was raspy and hoarse, but when he opened his arms, Colton threw himself into Ace's embrace, not caring about the tears that rolled down his cheeks. He was exhausted, and had had the life scared out of him. "It's okay," Ace purred softly. "We're okay." He rubbed soothing circles around Colton's back.

Colton pulled back, cupping Ace's face. "I love you, Ace."

"You do?" Ace blinked at him before his lips spread into a huge grin. "I love you too, Colton." He kissed Colton, and Colton melted against him, allowing Ace's warmth and affection to flood him.

LOVE IN SPADES   271

"Where's Ferris?" Colton asked. Not that he was concerned about the man's safety. Ferris had been a monster. Yes, he'd saved Lily's life, but he hadn't done it to help a little girl. He'd done it for financial gain.

King's gaze turned hard. "Sinking to the bottom of the ocean, I imagine. When the three of you fell over the edge, Lucky went in after you, and I went after Ace. I didn't see Ferris."

"His injuries were fatal," Ace said, his gold-green eyes clouding. "I made sure of it."

"Nolan," Colton gasped.

"He's in police custody."

"It wasn't his fault, Ace." Colton explained what had happened, but both Ace and King remained stoic.

"I understand what he did for his granddaughter," Ace said, his expression softening as he brushed his thumb over Colton's cheek. "But that doesn't excuse what he did to you. He signed your death sentence the moment he agreed to hand you over to Ferris. Baby, if they'd managed to get you to Colombia, you would never have made it home alive. They would have taken what they wanted from your father and then killed you, or worse."

Worse than being killed? Colton shuddered at the thought. "I know, but—"

Ace cupped the back of Colton's neck and brought him in close. "He had a choice. Instead of turning to the authorities for help, he chose to sacrifice you. That's not what family does, Colton. He needs to answer for his crimes."

Colton nodded. Ace was right. Of course he was right. Colton was just having trouble wrapping his head around everything.

"Come on," King said, helping them both to their feet,

then ushering them toward the stern. "We need to get you both checked out by the paramedics."

Ace wrapped an arm around Colton, pulling him close. They walked huddled together until they reached a sea of law enforcement. Police and SWAT had swarmed the boat, and were shouting orders at Ferris's men who were either on their knees with their arms zip-tied behind their backs or unconscious on the floor. Ace led Colton to the yellow stairs. By the time Colton reached the bottom, his knees were a little shaky. The events of the evening were beginning to catch up with him, and Ace was immediately at his side.

"You're okay, Colt. Everything's going to be okay." Ace led Colton to the back of one of the ambulances, and Colton sat, smiling his thanks at the nice EMT who wrapped him up in a warm blanket as she checked him over. In the ambulance to his right, Ace sat with his own blanket, those beautiful eyes on Colton.

"Well, someone's smitten," the EMT teased, motioning to Ace.

The butterflies fluttered like crazy in Colton's stomach despite the situation, and he let out a dreamy sigh, making her laugh. "Yes, well, the feeling is mutual."

Ace stood, said something quietly to the EMT, who nodded, before he made his way over. God, the man was sex on legs, his hair wet, his clothes molded to his powerful body.

"Hi," Ace said quietly, smiling at Colton.

"Hi."

"I'm, uh, going to go check on one of the other guys," the EMT said, sounding amused.

Colton moved over and opened one side of his blanket, his heart beating wildly when Ace sat beside him, wrapping the end of the blanket around his shoulder, his right arm slipping behind Colton, and tucking him against him. They pulled the blanket closed, and Colton turned his face to press his lips to Ace's. He wasn't sure if Ace might say something, considering how many people were around, including team members from his own company, but Ace didn't. Instead, he deepened their kiss, his mouth hot, and his lips soft. When they came up for air, Colton shifted so he could lay his head on Ace's shoulder. He was finally where he was meant to be.

In Ace's arms.

EPILOGUE

"ONE HELL OF A TURNOUT."

Colton couldn't agree more. The crowded club filled his heart with joy, and he beamed brightly at Frank, who stood beside him at the packed bar. "Even better than last year."

The annual Sapphire Sands Charity Masquerade was always a hit, but this year the tickets had raised more money than ever before, and because of that, a new LGBTQ youth center would be opening in Jacksonville in the fall, one that could help triple the number of youths than they'd anticipated, thanks to the generous donations of tonight's guests, many of whom happened to be clients of the Kings. Colton had a feeling his boyfriend might have had a hand in tonight's success.

The club was crammed with guests from all walks of life, all coming together to help LGBTQ youth. Frank had spared no expense in tonight's décor. It was elegant and all white, from the seating to the tall fiberglass palm trees strategically placed around the club, tiny crystals seeming to rain down from the ceiling. The white twinkling lights and neon blue lighting gave everything an ethereal glow.

"This is going to mean so much to these young people," Frank said, his eyes getting a little misty, and Colton covered Frank's hand with his own and gave it a squeeze. If anyone could appreciate the safety and support the youth center offered, it was Frank. He'd spent time on the streets as a homeless youth after his parents kicked him out with nothing but the clothes on his back. Frank was a survivor, a fighter, and he was determined to show the world it couldn't break him. Now the man was an ex-fireman who owned one of the hottest, most exclusive gay clubs on the East Coast. He'd accumulated a small fortune through his business prowess, and he used part of that fortune to help LGBTQ youth in the hopes they wouldn't have to suffer the way he had. Colton was grateful to have a man like Frank Ramirez in his life.

"I know how privileged I am," Colton said, his voice thick with emotion. "A rich white boy with an expensive college education he didn't have to pay for and wonderfully supportive parents. I was spared the horror and tragedy so many of our LGBTQ youth face. I know what it's like to be scared of admitting to the world who you are, but since I've never had to risk what these young people have, it's my honor to be able to help in any way I can."

"I'm so happy you're here, Colton." Frank grabbed him, pulling him off the barstool and into a tight embrace.

"You trying to steal my man, Frank?"

Frank laughed and turned to Ace, who winked at Colton as he stepped up beside him and wrapped an arm around his waist to draw him close against him. He placed a kiss to Colton's cheek. "I leave you alone for five minutes and already they're all over you," he teased before turning his attention back to Frank, poking his thick bicep. "You're looking exceptionally muscular in that Spartan costume."

The man did look particularly impressive. Frank always looked good, but he was never without his signature black suit, shirt, and tie. Now wearing nothing but a red cape draped around his shoulders, brown leather loin cover, and arm and leg guards, his chiseled physique was on display. You could bounce a quarter off the man's pecs.

"Yeah, um, it wasn't my first choice," Frank muttered, absently putting a hand to his bare chest. "A friend of mine's a costume designer, and when I asked for his help, this is what he insisted on. Usually the only ones this naked are the patrons after happy hour." He looked Ace over and whistled. "Well, damn, Sharpe. Don't you look pretty. The king of spades, huh?"

Ace chuckled. "It was Colton's idea."

"And a brilliant idea it was. He looks gorgeous." Colton didn't second-guess himself when it came to picking their costumes, because no costume would have done Ace justice like the tailored, specially designed three-piece suit. It was a rich black, hugging his broad shoulders, tapering at his waist, and enfolding his strong legs. The gold design was elaborate yet elegant and incorporated the card suit he'd been nicknamed after on each side of the suit jacket. His Venetian-style mask was black and gold, the top of which formed a kingly crown, the tips little spades. Colton had chosen a Regency era aristocratic riding outfit consisting of polished black boots, taupe-colored high-waisted pants, brocaded vest, and black tailcoat. He had a top hat and a riding crop that Ace seemed unable to stop touching. It was usually accompanied by a riding innuendo.

"You both look amazing," Frank said as Joshua appeared.

"Hey, guys." His gasp was echoed by Frank's as they stared at each other.

From next to Colton, Ace laughed, and Colton elbowed him gently to shush him. Ace loved taunting poor Frank. Though Colton understood why. He'd never seen two men more awkward around each other than Joshua and Frank. Joshua finally managed to snap himself out of it, and his smile stretched from ear to ear as he looked up at Frank.

"Hi."

"Hi," Frank replied, his voice low and gruff despite the crooked grin.

"You look great," they said at the same time, and Ace groaned. It was kind of sweet. Both men blushed, neither saying a word. Colton had never known Frank to get tongue-tied, but the big guy seemed to have trouble forming sentences when Joshua was around. Whenever Colton spoke to him, Frank always asked about Joshua and how he was getting along at his new job, how he was doing in general, and in his own Frank way, subtly inquiring as to whether Joshua had met anyone. Then when he was finally faced with the man, Frank's brain vacated the premises.

"You're looking very handsome," Colton told Joshua, who wore a costume that was reminiscent of a 1940s pilot. The tucked white shirt and vintage-style pants accentuated his slim frame, while the brown leather flight jacket with the cream-colored scarf draped around his neck made him look dashing. "Joshua?"

Joshua blinked and turned to Colton. "I'm sorry, what?"

"Baby, can't you see the poor guy was distracted by Frank's eight pack? By the way, you wearing anything under that skirt, Frankie?"

Frank groaned and covered his face with his hands while Joshua looked like he was about to pass out.

"Why don't we all go dance?" Colton suggested,

LOVE IN SPADES   279

pressing his lips together to keep from laughing when Joshua let out a squeak.

"Great idea!" Ace smacked Frank on the chest with the back of his hand. "Joshua can lend you his scarf to cover up your boy parts if things get a little awkward beneath your skirt. But hey, easy access, right?"

Frank growled and lunged for Ace, but he wasn't quick enough. Ace darted through the crowd toward the dance floor with Colton in tow.

"You're such an ass," Colton scolded, but his reprimand quickly gave way to laughter when Ace swung him around into his arms and started dancing with him.

"Yes, but I'm *your* ass."

"You are," Colton replied with a dreamy sigh. God, he was so stupidly in love with this man. His damned face hurt from smiling so much, but he couldn't help it. The more time he spent with Ace, the more trouble he had picturing his life without him. Before Ace, Colton had been married to his job, and he'd been fine with that. He worked extra hours because why not? It wasn't as if he had anyone to come home to. Not that he didn't enjoy having some time to himself. He'd never been lonely when he'd been in his house. But now that he'd experienced his home with Ace in it, he didn't want to go back. His job would keep him busy, especially once he took over from his father, but he'd make time for them. They'd already discussed it, how they'd build in time for each other despite their busy schedules. He understood Ace would have to be away sometimes for days on end, maybe longer, but they would always be coming home to each other.

"How's Red?" Colton asked as he slipped his arms around Ace's neck, their bodies pressed together as the lights hit the many crystals dangling from the ceiling, creating a blanket of glittering diamonds. The music was a heart-pounding dance beat, but Ace led him in a slow dance. He shook his head in shame, though his eyes were filled with amusement.

"I've never seen anyone look that happy while recovering from multiple gunshot wounds. Of course, that's probably down to your boy Laz. He's spoiling Red. Next thing you know he's going to expect us to fluff his pillows and read to him. It's very concerning."

Colton waggled his eyebrows at Ace. "Are you saying you wouldn't fluff my pillow?"

"Baby, I will fluff whatever you want," Ace growled playfully, nibbling at Colton's neck.

"Ooh, now that sounds promising."

"The movers won't be around with my stuff until Sunday, so you know, we have a whole day for fluffing."

Colton threw his head back and laughed. When he looked into Ace's beautiful gold-green eyes, his heart felt as if it was about to burst inside his chest. He couldn't remember ever being this happy, and he couldn't wait for Ace to finish moving in with him. It was a little quick, but a few days ago when Ace woke Colton up in the most sinful way, Colton let it slip how he wished he could wake up to Ace every morning. To Colton's delighted surprise, Ace agreed with him.

A part of Colton had expected Ace to balk at the idea, or at the very least need more time to consider it. Ace only lived a few minutes away from King and the rest of his brothers, so Colton understood any hesitation to move farther up the coast. But nope. Ace had been as excited as Colton, and he'd made the moving arrangements right away.

It felt right. Whenever he was with Ace, it was like he

LOVE IN SPADES   281

was drunk on life. He was at peace and excited about their future together. After everything that had happened, they were taking a few weeks off together. Not only had King been fine with it, he'd insisted upon it, stating he would seriously love it if Colton took Ace off his hands for a while. Apparently, Red was the buffer between Ace and King, so with Red on leave until he fully recovered, King needed Ace to be away from him. As much as King loved his best friend, he was very forthright about the fact Ace possessed a talent for driving even the most steadfast of men over the edge. If he needed Ace, he'd call, but in the meantime, Ace was to enjoy his vacation and "not wreak havoc."

"So, I was thinking that next week we could spend a few days celebrating this new chapter in our lives. Maybe Paris, Mumbai, or Spain. What do you think?"

Ace thought about it. "On one condition."

"Oh?" Colton loved the mischievous twinkle that came into Ace's eyes.

"That wherever we go, there's a big comfortable bed where I can have my way with you over and over. Also, room service, because we're going to need to keep up our strength."

"Deal, Mr. Sharpe."

"Oh, I already did, Mr. Connolly. And as you can see," Ace murmured, his voice sinful as he slid his hands down Colton's back to his ass before brushing his lips over Colton's, "I already won." Ace kissed him, all his love and affection coming through his passionate kiss.

Colton couldn't agree more. Ace had most certainly won this hand, but Colton had won something better. He'd won Ace's heart.

UP NEXT

Check out Red and Laz's story, *Be Still My Heart*, the second book in the Four Kings Security series on Amazon and KindleUnlimited.

A NOTE FROM THE AUTHOR

Thank you so much for reading *Love in Spades*, the first book in the Four Kings Security series. I hope you enjoyed Ace and Colton's story, and if you did, please consider leaving a review on Amazon. Reviews can have a significant impact on a book's visibility on Amazon, so any support you show these fellas would be amazing. Check out Red and Laz's book, *Be Still My Heart*, available from Amazon and KindleUnlimited.

Want to stay up-to-date on my releases and receive exclusive content? Sign up for my newsletter.

Follow me on Amazon to be notified of a new releases, and connect with me on social media, including my fun Facebook group, Donuts, Dog Tags, and Day Dreams, where we chat books, post pictures, have giveaways, and more!

Looking for inspirational photos of my books? Visit my book boards on Pinterest.

Thank you again for joining the Kings on their adventures. We hope to see you soon!

ALSO BY CHARLIE COCHET

FOUR KINGS SECURITY

Love in Spades

Be Still My Heart

Join the Club

Diamond in the Rough

LOCKE AND KEYES AGENCY

Kept in the Dark

COMPROMISED

Center of Gravity

TITLES COMING SOON

THIRDS

Hell & High Water

Blood & Thunder

Rack & Ruin

Rise & Fall

Against the Grain

Catch a Tiger by the Tail

Smoke & Mirrors

Thick & Thin

Gummy Bears & Grenades

Darkest Hour Before Dawn

Tried & True

THIRDS Beyond the Books: Volume 1

THIRDS Beyond the Books: Volume 2

THIRDS UNIVERSE TITLES

Love and Payne

SOLDATI HEARTS

The Soldati Prince

The Foxling Soldati

NORTH POLE CITY TALES

Mending Noel

The Heart of Frost

Vixen's Valor

Loving Blitz

Disarming Donner

The King's Courage

North Pole City Tales Complete Anthology

FALLEN ROSE

Roses in the Devil's Garden

A Rose by Any Other Name

THE AUSPICIOUS TROUBLES OF LOVE

The Auspicious Troubles of Chance

The Impetuous Afflictions of Jonathan Wolfe

STANDALONE

Forgive and Forget

Finding Mr. Wrong

Between the Devil and the Pacific Blue

Beware of Geeks Bearing Gifts

Healing Hunter's Heart

Love in Retrograde

AUDIOBOOKS

Check out the audio versions on Audible here.

ABOUT THE AUTHOR

Charlie Cochet is the international bestselling author of the THIRDS series. Born in Cuba and raised in the US, Charlie enjoys the best of both worlds, from her daily Cuban latte to her passion for classic rock.

Currently residing in Central Florida, Charlie is at the beck and call of a rascally Doxiepoo bent on world domination. When she isn't writing, she can usually be found devouring a book, releasing her creativity through art, or binge watching a new TV series. She runs on coffee, thrives on music, and loves to hear from readers.

www.charliecochet.com

Sign up for Charlie's newsletter: http://bit.ly/CharlieCochetNews

facebook.com/charliecochet

twitter.com/charliecochet

instagram.com/charliecochet

bookbub.com/authors/charliecochet

goodreads.com/CharlieCochet

pinterest.com/charliecochet

Printed in Poland
by Amazon Fulfillment
Poland Sp. z o.o., Wrocław